OF SAND AND
BLOOD

a novel

MICHAEL ROYEA

Relax. Read. Repeat.

To Pat
all my best

OF SAND AND BLOOD
By Michael Royea
Published by TouchPoint Press
Brookland, AR 72417
www.touchpointpress.com

ISBN-10: 1-946920-34-7
ISBN-13: 978-1-946920-34-8

Editor: Melody Quinn
Cover Design: Colbie Myles, ColbieMyles.com

Connect with the author at http://www.michaelroyea.ca/

First Edition.

Printed in the United States of America.

CHAPTER 1

...uri, vinciri, verberari, ferroque necari patior
...to endure being burned, bound, beaten, and slain by the sword

THE FIRST LIGHT OF DAWN PIERCED THE CRACK IN THE MUD-BRICK wall and illuminated the tiny room. Alexandros slipped out of bed and dressed in anticipation of the day that lay ahead.

"Alexandros," his father called as he walked into the cool morning light.

"Good morning, Father."

"Excited about your journey to the market?"

"Yes. But don't worry; I will get a good deal for the goats."

This was to be his second trip to the market in Tricca by himself, which was a half day's walk from their small farm.

"I know you will do well, but I fear you going that far by yourself. I could get your uncle to accompany you."

"I will be fine, Father. I'm nearly sixteen. It's time for me to take on more of your burden."

Alexandros did not mention what they both knew: his father was ill. He was tall, thin, and walked hunched over with much difficulty. He attempted to hide his condition from the family, but it was obvious to everyone.

"You best leave right after breakfast. Come in as soon as you finish your chores, and give the dogs extra," his father told him. "It will be a long walk for them too."

Alexandros hurried into the little barn, released the dogs, and fed them. Then he gave hay and water to the young goats. When he returned to the house, the table was covered with bread, yogurt, cheese, and honey, and, as soon as his sisters had finished milking the goats, fresh warm milk. After they had finished breakfast, Alexandros received a lunch of bread and cheese for the journey. With a final hug from his mother, he returned to the barn and let the goats loose. The dogs herded them into a bunch and waited for their commands.

"Remember, Alexandros, to the market and back. Don't stray off the trail and beware of strangers selling goods on the edge of Tricca," his father said.

"Don't worry. I will come directly back with the money. I know how much we need it."

"And one other thing, if you find out who that young girl is, I will try to meet with her parents to arrange a dowry."

"How do you know about her?" Alexandros asked. "I told no one."

"I have my ways." He smiled. "It's time you had a wife. Now go along. You want to be back before dark."

Alexandros hugged his father then whistled to the dogs. They sprang up and began to move the small herd of goats along the road. He hurried to catch up, glancing back at his village of Gomphoi one last time.

It was a good day to be alive. A gentle breeze rippled across the tops of the grain like waves on the sea. The sun was warm, the sky a soft blue, and clouds billowed along the horizon. He was lost in thought and whistling softly to himself when a familiar voice rang out from behind him.

"Wait for me!"

"Good morning, Georgios."

Georgios was his best friend who lived on the neighboring farm. He was a year younger than Alexandros.

"I wish I could go with you," Georgios said.

"You're too young," Alexandros replied. "And besides, I'm mad at you!"

"For what?"

"I told you about that girl I saw in Tricca in confidence, and you told my father."

"I had to. You're too much of a coward. How else would you ever get her?"

"I am not a coward! But you still can't come to Tricca. Maybe I will bring you next year. Best hurry back before your mother gets worried."

"You can tell me all about it tonight!" he yelled as he ran back toward Gomphoi. "Especially that girl!"

Alexandros went on alone and soon came to a group of trees that followed a small, dried-up creek. On the other side was the vast plain of Thessaly that stretched to the Peneios River. Tricca, the largest town in the region, was just across it. The flatlands seemed like an endless sea of grain with an occasional grove of trees dotting the landscape. The plains ran to the sea in the east and were abruptly stopped by mountains in the west.

He had walked for several hours when his belly began to growl, and he decided to stop for lunch. The five goats had discovered a patch of green grass and were nibbling away while the dogs eyed them and waited for signals from their master. The youth sat beneath a tree as he ate his lunch. He thought back to the festival of Artemis last fall when, for the first time, his father had passed on to him the honor of performing the blood sacrifice.

His father, one of the most respected men in the community, had been selected many years earlier to make the annual offering to the goddess. Alexandros had assisted in the rites several times and had begged his father to allow him to wield the knife. Finally, his father had agreed. But the youth could not do it. When Alexandros looked into the eyes of the goat, he could not bring himself to slit its throat. Instead, he had collapsed on the ground with tears streaming down his cheeks. Unseen by the spectators, his father had taken the knife, made the cut, and then covered his son's hands with blood. Alexandros was more determined than ever to prove he was a man. Next time he would draw the knife.

Alexandros held out a few breadcrumbs in his hand and sprinkled them on the ground as an offering to Hera, his family goddess. He had a special request for her—to see that girl at the market again. She was the prettiest girl he had ever seen. This time, if she was there, he would smile and maybe even talk to her. He wouldn't return to Tricca until next spring, so he had to find out who she was today.

He finished his lunch, took a long drink of cool water, stood up, and stretched. The goats and dogs had also found a bit of shade to rest, but it was time to move on. He called to the dogs. They rose and began to move the goats. Alexandros had almost caught up to them when something spooked the small herd and they scattered.

The youth grasped his heavy stick with both hands and scanned the surroundings. He whistled commands to the dogs and strained to listen for any sounds. There was a thumping noise in the distance. Several men on horses burst out from the tree line in the distance and were headed toward him. As he turned to search for the herd, which was nowhere in sight, more riders came from the opposite direction.

Alexandros turned and began to run as fast as he could, but the riders advanced on him. As he looked back at them, he tripped and hit the ground hard then gasped for breath and struggled to get up. Before he could regain his footing, a net entangled his arms and legs.

Two men grabbed him and pinned his arms.

"Let me go!" he screamed, but they replied in an unintelligible language.

They tied a rope around his body, attached the other end to a horse, and headed west. He tried to free himself, but it was useless. Soon they arrived at a road where a cart was waiting. The back was enclosed with iron bars. His captors threw him into the cage that held several other men. He lay on the floor, casting his eyes around at them. A few had the hope of youth etched on their faces, but the majority were wrinkled and tanned from many years in the fields. No one acknowledged him as they sat in silence staring off into the distance. He tried to speak to them, but the guards yelled and thrust a wooden pole into the cage. He winced and drew himself into a tiny ball, too afraid to move.

The road was rutted, and the cart bounced hard as they moved out of the rolling countryside and into the mountains. Along the way, a few other carts joined the caravan. As dusk began to fall, they came to a halt. The occupants were pulled out one by one and shackled to trees. Armed guards paced around them. Few slept.

Alexandros tried not to think about his family, but it was difficult. He pictured his father and mother in their kitchen sick with worry, unable to search for him until morning. He scratched up some dirt and squeezed it in his hands, determined not to cry. He tried to work on the leg iron, but could not free himself. He didn't think the night would ever end.

At first light, some soldiers threw hunks of bread on the ground near the prisoners. The other men fought over the food, but Alexandros was too scared to eat. Then a young boy passed around water. Guards pulled the prisoners to their feet and herded them onto the carts once more, and their journey continued.

By midday, Alexandros had seen four prisoners faint from the sun. Others cried out for water and were hit by the guards. The youth noticed the older man next to him hadn't moved for a long time, but his attempt to tell the guards was met with a blow from a club. They stopped again at dusk and repeated the routine.

By midafternoon the next day, Alexandros caught his first glimpse of something he had only heard tales of—the sea. It was so flat and vast; there seemed no end. His father had told stories of how one would fall off the edge of the world into eternity if you traveled too far on the sea. Alexandros thought it beautiful yet frightening. The caravan passed through a village near the water where the people averted their eyes and scurried out of sight.

They came to a halt on the dock. Alexandros' mind reeled as he gazed in wonder at what must have been the ship Odysseus sailed in on his adventurous return from the Trojan War. The prisoners were dragged out of the cage and pushed across the dock and up a wooden plank onto the ship. They were then forced to climb down a ladder into the hold. When one boy balked at the feat, he was pushed in. His scream was interrupted by a loud thud, and then all was silent. As Alexandros descended the ladder, he saw the motionless remains of the boy illuminated by the shaft of light that entered the small hatch. No one bothered to help the boy or even move his body.

A putrid stench rose from the bowels of the ship as Alexandros descended ever lower. It took some time for his eyes to grow accustomed to the dimly lit interior. He could see people everywhere, and yet more were being forced in. He searched for a place to sit before being pushed from behind by the next man. He lost his balance and fell on someone who swore and pushed him off. He was shoved by another and another until he finally came to rest on the hard planks of the floor. He pulled his knees under his chin, shivering with fear. The heat was overwhelming, and the movement of the ship made him queasy.

It only grew worse when the hatch was closed and darkness enveloped the interior. Alexandros thought of the underworld and believed it was no worse than this. As the ship began to move, he could hear the moans and cries in the dark of fellow prisoners. People vomited, yelled, cursed the gods, beseeched the gods, screamed, and pleaded. The youth was never sure if he was awake or asleep, or whether this was reality or a nightmare. He couldn't tell how long they had been sailing. Time stood still. He threw up what little remained in his stomach and held in his urine until he felt his sides would give way. Alexandros grew used to the smell, but not the sounds of suffering from those around him.

After a while, Alexandros reached out to the gods and offered a vow to Hera, his family protector, to sacrifice a fine goat to her should she help him return home, though he couldn't help but wonder why she seemed to have abandoned him. Thoughts of his family filled him with strength and concern.

A sudden jolt signaled their arrival at a dock. Sounds of men working filled the darkness and the occupants became restless. They shoved one another and stumbled in the dark trying to find the ladder. Someone stepped on Alexandros. He grimaced in pain while he attempted to push the large individual away.

Alexandros blinked as the morning sun flooded the interior from the open hatch and tried to avert his eyes from the contorted and bloated corpses of those who had not survived. Guards were yelling from above. He joined the line of prisoners who were ascending the ladder. Wherever they were going had to be better than where they were.

When he emerged onto the deck, Alexandros was dragged down the gangplank and loaded into another wheeled cage. The dock was crowded with people coming and going, but none paid any attention to Alexandros or his fellow prisoners. Several soldiers escorted them into the unknown city, which was even noisier and more bustling than the docks. Despite his fear, he was enthralled by the vast number of buildings and countless people. There were more people on one street than in his entire village. They headed straight toward a large structure on the outskirts of the city.

Alexandros stared in awe at the building, which rose into the sky and had numerous doors along its oval exterior. Pillars separated the arched doorways on the ground floor; columns divided the openings on the second. He was pulled out of the cart and herded into one of the many entrances that revealed a long cavernous tunnel lit by a few lamps on the walls. Prison cells lined both sides of the hallway. Most were crammed with forlorn-looking people, but he noticed that some had only one occupant. These men appeared very different from the others. They were large, well-muscled, and wore tunics of fine cloth. A few even smiled at him as he passed. His leg irons were removed, and he was pushed into a cell.

There were four others in the tiny cell; two older, gray-haired men, a youth around his age, and a boy who appeared about ten years old. The boy was huddled in a corner and had his head buried in his knees.

"Are you Greek?" one of the older men asked.

Alexandros nodded.

"What's your crime?"

"Crime? I was on my way to the market with some goats when Roman soldiers grabbed me. I committed no crime."

"Sure you did, the crime of being caught!"

"How is that a crime?" Alexandros asked in bewilderment.

"The Romans need meat for the slaughter."

"What do you mean? What is this place?"

"Hades, and we're about to enter Tartarus."

"Tartarus? My father says that is only for those who offend the gods and I've always made my offerings to them."

"Ahh, but these are Roman gods, the rulers of the world! We offend them by existing."

"I don't understand."

"You will soon enough, boy. When the sun is high, you'll understand." The old man slumped to the floor and Alexandros could see he didn't want to talk any more.

Alexandros lay on the hard, cold floor, drifting in and out of sleep. At one point, young men came around the cells with water and some kind of gruel. The youth drank some water and forced down a bit of the vile concoction. He tried to think of what he could have done that was so bad as to deserve this. Why did the Romans have different gods? Maybe if he could find someone who understood him and explain it was all a mistake, then everything would be alright. He had spoken to the young man with the water but was met with bewilderment. None in his cell would speak to him again.

Alexandros was awakened when someone began to shout and hit the bars of the cells. He looked around at the other occupants of his cell who were more frightened than ever.

"What is it?"

"The boatman approaches!" one of the old men cried out in fear.

"The boatman? I don't understand. What boatman? What's going on?"

"Charon!"

"Charon? But he ferries shades across the Styx. He can't be in this place," Alexandros told them.

"He's right!" another shouted. "We've already crossed the Styx!"

The cell door opened. Several large men with wooden clubs stood outside. One pointed to the young boy and Alexandros. Both were grabbed by the guards and dragged from the cell. Alexandros protested, and the boy screamed.

They were led along another tunnel. Alexandros could see a shaft of sunlight that pierced the muted light of the interior through the cracks of a door and was reminded of his bedroom. The door flung open, and Alexandros was blinded by the bright noonday sunshine as they stepped outside once more.

They were no longer in the streets of the city.

Alexandros looked around in awe. They were walking on sand in a massive oval-shaped space surrounded by a crowd of people seated on benches. The murmur of the vast number of spectators sounded like a swarm of bees that had been disturbed by the stick of a mischievous boy. Never had the youth seen so many people. Not even at the festival of Zeus when his entire village, and those of two neighboring towns, would gather to celebrate.

Three prisoners had been brought out: Alexandros, the young boy, and a man in his twenties. The young boy was dragged, and two burly attendants had to force the man along, but Alexandros walked on his own and gazed at the spectacle. His father had once traveled to Delphi to witness the oracle, and the youth had sat mesmerized at his retelling of the adventure, especially his description of the temple of Apollo, the theater, and stadium which flooded back to him as he took in this wondrous structure. He was too preoccupied to notice the three stakes driven into the ground in a row along the center of the arena, or that each had a length of chain attached to it. He barely noticed as they fastened his leg to the one on the left. The young boy was hitched to the center post and the man to the one on the far right.

The crowd was restless. They moved around, talked, laughed, shouted, and threw objects, but were oblivious to the three chained prisoners. Alexandros turned to look behind him when he heard the door through which they had been brought open again and saw a man enter carrying three swords. He walked to the prisoners and dropped one sword near each, then retreated into the safety of the tunnel as a rat scurries for cover at the approach of a man. The youth turned his attention back to the crowd. He was staring intently at first one person then another when a roar like the thunder of Zeus shook the foundations of the arena. He couldn't understand why the crowd had erupted until a deep guttural roar came from behind the prisoners. Alexandros slowly turned around.

The youth would never have believed anyone could be so big. The man was almost seven feet tall with massive arms and legs and a chest that was made even larger by the breastplate he wore. Greaves covered his shins, and bronze armor protected his lower arms. The iron helmet that sat on his head glistened in the sun; a tall horsehair plume adorned the top. He held a trident in his right hand. Every time this giant of a man thrust his arms into the air and roared, the crowd went wild. They shouted and stamped their feet.

The Giant strode around the arena, close to the crowd, with his arms above his head and thought how much he would miss the adulation of the crowd, the pleasure of victory, and the thrill of the kill. The people began a rhythmic chant of "*Gigas! Gigas!*" This was his last appearance in the arena, and he was going to enjoy every moment of it. He would have preferred to finish with a real match rather than executing prisoners, which was more like swatting flies, but he would still make a show of it.

And besides, this way he was able to wear his armor. As a retiarius, he had always fought with a trident and net, but no helmet. His only armor had been a shoulder shield. The Giant's immense size was but one of the elements that had made him so famous, and the Master had decided it would be a shame to cover his handsome features with a helmet. But today he could wear his Trojan armor that had been specially commissioned by a wealthy fan just for him. The breast plate carried scenes of the Trojan War. His favorite depicted the Trojans as they stormed the Greek camp and pushed them back to the sea. The Giant fancied himself another Hector with his bronze helmet and tall horsetail plume that danced in the air every time he tossed his head. Today he was a Trojan. Oh, how he hated Greeks.

After walking twice around the arena, the Giant stopped and turned to face the prisoners, a broad smile on his face. He cast his gaze at each in turn. The man glared at him, the boy lay curled up on the ground, and Alexandros began to feel sick. The Giant focused on the boy and in a few strides loomed over him. The boy lifted his head from the protection of his hands and looked up at the Giant. He was trembling so violently that he could barely breathe. Alexandros could see a growing spot on the front of the boy's tunic.

The Giant raised his trident. The boy jumped up and began to run away, only to scream in pain when he reached the end of the chain that grasped his ankle. A trickle of blood ran across his foot. He reached down to rub his injury, tears flowing down his cheeks. The Giant bent down, grasped the chain, and snapped it toward him. Alexandros heard the crack of the bone as the boy's ankle shattered. He screamed and dropped to the ground. The Giant picked up the sword and moved within striking distance of him. The massive man loomed over the helpless boy who fell silent. Fear trumped pain, and he attempted to crawl away. With a mighty blow, the Giant brought the sword down and struck the broken leg below the knee, severing the limb.

Never had Alexandros heard such a scream as pierced the arena. The boy grasped the stump of his leg with one hand while he pulled himself with the other toward the door. The Giant grabbed the chain which held the severed leg, raised it over his head, and spun the appendage in the air. The shouts of the spectators and pounding of feet on the wooden bleachers were deafening. Blood drops from the severed leg splattered on Alexandros' face; he vomited.

The Giant dropped the chain and thrust his arms in the air. He turned toward the man who brandished a sword. Perhaps he would make a fight of it for the crowd. As the Giant moved in closer, the man jabbed with the sword. He easily sidestepped the maneuver. Much to the chagrin of the man, the Giant was quick and agile. Now the Giant moved in close and baited the man, who thrust the sword again. The crowd gasped as it appeared to slice deep into the Giant's left side just below the breast plate, but the razor-sharp blade had passed harmlessly between his left arm and rib cage. As the man retreated, the Giant brought the trident's handle down across the sword and knocked the weapon from his hand.

He recovered the sword and lunged at the Giant once more. The Giant twisted his body to avoid the blow and, with his opponent off balance, brought the handle of the trident down hard on his back, plunging him face-first into the sand. He turned his back on the prone opponent and raised his arms. This was the move the crowd expected from him; exposing his naked back to a down, but still dangerous, opponent. It had helped make him famous as a gladiator and a star of the arena.

As the deafening noise filled the arena, the young man lay on the sand gasping for breath. He could see the immense shadow just ahead. He had dropped his sword and groped the sand for it, but by the time he found it and regained his composure, the Giant faced him once more. He struggled to his feet and retreated to the end of his chain, but the Giant followed. The man had served two years in the army and was proficient with a sword, but had never fought a man with a long-handled trident.

The man rushed his opponent. The Giant thrust the points of the trident under the man's chin and lowered the handle into the sand. The young man's momentum raised him off the ground, suspended by the points of the trident stuck in his throat. His feet dangled comically in the air. The sword fell from his hand, and he grabbed fruitlessly at the points driven deep in his neck. The Giant knew precisely where to place the trident so that the blow would be fatal, but the death slow. The young man gasped as blood squirted from his nose and mouth. His chest heaved as he struggled to breathe.

***

From the edge of the arena, Lucanus shook his head. He nudged the Master with his arm. "You should hurry him up. There's still many to go. At this rate, we'll be here all afternoon."

"Leave him be," the Master said. "This is his time. Let him enjoy it. See how the crowd loves him?"

"He is a favorite. Are you really going to free him after today?"

"This is his last performance in the arena."

"But why are..." Lucanus stopped short before he felt the Master's hand across his face. He, and everyone else, knew why the Master was giving the Giant his freedom, but none dared speak the reason.

The Master was the lanista, a former gladiator who had won his freedom in the arena, become wealthy, and now owned a stable of gladiators that included the Giant. He was still muscular after several years out of the arena. He cared for his charges but was brutal to those who disobeyed. Lucanus had once seen him slice off the head of a gladiator who refused to fight his friend. And then the Master killed his friend. He struck fear in those around him.

Lucanus was the Master's assistant. Blind in one eye and with a gimpy leg that caused him to walk with a pronounced limp, the Master kept him for his ability to spot new talent. Together they scoured the slave markets for the next great gladiator. The Master valued Lucanus' opinion and rewarded him handsomely when he was correct. After all, Lucanus had chosen the Nightman from a crew headed for the mines, and now he was the next in line for greatness after the Giant retired. However, Lucanus also knew he was but a whisper from the slave market himself if he disappointed.

Lucanus, born the son of a slave and her master, had been treated kindly by his owner. When he was fifteen, a beautiful girl was brought into the household as the owner's pet and Lucanus, young and handsome, fell in love with her. He had been severely beaten when the owner caught him making love to the girl. Sold to the owner of a school of gladiators, Lucanus did anything and everything to survive, and he was always assigned the worst jobs.

It was only after the school was bought by the Master that Lucanus' uncanny talent to spot aspiring combatants was recognized. From that point, his life became much more tolerable and, after successfully selecting three winning gladiators for the Master, he ascended to the role of the Master's trusted adviser. Lucanus had grown bolder as time passed and was one of the few who could speak honestly to the Master without being beaten, or worse, though even he feared the Master's wrath.

***

After a few minutes, when the crowd had tired of the spectacle, the Giant released his grip on the trident and let the young man fall to the ground. The Giant now turned his attention to Alexandros. As he approached, the youth began to tremble uncontrollably. His knees grew weak and his bowels voided. The Giant motioned to the sword that lay near the youth's feet, but he feared being unable to rise if he knelt to pick it up. Tentatively, he reached for the handle. The Giant stood watching his every move, the smile still on his lips.

The crowd began to laugh as they could see the sword shaking in the hand of this unkempt, dirty youth. They found his fear amusing, as did the Giant. Gladiators were trained to face death without fear. The youth could see him laughing under his helmet as he made a pathetic jab at the Giant, who stepped out of the way and then clubbed the youth on the back with the trident. Alexandros hit the ground hard. Everything went black before he could see again. The Giant raised his arms and turned his back on Alexandros. This was the best day of his life.

The sword entered his lower right side at a steep upward angle, sliced through a kidney, intestines, the esophagus and left lung, but stopped short of the heart. It was a fatal blow, but death would not be quick. Most spectators didn't see the blow delivered and continued to cheer for the Giant as though everything was fine. Even the Master and Lucanus saw nothing amiss. They became aware that something was wrong when the trident dropped from the Giant's right hand and hit the ground with a thud. Then, arms still raised, he fell onto his knees.

Alexandros, who stood directly behind the Giant, could hear his labored wheezing as he gasped for breath. His monolithic chest rose and fell with great effort. He would not give up life easily. After what seemed an eternity, he fell face down into the sand. A cloud of dust rose around the gargantuan man. The horsehair plume on his helmet continued to quiver long after his body became motionless. Blood oozed from the wound and flowed from his mouth and nose as his life drained into the sand. As the mighty Hector had fallen, so did the Giant. A deafening silence enveloped the arena.

Alexandros stood frozen, unable to turn his head as someone approached from behind. He stiffened in preparation for what he believed would be a fatal blow.

"Raise your arm!" the Master said. The color had drained from his face.

Alexandros remained still.

"Raise your arm, boy!" He grasped the youth's right arm and thrust it in the air.

The crowd erupted in a huge roar; the entire arena reverberated to the sound. Alexandros stood dumbfounded, unable to comprehend the scene. *Why are they cheering? I killed a man.*

Still holding his arm, the Master turned to face the editor for a decision. This was rare. A prisoner condemned to die in the arena at the hands of a trained gladiator had not only survived but killed his executioner. The usual outcome was death for the prisoner, no matter the circumstances, but this was different. The Giant had been a favorite of the people, yet, at his death, they cheered the one responsible.

For some unknown reason, the Master saw something in this decrepit youth. His most skilled champion was dead and, while he had another to replace him, times were tough, and the spectators loved the youth. He doubted the boy could last in a match, but that didn't matter. Perhaps he could get one good payday before his death. However, the decision as to whether or not this youth survived was for the editor to make, not the Master. So the Master held Alexandros' arm high and encouraged the crowd.

The editor of these games, Lepidus Salvius Capito, was a wealthy shipping magnate in the city of Brundisium who controlled most of the goods that were shipped into or out of the port. He was a cruel man; his wealth was only exceeded by his lust for power. To those ends, Lepidus was putting on these games for his clients and supporters. The day had included a small beast hunt in the morning, followed by the prisoner executions during the midday, and, finally, the gladiatorial bouts in the afternoon. The Master had wanted to supply all the gladiators for the show, but Lepidus had contracted with a troupe from Capua, renowned for its gladiatorial schools, and left the Master to supply a few men to execute the prisoners and a half dozen to fight, including the featured performer, the Nightman.

Lepidus stood and surveyed the crowd, who would not be silenced. The people couldn't get enough; this boy had slain the Giant. No one had ever defeated him; now he was dead, and they had had the privilege of seeing it. There was no way they were going to let the editor execute this young man. Perhaps the gods were protecting him. How else had this mere boy killed the Giant? There could be no other explanation.

The noise intensified, and the editor realized all the goodwill he had gained with these games would be lost if he ordered the death of the youth. The boy must live.

Lepidus held out his arm, fist clenched, thumb straight, then slowly turned the thumb down.

The Master looked at Alexandros. "You live!"

Alexandros felt something on his leg and realized someone was removing the chain that bound him. The Master pulled him by the arm toward the entrance gate. They walked past the boy who lay motionless at the end of a line of blood that crossed the sand like the slim trail left by a slug from the point where his leg was amputated. When they arrived at the gate, the Master spoke to Lucanus. Alexandros couldn't understand anything he said.

"Go with him!" the Master ordered while pointing at Lucanus.

In a daze, he followed Lucanus past the crowded cells to an empty one. He stood for the longest time, his knees too weak to go further, then finally collapsed onto the floor and lost consciousness. He wasn't sure how long he had been laying there when he heard voices.

***

The Nightman stood stoically before the arena gate. From the corner of his eye, he could see the towering figure of a man who stood silently beside him. Butterflies churned in his stomach. He grasped the handle of his shield tight to prevent any shaking. A sliver of late afternoon sunlight shone through the crack in the gate and sliced vertically through his opponent's face. The man was from the Capua school and unknown to him, but he suspected it wasn't going to be easy. As the Nightman's reputation grew, the most skilled sought him out. Everyone believed he was destined for the Imperial games. A victory over him would raise a winner's status.

The gate flew open, and both men strode into the arena, the Nightman to the left and his opponent to the right. The crowd chanted his name as he held his helmet high. He walked clockwise around the large arena, soaking in their adulation, which would only continue if he won. They stopped in front of the editor's box where their weapons lay spread out on a table. The Nightman picked up his short, slightly curved sword and examined the razor-sharp edges, signaled his satisfaction to the editor, then held it out to the referee for his approval.

Next, his opponent, a murmillo named Astus, examined his straight short sword. The weapons were placed on the table as the two men put on their helmets. The Nightman's was broad-brimmed with steel mesh covering the face, an image of Nemesis carved in high relief on the front, and a tall crest on top that ended in the head of a griffin. His shield was small and rectangular, and iron greaves covered both legs to his knees. Astus' helmet was similar in shape, but the top held carvings of several gods. The crest was low and thick and ran from front to back with more figures carved on each side. His shield was long, heavy, and rectangular, and reached from below the knees to his neck. The two men picked up their weapons once more, saluted the editor, turned, and walked to the center of the arena.

Everyone knew the Nightman was better than most, but in matches between a Thracian and murmillo, Thracians, like the Nightman, nearly always lost. The Master was seated to the left of the editor, a man he despised, as he did all free men. Gladiators were loved in the arena and spat upon in the street, but the Master was one of the few to survive, become wealthy, and gain his freedom at the end of a blade.

Astus was confident and experienced. He had a history of fourteen matches, had only lost two, and was spared both times by the audience for his entertaining performance. He was strong, well-protected by the large shield, and ruthless. But he wasn't taking the Nightman lightly. His reputation preceded him. He had fought nine bouts over five years with no losses, and seven of his victories had resulted in the death of his opponent. The crowd was divided in loyalties between the two gladiators, though alliances could change during the heat of battle.

The Nightman rushed at his opponent, who met the charge with a thrust of his sword that was parried by the Nightman's shield. He pressed Astus and struck shield on shield while searching for an opening. Several times his curved blade just missed flesh and each time the crowd responded with growing excitement. A good show was important because it might save the loser's life.

The men exchanged blows with both swords and shields as the late fall sun beat down on an unusually hot day. Sweat poured off the Nightman's forehead and into his eyes under the stifling iron helmet.

Astus struck a blow with his shield. As he pulled it back in place, the Nightman threw himself against Astus and, at the same time, sliced around the shield and struck his opponent's left arm. It was superficial wound, but the crowd jumped to their feet at the sight of blood. Now the Nightman pushed his advantage and struck Astus' shield and sword with quick blows that kept him off balance and retreating. Astus thrust his sword, but the Nightman stepped to his right, moved in close, and dragged his sword across the back of Astus' left leg. The iron bit deep, cutting the flesh to the bone and nearly severing his leg. Astus fell back onto the sand. The referee hurriedly stepped between the two gladiators and signaled the match over.

Lepidus rose, held out his right arm, listened as the crowd shouted their approval for Astus' valiant fight, and turned his thumb down. The crowd applauded his decision. The Nightman turned toward the editor and raised his arms in victory. The Master stared at the editor, unsure what he would do, and again Lepidus eyed the spectators who were standing when another chant of "Nightman" filled the arena. The Master relaxed knowing Lepidus would not go against the wishes of the crowd. With a quick gesture, he turned his thumb down again.

The editor passed a palm leaf to an assistant in the arena, who in turn handed it to the Nightman along with a small silver plate. Next, the assistant counted out ten gold pieces, half of which the Nightman would keep. The remainder would go to the Master along with the silver plate.

As the Nightman paraded around the arena in triumph, men with a stretcher ran in to collect Astus and take him to the medicus. Unfortunately, even though the people had spared his life, the blood loss was too great for the medicus to save the murmillo's life.

***

"Boy! Do you want anything? Water? Food?"

Alexandros slowly turned his head to see a dark-haired muscular man standing by the door. His face was obscured by a scraggly beard. Sweat ran down his forehead.

"Water," the youth responded meekly.

The man nodded his head, and a servant extended a container of water through the bars of the cell. The youth reached up, grasped the vessel, and began to drink greedily.

"Not too fast!" the man said. "You'll be sick. Sip the water." His voice was forceful but soothing.

After quenching his thirst, he stared up at the man. "You're Greek?"

"Yes."

"From where?"

"Athens. And you?"

"Thessaly."

The man began to laugh. "Not many gladiators from Thessaly. Just pig farmers!"

Alexandros didn't understand. "What is a gla-di-a-tor?"

The man stopped laughing. "It's a dead man, boy. A dead man."

He still didn't understand but thought it best not to ask again. "What is your name?"

"My real name is Miltiades, but I am known as the Nightman."

"Miltiades of Marathon, a fine name. But I don't know what the other means."

The Nightman had pronounced his name in Latin. He tried to translate it to Greek for the youth.

"Why do they call you 'Nightman'?"

"Because anyone who faces me in the arena sees only eternal night." Seeing the perplexed look on the youth's face, he continued, "I kill those I fight."

"And make a lot of money doing it!" the Master said as he approached. "What's your name, boy?"

"Alexandros, son of Leontis from the village of Gomphoi, south of the river Peneios."

"Like the 'Great'?"

Before he could say anything else, the Master continued, "You don't look so great to me. From now on you will be known as the 'Greek.' Understand? Your name here is the Greek." He turned his attention to the Nightman. "Be prepared to leave immediately."

"We're going back in the night?"

"There have been some problems with the fees, and I might have to 'persuade' the editor to come up with all the money owed. I want to leave before he has time to bring in reinforcements."

"What about the wounded?"

"Drag them onto the carts. The medicus can treat them on the road."

"And this one?" the Nightman asked, pointing at Alexandros.

"He's your responsibility. He doesn't speak Latin. You and I are the only ones he understands, so keep him with you. Now go!"

As the Master hurried away, the Nightman motioned for a guard to open the cell. "Can you walk?" he asked Alexandros. He struggled to his feet and staggered out. The Nightman supported him as they walked through the corridor, Alexandros could feel the man's strength. The cells that had teemed with life when the youth arrived were now eerily empty. He could see a few other men walking ahead in the dim light. The young Greek was loaded into another cart surrounded by bars, but there were benches to sit on. The Nightman sat across from him. He could sense Alexandros staring at him as the caravan departed.

"Where are we going?" Alexandros asked.

"Home."

"Thessaly?"

The Nightman glanced at him. He didn't know whether the question was funny or sad. "No, boy. We're headed to your new home, the one you'll never leave. At least not alive."

"But I want to return to Thessaly, to my family. Why can't I go? I did nothing wrong. Why am I here?"

"Entertainment—the same reason the rest of us are here."

"I don't understand."

"Neither do I, Greek. Neither do I."

CHAPTER 11

THE MASTER THREADED HIS WAY THROUGH THE MAZE UNDER THE seats of the amphitheater until he reached the offices of the attendants. After a bit of searching, he found the editor sitting behind a small table in one of the rooms. A large man stood on each side of him.

"Here for your fee," Lepidus stated. "A fair show. It's a pity about the Giant though, and on his last appearance. He must have offended the gods, don't you think? Or perhaps that stripling is descended from them?"

"Descended from the gods? I didn't know you were of such a mind, Lepidus, as to believe the gods walk among us."

"Who are we to know their designs? Perhaps your boy is another Hercules."

The Master forced a smile. "Enough. Now for the balance of my fee."

"Yes, straight to the point. I admire that in you, Master. You would have gone far in business if you were," he hesitated, "a free man."

"I am as free as one needs to be. You had five gladiators second class and, of course, the Nightman, a first class. Two were wounded and one killed. The death increases the price, but, as it was during the match and not on your order, it will only be another 3,000. Plus three for the executions. The total is 26,000 sesterces. You gave me 5,000 for the deposit, leaving 21,000 sesterces, or 210 gold pieces if you prefer."

"Yes, about the fees. They seem a bit excessive given the conditions in the empire."

"They are the lowest you'll find for each class."

"But there is the matter of the Giant's unfortunate death. As it was caused by a prisoner, there should be no fee. It was an unforeseen circumstance for which I hold him entirely responsible. The Giant made a mistake, and I am not paying for his error."

"Fine, I'll reduce it by 1,000."

"And there's the matter of the boy. After all, I paid good money for those prisoners with the intention they be executed. Instead, you claim one of them. For all I know, he will become a star in the arena. You can't expect me to give him to you."

The Master leaned menacingly on the edge of the table directly across from Lepidus. "What you say is true. You should be compensated for a slave. I'll purchase him for 50 sesterces."

"Fifty!" Lepidus burst out laughing. "That doesn't even cover storage fees. I had to hire a ship to bring those prisoners from Greece, bribe the soldiers who captured them, and now you expect me to give one to you for 50? I want 5,000!"

"Five thousand! You're mad! That is the rental fee for a first-class gladiator."

"And the matches weren't that impressive. The man killed was third rate. He looked diseased to me. I think you put him in there to dispose of bad waste expecting me to compensate you at double the price. I will not pay the extra."

The Master glared at Lepidus and leaned closer, which caused the two bodyguards to step forward.

"I believe 15,000 is a fair offer and, as you've received 5,000, I will give you the remaining ten. Of course, if you're not satisfied, you are welcome to lodge a complaint with the Brundisium council or the local senator."

"All neatly in your pocket," the Master growled.

"Come now. You give me too much credit. I'm but a humble merchant." Lepidus threw a bag of coins on the table. "Ten thousand. Count it if you want, but not here." When he raised his hand, the bodyguards moved toward the Master.

Before either could react, the Master pulled a dagger from his sleeve, sliced open one man's throat, and slashed the other across the face. One fell on the table and splattered Lepidus with blood. He jumped up from his seat. The Master waved the dagger before Lepidus' face and smiled ever so slightly; how he enjoyed the look of fear in an opponent's eyes. Once a gladiator, always a gladiator. "Perhaps you wish to reconsider your offer?"

Their eyes locked, but, being a sensible man, Lepidus knew when he was defeated. "Of course, Master, a misunderstanding. I never intended to slight you. 26,000 it is, less the 50 for the boy. After all, he'll never amount to anything. On second thought, consider him a gift," Lepidus continued, all the while counting out coins on the table. "I believe you will find the additional amount there."

The Master picked up the two bags of coins, withdrew a few, and dropped them on the table. "For them." He motioned at the two bodyguards.

Lepidus forced a smile. "It has been a pleasure doing business with you. No hard feelings over the misunderstanding?"

"None. I hope you will consider my humble troupe for any future games you sponsor."

"You're always my first choice."

The Master backed out of the room and hurried into the night.

***

The small caravan followed the rutted road across the countryside heading north. A wave of sadness overcame the Greek when he thought of his family, his dogs, and home. His curiosity as to where they were going did nothing to ease his apprehension and fear. The events of the day spun in his head, and he felt remorse at having killed that man. Maybe he had survived. Alexandros had never stabbed anyone before. The big man might still be alive. The thought cheered him somewhat, though deep down he knew the Giant was dead.

The caravan continued moving through the night because the Master was worried about the actions of Lepidus. The merchant wasn't a man to take an insult with grace. The Master sent scouts ahead and behind to watch the road. Even though he had well-trained gladiators, they were a small group and vulnerable to attack. All the territory north of Brundisium was controlled by Lepidus, and he could easily send word to his allies to retrieve the gold he had paid against his will.

When dawn spread across the horizon, they had put enough distance between their wagons and the long reach of Lepidus that everyone was beginning to relax. Soon they would be in the region under the control of Senator Flavius. He was a harsh man. Even Lepidus would not dare offend him. Around midmorning, they approached a small inn where food, water, and fresh mules could be acquired. The Greek hadn't slept much on the journey. He could sense the unease of the Nightman, who had remained vigilant all night. The Nightman was let out of the cage when they stopped but returned in short order with food and water for the youth.

It wasn't long before they continued their journey, but another day was needed to arrive at their destination. The Master was always nervous on these long trips, especially after the recent escape of Pugnax. The caravan stopped for the night at another inn where the gladiators were led into the stable and secured with leg chains. The Nightman was the only gladiator who remained free. Food and water were brought, and the Greek was able to sleep in warm straw. The fact they were surrounded by animals comforted him.

Everyone was roused before daybreak as they were only a few hours from the safety of the Master's school. One of the wounded gladiators had died during the night. The Master decided to bury him before they left. The Nightman and two others dug a shallow grave behind the inn where the body was placed. Then everyone was brought out to witness the burial. All stood in silence. The Greek found it strange that no words were spoken over the deceased nor were the proper rituals observed. They left without breakfast. The Master didn't want to spend any more than necessary.

The Greek admired the rolling country covered with grape vines

and olive trees that varied from the plains of Thessaly. It wasn't long
before he could see a large, walled compound atop a low hill in the
distance—the Master's gladiatorial school. Upon entering the
enclosure, Alexandros could see the stables on the left and beyond
them a two-storied villa. There was an open area to the right and in
the center stood a tall cross on which hung a decomposing body. The
Nightman caught the youth staring at the cross.

"That's what happens to the ones who try to escape."

As Alexandros stared at the corpse, he wondered what kind of
place this was. The cart passed through a second gate and stopped
in a rectangular courtyard that was enclosed by a covered portico
around the interior. The roofs sloped down into the courtyard.
Behind the portico were a series of doors. There were no windows.
Spaced at random intervals in the courtyard were wooden posts
about the height of a man. Alexandros followed the Nightman out
of the cart to where several slaves were waiting.

He spoke to one of them and then turned to the youth. "Go with
him to the bath. Afterwards, have breakfast and then rest."

Alexandros followed the slave into a building at the end of the
courtyard. A simple alternating black and white mosaic covered the
floor of the apodyterium. A bench was attached to three of the walls
with a shelf above. The slave peeled off the youth's soiled tunic and
threw it on the ground outside the door, then pointed to a square
basin sitting on the floor and indicated the youth should stand in the
water. As soon as he did, the slave began to wash his feet. Next, he
was led to a round marble basin that was waist height in which he
washed his hands. Following this, they went into the tepidarium
where Alexandros stepped down into the warm water. He was
immediately struck by the beauty of the images on the tiled floor of
the bath. Sea creatures swam around a central image of a god—a
male figure with tentacles for legs which he recognized as Triton.
The slave pushed him farther into the water and began vigorously
scrubbing his soiled skin.

After this, the attendant gestured for Alexandros to go through yet another door. The youth stepped out of the water and into the second room, but jumped back as the floor scorched the bottoms of his bare feet. In his haste, he hadn't noticed a pair of wooden sandals by the doorway. Alexandros placed them on his feet and re-entered the caldarium. He was overwhelmed by the heat; he would have collapsed onto the fiery floor had the attendant not caught him and pulled him out.

They returned to the changing room and entered a second door that lead into the frigadarium. This room was smaller than the others, and the floor was covered in a black and white leaf-shaped pattern which gave the illusion of walking on a three-dimensional surface. Alexandros found this disorienting; he felt as though he were about to step into a multitude of holes. There was a pool at one end, though the youth retreated quickly when his feet entered the frigid water. The slave pushed him forward. He was covered with goose bumps upon exiting, but the experience had revived him. He was glad for the warmth of the changing room. The slave dried him and gave him a massage.

Alexandros' soiled tunic was replaced by a clean one. Then he was led to the dining hall—a long narrow room next to the baths. Only a few occupants were eating. He sat and another slave placed a bowl of barley porridge, a chunk of bread, and a ceramic goblet that contained a dark liquid with bits of something floating on top of it on the table in front of him. He took a sip and grimaced. Another servant poured honey into the mixture, creating a much more appetizing concoction. He ate this first meal greedily and drained the goblet, bits and all.

The slave who had bathed Alexandros waited for him to finish eating before leading him to one of the cells along the portico. The tiny room had a single bed against the wall. There was also a table and one chair to the left of the bed. A chamber pot sat on the floor next to the table. A small slot in the door allowed light to enter the room. When opened, a shaft of light streamed through and illuminated the interior. The Greek moved to the bed, laid down, and thought of Georgios.

***

The next day found the Master in a foul mood. He was still angry over the incident with Lepidus. Times were hard, and the Master needed every denari.

And then there was the senator. Marcus Quintus Flavius would soon arrive to discuss the funeral games for his son, and the Master loathed the senator. He hated all free men who continually looked down on him and his kind, no matter their earned status. Once a gladiator, always a gladiator. But he needed men like the senator to survive. Emperor Tiberius refused to sponsor Imperial games, and in the climate of fear amongst the upper classes of being too ostentatious, there wasn't much demand for his stable of gladiators. The Master could barely afford to feed and train them. If things didn't improve, and fast, he would be forced to sell some of his best. In better times, he would never have agreed to execute prisoners for anyone and, had he not gone to Brundisium, the Giant would still be alive.

The Master observed the men in the training yard from his second story office window. He watched the Greek toy with a wooden sword and was deep in thought when a knock startled him.

"Enter!"

"The senator is at the gate," Lucanus informed him. "Are you going down to meet him?"

"You go. And bring the fat pig up here. Make him sweat coming up the stairs."

"He will be insulted that you send a slave to fetch him."

"Then piss on him! Now go!" the Master said. "And have wine sent up. Lots of it. The cheap stuff with plenty of water in it!"

The Master could hear the senator as he puffed and complained.

"Senator Marcus Quintus Flavius to see you," Lucanus said.

"Senator Flavius, dear friend, it is *so* good to see you," the Master said. "It has been far too long since we've seen one another."

"Master, you must... excuse me... too many steps... for a man...

my age."

"Forgive me, Senator. I would have come down to meet you personally but my idiot slaves did not inform me soon enough."

"Ah yes, it is hard to find good help these days," the senator replied as he caught his breath. "It has been over a year, I believe, since last we met. At the races in Pompeii, wasn't it?"

"How is that beautiful wife of yours?"

"Still grieving, I'm afraid."

"Oh yes, I'm sorry for your loss. Your son was a magnificent specimen of a man. He will be missed." The Master grasped the senator's arm. *It's too bad he was fatter, lazier, and twice as ugly as his worthless father,* he thought.

The senator was short and pudgy, with a nearly bald head and stubby fingers. He always reeked of fish.

A slave arrived with the wine.

"Here we are, Senator. Sit. Have some wine to quench your thirst. It's some of my best." After handing him a cup, the Master sat down opposite him and continued. "Tell me, have the conditions in Rome improved?"

The senator looked around the room, saw they were alone, and leaned in close to the Master. "If by improvement you mean 'Tiberius is dead,' then I'm afraid not." He leaned back in his chair.

"But he is old now, so there's hope?"

"Sometimes I believe he will live forever! There was a rumor in Rome not long ago that he had died. People were celebrating in the streets until the Praetorians arrived and rounded up a bunch of them. No one has seen them since! Some of us think he started the rumor himself."

"Is he in Rome?"

"No. He stays on Capri fiddling children while slaves run the empire."

"But who would replace him?" the Master asked.

"My money is on Gaius."

"Gaius?"

"Caligula. He seems to be intelligent, and he has a nice disposition to govern. He's an exceptional member of the Julio-Claudian family."

"Your endorsement of Gaius is enough for me, as long as he brings back the Imperial games."

"Ah, yes. It has been awhile. You fought there if I'm not mistaken?"

"In front of Augustus, no less. One hundred pairs of us, some of the greatest gladiators in the Empire. Augustus granted my freedom for a victory over one of his men."

"Enough politics. To the business of my coming here."

"Yes, of course."

"I wish to celebrate games in my son's honor so, naturally, you were my first choice to supply the gladiators. The fact that you have the best in the Empire doesn't hurt."

"You flatter me. But I do pride myself on producing superior combatants for the arena."

"However, I have had the good fortune of acquiring several wild beasts from a close business acquaintance of mine, surplus from the imperial gardens, so my budget for the gladiators is somewhat limited."

This concerned the Master. "You know as well as I that even with a beast hunt, people are expecting gladiators. It would be an insult to your son's memory to exclude gladiators."

"Oh, of course there will be gladiators. A few."

"What do you mean by 'a few'?"

"Perhaps five pair."

"Five pair! That wouldn't cover my costs. I do not offer charity!"

"Calm down," the senator urged him. "Perhaps a few more. And the venue is close."

The Master regained his composure. "I couldn't make money with less than twenty pair, and that is only because it is less than a day's ride."

"Ten is as high as I can go. You know as I that times are hard, even for senators."

The Master hated to accept, but at least he would make a small profit. "I would do this for no one but you. Ten pair."

"And, of course, I expect the Nightman."

"Impossible! He fought two days ago."

"I heard it was a lackluster performance against an untrained slave."

"Hardly! It was a fine murmillo from the Capua school and a real test of his abilities."

"Was he wounded?"

"No, but he—"

"That's the deal. Ten pair, including the Nightman, or nothing."

The Master glared at him. "On the condition you pay half now."

The senator smiled and stood up. "I am glad to pay you an advance of, say, twenty percent." He pulled a small pouch out of his tunic and offered it to the Master, who grudgingly accepted it.

"Now if you'll excuse me, I must attend to urgent business. Lucanus!"

Lucanus, who was listening outside the door, stepped into the room.

"Show the good senator to the gate."

"Oh, one final point. All bouts are *sine missione*."

"That will be ten times more for the ones killed!"

"I will pay you 5,000 gold coins, not a sesterce more."

"That's robbery! I should get that without their dying."

"Accept or I will contract to the Capua school. They are quite willing to travel here for that sum."

The Master knew the senator was right. With few gladiatorial games, this would be a good opportunity for the school. And besides, he could send out some new men, cheap men as sacrifices. It wouldn't be too bad.

"I reluctantly agree to your offer."

"Good! I will see you in three weeks. I look forward to your show."

"We won't disappoint. Tell your friends about us."

"Oh, I shall. Good day." The senator turned toward the door, dreading the long climb down.

"Lucanus, return to me after the senator is gone," the Master whispered.

* * *

Alexandros had been in the courtyard all morning admiring the others as they trained. Everyone was so big compared to him, and their technique with the wooden swords astounded him. An older man, a trainer, had given him a weapon and was trying to show him how to use it. He had to use a lot of gestures because didn't speak Greek. Alexandros swung the wooden sword, shifted it from one hand to the other, and at times juggled it all to the frustration and amusement of the trainer. The Master was watching him from the tower when Lucanus returned.

"Sent the fat shit on his way?" the Master asked without removing his gaze from the boy.

"We're going up there with ten pair?"

"Money is money, and we need anything we can get now. What do you think of the Greek?"

"Who?"

"The youth I brought back. What do you think of him?"

Lucanus joined the Master and observed the boy. "Too small and weak to be a gladiator. He has some quickness about him, but wouldn't last through his first bout. It was a fluke. He's no match against a trained gladiator. You should have left him there for someone else to finish off."

"He's going to the senator's party."

"What? You can't be serious. If you do plan to make something out of him, maybe in a year or so, we could fashion him into—"

"He fights in three weeks! Come with me to the yard."

Lucanus knew the Master well enough to remain silent.

"Do any of the trainers speak Greek?"

"I don't think so, but I can check," Lucanus said.

"Where's the Nightman?"

"Probably sleeping."

"Send for him."

They descended the winding stairway, but instead of going straight into the courtyard by the stables, they turned left and stopped in front of a locked metal gate.

"Open it," the Master ordered the guard on duty.

The gate swung open, and they entered the training yard. The Master went directly to the Greek. Lucanus left to find a slave to send for the Nightman.

"Boy, Greek," the Master called to him.

Alexandros turned toward the Master. "Why are you keeping me here? Why can't I go home?"

"You want to go home? All you must do is win. Win, and you will be free."

"Win what?"

"Your match in the arena."

"I don't understand."

The Nightman had arrived.

"You will train to be a gladiator and fight in the arena. Win, and you will gain your freedom. Then you can go back to Thessaly," the Master told him.

"I do not want to fight! I will not fight!"

"Do you have a family in Thessaly?" the Master asked.

"Yes, my parents and two sisters."

"If you do not fight, I will send my men to your home, kill your parents, rape your sisters, and then bring them back to Italy and put them in a whorehouse to be raped over and over by Roman soldiers. Is this what you want? Or do you want to fight and win your freedom?"

Alexandros glared at him. "No one would do such a thing!"

"You trust him?" the Master pointed to the Nightman. "Tell him."

The Nightman sighed and turned to face the Greek. "He would do such a thing."

The Greek's heart sank. He did not want to fight anyone, but what choice did he have? He must protect his family. "If I win, you will free me?"

"I will even arrange transport to Thessaly."

"Then I will fight."

The Master now addressed the Nightman in Latin so the Greek wouldn't understand. "You will train him."

"Me? Why?"

"None of the trainers speak Greek."

"So you expect him to fight as a Thracian?"

"No, a dimachaerus."

"I know nothing of that style."

The Master ignored him and continued, "He fights with two swords, straight not curved. And no armor. He wears only a loincloth, barefoot, and don't cut his hair. He will be the Greek Wildman—a boy captured in the deep forests of Thessaly and turned loose in the arena."

"I will do my best, but Lucanus says I fight in three weeks. I won't have much time."

"Don't worry about your match. It will be soft, an easy kill. Prepare the Greek for the same games."

"Three weeks? Impossible! It will take months to prepare him for his first match. You are offering him as a sacrifice!"

"Three weeks! And the bouts are *sine missione*." With that, the Master and Lucanus left the yard.

"What did he say?" Alexandros asked the Nightman after they were gone.

"You will fight in three weeks, and I will train you as a dimachaerus."

"What's that?"

"A man who uses a sword in each hand and wears no armor. The match is *sine missione*. It means without mercy, the loser of each bout dies. And if you don't please the audience you will die, even if you win."

"But he said I would be free if I win! They can't kill me if I win."

"They can do whatever they want."

"But he promised—"

"Look, boy, don't believe everything the Master tells you! The only way most of us will ever be free is when we walk in Hades."

"But he said..."

"We won't have time to improve your strength, so we will concentrate on handling the swords. You must rely on speed and movement to win. You will probably fight a heavily armed man who moves slow, so speed is your advantage. I saw you playing with the sword. Where did you learn to do that?"

"One time a troop of entertainers came through my village. They had two jugglers. I watched them perform and practiced after they left. I juggled eggs from my mother's chickens, but she was upset when I dropped some."

"Juggling the swords will please the people. It's different. But you must be cautious and not lose sight of your opponent."

"Don't worry, Miltiades. I will win. I must, for my family."

The Nightman stared at him. *He has no chance.* "Don't call be Miltiades. I am the Nightman."

"How long have you been a gladiator?"

"Five years."

"Are you a dima..."

"Dimachaerus? No, I fight as a Thracian with one sword, a small rectangular shield, arm guards, greaves and a helmet."

"That big man, the one I stabbed—"

"The Giant."

"Was that his name?" Knowing made the pain worse.

"That was his name. What about him?"

"Was he your friend?"

"Gladiators have no friends."

"Why?"

"Because you may have to kill anyone here. Never make friends. Never care for anyone. Everyone is your potential enemy."

"That seems a terrible way to live."

"No one lives here. This is a place of death. I told you before— we're dead men. What did you want to know about the Giant?"

"I thought...I hoped maybe he would be alright."

"Hope is for fools!" the Nightman snapped. "You drove a sword through his back. What do you think? The best a gladiator can hope for is a quick death. That's all there is for us."

"Why do you stay if it's that bad?"

"We are all slaves. Few are here by choice. If anyone tries to leave they will be caught and end up on a cross like the man by the gate."

"Who was he?"

"Pugnax, a Thracian like me. He was good, but he missed his family. He was taken prisoner in Germany, and the Master bought him at the slave market in Brundisium two years ago. He fought several times and won most, but he couldn't get over his family. The Master laughed when he said he wanted to buy his freedom. The next week he escaped. No one knows how he got away, but he was found three days later, beaten, and brought back. A few days after that they nailed him to the cross."

"This is a terrible place, isn't it?"

The Nightman walked away.

My father was wrong, Alexandros thought, *there is a place worse than Hades.*

***

After dinner that evening, Alexandros was feeling better. He would soon be free. It concerned him that the Nightman didn't seem too optimistic about his chances, but he would do whatever it took to win, even if it meant killing another man. He would live with the consequences as long as he could return home. He had been in his room a short while when the door opened.

"You're the one who doesn't speak Latin," a soft female voice spoke. "Don't worry. I speak the universal language."

She was illuminated by the light from the small opening in the door. Alexandros could see her long dark hair and slim body under a thin tunic, but her features remained vague. Then she removed her tunic. He had never seen a naked woman. He stood up from the chair with his back against the wall.

"Don't be shy," she said, moving against him. "You're young.

Ever been with a woman?"

He pressed back against the wall as she grasped his hand and placed it between her legs. It was warm and moist, and he could feel something flowing down the inside of her leg. With her other hand, she latched on to his penis and began to stroke it. It quickly grew erect. She pushed her body against him and kissed him softly on the neck and lips. After a few more strokes, he released himself onto her hand. He barely felt anything.

"Good boy," she said, wiping her hand on his tunic. "You're my sixth tonight. Wish they were all this easy. Guard!" she called after putting on her clothes.

The door opened and she left without another word. Alexandros stood against the wall, unmoving. He heard the door of the next cell open and close, then muffled noises followed by the woman screaming, furniture being banged around, someone being slapped, more screaming, and, finally, crying. Then silence once more. He wiped his sticky hand on his tunic and lay down on the bed. He thought of that girl at the market.

***

The next morning, Alexandros began a training routine the Nightman thought might help him survive his match. First, it was up early for a breakfast of barley porridge and a warm cup of the dark liquid with floating bits, which he had discovered was ash. Then the Nightman led him out to the yard.

"We train with wooden swords that are twice the weight of the real ones. This improves your strength," he explained, handing Alexandros two swords. "Grip them tight and keep your hands out from your body. Constantly move the swords. Not a lot. This will keep your opponent guessing. But first I want to see how fast you are. Stretch your arms straight out to the side."

As he stood there, arms out, the Nightman drew a circle in the sand with his heel around the exterior of Alexandros' reach. "The object is to stay inside the circle but not be hit by my sword. Ready?"

"Yes."

The Nightman took up a position facing him. Without warning, he thrust his sword at Alexandros' belly, but when his arm had extended, Alexandros wasn't there. He had easily sidestepped the blow and was waiting for another. The Nightman thrust again and again; right, left, up or down, it didn't matter. Alexandros dodged the sword with ease. Only occasionally was he hit, but never enough to do any harm.

Both were sweating heavily an hour later when the Nightman stopped. "I've never fought anyone as fast. How did you learn to be so quick?"

"I don't know. It seems easy."

"You need to be quick. But to win, you must fight back. Rest for a bit, and then you'll use the swords."

The Nightman sat in the shade. Alexandros seemed to think this was a game. He twisted and turned the swords in circles, then attempted to juggle them, with limited success. He continued to the amusement of the Nightman, who finally grew bored, stood up, and walked out into the sun.

He picked up a wooden shield and motioned for Alexandros to join him. "Now we'll see what you can do with a sword. When I thrust at you, guide the blow away from your body with one sword and try to strike me with the other."

Alexandros' coordination wasn't as good as his speed, and he often clashed the swords together or moved the wrong way, deflecting the Nightman's sword into himself. The wooden swords did not cut, but could, nevertheless, be painful. Finally, the morning workout was finished.

The Nightman took him back to the dining hall where he ate a lunch of barley porridge mixed with beans and bread and, of course, the dark liquid with the floating ash made barely tolerable with honey.

After a short rest, the Nightman began an afternoon of sparing with Alexandros. He pushed the youth back with his sword and shield without pause, which kept him off-balance and retreating.

Both grew tired as the afternoon wore on, but they continued with only a few short breaks until late in the day. The Nightman showed him the standard series of moves the audience would expect, but also a few tricks he had learned over the years. He was a quick study, but the Nightman knew his life was at stake.

Alexandros was exhausted. Though used to working in the fields day after day, the movements of the gladiator were completely different. The bath felt good after such a workout, and the massage soothed his tired muscles. Dinner consisted of more barley porridge and vile liquid, vegetables, and a little meat. He noticed many of the other gladiators staring at him.

"Why is everyone interested in me?" he asked the Nightman.

"You're new, that's one reason. The other is what happened to the Giant."

"They stare because I killed their friend?"

"There are no friends here. And don't mention the word killed, or anything to do with death, understand?"

"Why?"

"We all know our fate, but speaking of it is bad luck. Never mention anything about death, especially anyone you have killed in the arena."

"Which god do you make offerings to?"

"Silvanus, god of the collegia of gladiators. There are shrines at the south end of the courtyard. There is also a shrine to Nemesis, but beware her power if you sacrifice to her. She is a dark goddess from the underworld."

"I usually offer to Hera. Is there a shrine to her?"

"No, but we can set up one if you want."

"Who is Silvanus?"

"He is an old Roman god of the forest and hunting, a god of agriculture, a god of the earth, the sand. We live or die on the sand. It steals our blood. He is also a dark god, but if he rides on your shoulder, you will not fall to the sand."

"I want to make an offering to Hera, a goddess of light."

"Be careful not to neglect the dark gods, or you might pay with your life."

***

Alexandros was awakened by the sound of his door opening. Sitting up on the bed, he could see the Nightman silhouetted in the door frame.

"Come with me."

He followed the Nightman along the portico to the end of the courtyard by the gate. On the wall was a rectangular wooden box, pointed on top like a house roof. He looked at the Nightman, perplexed.

"Here." The Nightman handed him a small roughly carved figure. "Hera, this is her shrine. I managed to get a bit of wine for your libation."

Alexandros smiled at the gesture. He took the figure and placed it carefully in the box, stepped back, and held his arms straight out in front, palms up.

"Greetings, Hera," he began in a low voice. "I have a humble offering and ask that you protect my family, as you are able, and protect me, as you are able, and bind the opponent I am forced to fight, as you are able. Do these and I will sacrifice a fine ram to you when I return home."

He took the jug from the Nightman and poured the contents onto the ground and shrine. He handed back the empty container, looked at the Nightman, and smiled.

CHAPTER 111

THE MASTER SEEMED TRANSFIXED AS HE STARED OUT THE TOWER window day after day and watched the Greek train. He had a natural ability for handling the swords. After two weeks he moved like he had been born with a sword in his hand. Even the other men in the yard would stop and watch. Unfortunately, he was a better entertainer than gladiator.

"He has some talent," Lucanus observed.

"Are you changing your opinion of him?" the Master asked.

"Given enough time, perhaps we could make something of him. But not three weeks." Lucanus knew the Master well, but he couldn't understand his plan. Whatever it was, he was sure it would not end well for the boy. "Who will he fight?"

"A murmillo—the Bearman."

Lucanus wanted to say something, anything, but held his tongue. The Bearman was an experienced combatant with over twenty bouts. His superior strength and skill would overwhelm the Greek. He had hoped the Master would pair the Greek with an easy match, but now he knew better.

Alexandros liked to train. It made the days pass quickly, bringing him ever closer to the match and freedom. He also discovered that he enjoyed entertaining others. When he would juggle the swords or attack the straw-stuffed dummy, his fellow trainees would gather to watch. He would smile, feign being wounded, and fall to the ground in dramatic fashion that usually elicited laughs. It was all a game to him.

But it wasn't a game to the Nightman, who would berate him like a father scolds his son. The Nightman knew it was all too real and, try as he might to remain aloof from the youth, he felt a responsibility for him. Men would die in the arena, and he was working hard to prevent the Greek from being one of them.

Alexandros began to feel overwhelmed as he tried to absorb the Nightman's years of experience in three weeks. He found many of the points of little value. As he grew in proficiency and drew more attention from others, he became cocky and believed that not only would he win, but it would be easy.

The men would rise at dawn, eat a light breakfast, and then train. Their regimen began with assaulting a six-foot-tall wooden post to warm up, followed by fighting a practice dummy filled with straw, and then, for the Greek, dodging swords used by the Nightman to improve his mobility and speed. In the afternoon, the Greek would spar with others. The Nightman could not discover what type of gladiator the Greek's opponent would be, so he could not tailor the training. He thought it might be a fellow Thracian, but his instincts told him the Master had something else planned. The Nightman was growing more pessimistic as to the Greek's chances of survival.

One week before the match at the funeral games, a tall, muscular stranger arrived at the school and asked to speak with the lanista. Lucanus brought the man into the garden where the Master soon joined him.

"My name is Maecenas Canuleius Zosimus. I am a free man and wish to become a gladiator in your school."

The Master eyed the man suspiciously. "Why do you want to become a gladiator?"

"The goddess Fortuna has sent me to poverty. I was a prosperous merchant when my warehouse burned. With no insurance, I lost everything—my goods, my family, even my name. I was respected, but now my name is cursed, and I am forced to beg in the street. I would rather die in the arena."

"Where are you from?"

"Tarentum."

"You are aware that you will sell yourself to me for a period of time and the contract cannot be broken? Only if you make enough to buy back the contract, if I agree to sell it, can you leave here."

"I am aware of the contract terms."

"You must swear an oath to be burned, bound, beaten, and slain by the sword if you do not follow my orders at all times. You will become my slave, and I can legally do to you what I want."

"I will swear. How much do you pay?"

"Times are hard in the empire for lanistae. The emperor refuses to give Imperial games and the wealthy cower likes dogs lest they appear to compete with Tiberius, so we are thrown scraps. I recently traveled all the way to Brundisium to execute prisoners, and in one week I supply ten pair to a senator's funeral games, but it is barely enough to turn a profit. The most I could offer is 15,000 sesterces for five years of service. Plus you keep half of the prize money."

"I was hoping for more, but times are hard for everyone. How much is the prize money?"

"It depends on your class. You would start at third class, that's around 200 sesterces for each win, but as you win, you go up in class. A first class gets at least 400 or 500, sometimes 1,000. I could offer you a match in one week if you think you're ready."

"I served time in the army and know how to handle a sword. I can fight in a week."

"Good. My assistant will draw the contract. Oh, there is one small point. I won't be able to pay you the 15,000 until after the match. The senator hasn't given me any of the fee yet, and I cannot come up with that amount until he pays. But don't worry, it is for Senator Flavius. He is good for the money."

"Agreed," Maecenas replied, extending his hand to the Master.

"A slave will take you to your room. You will begin training immediately with the best trainer I have. Lucanus!"

Lucanus appeared out of nowhere.

"Have someone take this man to a cell. And draw up the contract for a free man."

Lucanus nodded and led the man into the house, then returned to the Master. "A contract for 15,000? Where are we going to come up with that?"

"We're not. Did you look at him? He thinks he can fight because he was a soldier but is soft and flabby."

"You're going to sacrifice him?"

"The matches at the senator's are *sine missione*, so we need ten to eliminate. I told him I can't pay until after the match but by then he will be dead. I save one of my gladiators, and it costs me nothing. See how he spars. If you believe he is poor, I'll match him against the Nightman. But it must look good. If not, I'll put him against someone else. Understood?"

"Yes. I'll try him out right away and let you know," Lucanus said. A sad feeling overcame him, despite the fact he knew better than to become attached to any of the men. Lucanus now understood the Master's plan for the Greek; he was to be sacrificed so that the Bearman might live.

***

The trip to the senator's venue began early in the morning, though it was only a half day's journey. The Master wanted everyone to be settled in and prepared for their matches because this was important for his financial situation. There would be knights and probably other senators at the games and that would give the Master an opportunity to showcase his talented stable.

Alexandros was excited and a bit nervous. He would have liked to attend the banquet that evening for the gladiators but was advised against it by Nightman. Instead, he had a light dinner and tried to sleep. The excitement of returning to his family had made sleep difficult the past few nights. He was much less concerned with his bout now than when he began training, though the Nightman continued to stress the danger. He saw it as a minor inconvenience to overcome before regaining his freedom.

Early the next morning, after a restless night, Alexandros and the other gladiators were given instructions for the pompa, their order and pairings, and when each would fight. The men were restless in anticipation as they stood in the corridor near the entrance gate. Silence gripped the arena as the gate opened and the long procession began. First to enter were the lictors, the closest associates of the editor, who carried his symbol of power, the fasces. Next came four trumpeters, followed by six guards that surrounded two blacksmiths whose job was to guarantee the quality and sharpness of the gladiators' weapons. The next three men were a record keeper and those charged to handout the prizes—an olive branch and gold coins. Following them came Senator Flavius, the editor of the games, resplendent in his toga. Behind the senator were twelve servants carrying the shields and helmets of the gladiators who were to fight that afternoon, followed by two more trumpeters. After this group had stopped in the center of the arena, a flourish of trumpets and flutes signaled the entrance of the gladiators. They walked in two by two beside their opponent of the day. They wore no armor, only loincloths and sandals so that the spectators could admire their faces and bodies unencumbered by the trappings of their profession.

The Nightman led the procession, and the crowd's volume rose as he entered. Striding with confidence, he waved to the crowd, acknowledging their respect and admiration. The new man, Maecenas, walked by his side and also waved to the people, oblivious to his fate. Others were picked out for special applause as the crowd recognized individuals. When the Greek entered, little heed was taken; his small size and novelty led many to surmise he was but a sacrifice. But this didn't lesson the excitement for Alexandros, who reveled in the atmosphere of the packed arena. He strolled in a daze as though he was in the middle of a dream.

The gladiators walked slowly around the stadium and circled the first members of the pompa, who stood in the center of the arena. The senator waved to the large crowd and acknowledged the applause and cheers for himself, though in reality it was for the gladiators. After they completed the circle, the gladiators stood in a line by the gate to give the audience one last look, then marched into the galleries beneath the stands to prepare for their bouts. The senator and his entourage departed through another gate, and he made his way to the editor's box where his wife, still dressed in mourning black, was waiting. The Master was seated behind and to the left of the senator. When everyone had taken their seats, Senator Flavius stood and silenced the crowd.

"Friends and supporters, welcome to these humble games I offer you in remembrance of my son." A murmur of laughter flowed through the arena. He ignored it and continued. "In the tradition of games, we begin with a beast hunt followed by a special treat at midday—the execution of a slave who befouled his master's wife." A shout of approval rose at this announcement. "Then a special presentation of gladiatorial matches featuring the Nightman." A thunderous cheer greeted his name.

At a signal from the senator, a gate opened and a venator entered the arena. He wore a helmet and cloth wrappings on his legs and carried a large square shield and long spear. He walked around the arena then stopped in the center. The audience grew quiet as another gate opened. People strained to see into the darkened tunnel, anxiously anticipating the type of animal that would emerge. Attendants could be heard yelling in the tunnel and, finally, a bear sauntered into the arena. He had large bare patches all over, one eye was swollen shut, and he limped. It was one of the worse cases of mange the Master had ever seen. It looked like gold in his pocket.

The venator approached the bear. The creature was uninterested in the man. When he poked the bear with his spear, it merely walked a few feet away and lay down. The crowd began to boo and whistle. The senator shifted in his seat. Unable to make the bear move, the venator drove his spear into its heart. The gate opened again and, after a few minutes, another bear was dragged in by several slaves. He was lethargic and wouldn't even stand up, so the venator put him out of his misery. The crowd was growing hostile, stamping their feet and hurtling insults at the senator.

The next bear ran into the arena, but, unfortunately, rather than attack the venator, the bear was terrified of him. The venator cornered and quickly speared it. The senator had seen enough and ordered the venator removed, which caused a loud cheer.

For the next event, two bears were brought in to fight, but they lay down on the sand and refused to acknowledge the other's presence. To try and liven up events, a small herd of goats was ushered in and then another bear. The senator hoped the starving animals would attack the goats, but they appeared too weak for such a feat, and members of the crowd began calling out bets on which bear the goats would kill first. The senator was growing extremely concerned and silently vowed revenge on the supplier—a wealthy businessman from Venusia named Scelestus.

After the bear fiasco, a pair of ostrich were brought in and strangled, something that usually pleased an audience. A wave of whistles and obscene calls were hurled at the senator. It was midday when the senator declared an end to the debacle and called a short break to allow the arena to be cleaned and prepared for the execution. There was one bear left, and the senator pleaded with the gods that it was healthy.

The attendants dragged the dead animals from the arena and spread clean sand over the blood before driving a stake in the center. A naked man was dragged into the arena and hitched to the stake. The senator stood and silenced the crowd.

"This man, a slave, was caught in the act of raping his master's wife." This brought out a chorus of shouts and whistles from the people. "And he was condemned to death by beasts in the arena." A cheer went up.

A gate opened, and the last bear ran into the arena. It looked promising, but the bear had no interest in the man. Even with several slaves prodding him with spears and hot pokers, the bear would not attack the prisoner. Finally, the exasperated senator ordered the bear driven out. Wood and brush were brought into the arena and placed around the bottom of the stake by the slave's feet. He pleaded his innocence and begged to be released, but the tinder was set alight. It was pleasing to the audience, but also a disappointment.

Instead of a gallery of exotic beasts, the pathetic spectacle had embarrassed and humiliated the senator. The Master, however, was glad, for he had brought several extra gladiators, as well as four pair of novices. Not only was the senator grateful, but his grimace was barely noticeable when the Master tripled the original price for the extras, to be paid in full before one single match was fought.

The first four bouts had been fought by the novices using wooden swords and, while entertaining, the crowd was beginning to crave blood. The praegenarii were next, but they fought with clubs, whips, and shields, so there was still no bloodshed. The senator began to worry about his political fate as the crowd grew restless.

***

Frontis was visibly excited as he hurried toward the arena for Senator Flavius' mortuary games. The senator's son had been a worthless piece of horse dung, but that didn't matter. Any excuse to see gladiators had its merits, and the fact that it was in the local amphitheater was a bonus. Frontis dutifully stood in line nearly every morning outside the senator's villa at first light to receive his pittance from the man and pledge his allegiance. Though usually only a few denari, Frontis now held two prized tickets to the games in seats among the togas. With little interest in the beasts or executions, Frontis had planned to arrive just before the afternoon sand. The crowds thickened as he neared the arena and began to search for his best friend, Actius. The smell of sausages cooking in a small tent near one of the entrances mixed with the first aromas of blood from the morning events.

"Ticket, sir?" a hawker called as he approached Frontis.

"Piss off, boy. I got tickets."

"Hey, no need to be rude!"

"Move, or I'll call a centurion."

"Enjoy the show," the hawker grumbled. "Hope you get a splinter up the ass!"

Ignoring the comment, Frontis continued toward the fourth entrance where Actius should be waiting.

"Frontis, here!" Actius called out.

He turned to see his friend running toward him.

"Am I late?" Actius asked.

"Just arrived. Come on. We're in G section, third row."

"Third row? Senator Fat-ass gave you seats in the third row? With the togas?"

"With the togas. Close enough to spit on a gladiator," he said, starting up the stairs.

"How many times did you have to suck him for these tickets?"

"Hear that?" Frontis asked of the clacking sound. "That's the wooden clubs of the praegenarii. They must be almost finished, which means the first bout is about the start. Hurry, I don't want to miss that new boy."

"You don't think he has a chance, do you?" Actius asked as they threaded their way through the crowd to their seats.

"He's one of the Master's men, and you never can tell with him what he's up to."

The two men found their seats, placed small cushions on the hard wood, and settled in.

"Did you get a program?" Actius asked. "Who is this Greek fellow fighting?"

"Here, first match. The Bearman," Frontis said, handing him the *libellus munerarius*.

"The Bearman? No chance."

"Bet?" Frontis asked.

"How much?"

"Ten sesterces."

"That the Greek wins? Easy money, but I hate to take advantage of a friend."

"Shut up and bet, good?"

"Ten pays twenty if the Greek wins."

"Done!"

"Wait, what have you heard about this Greek? You heard something, didn't you?" Actius asked, suddenly nervous.

"I know as much as you. I just have a feeling. After all, he did kill the Giant in Brundisium. And with no training. I heard he might be some kind of god-son or something."

"A god-son? Some of the Master's bullshit more like it."

"Want to cancel the bet?" Frontis asked.

"Why? You not sure of the boy now?"

"I don't want to steal your money."

"Save your pity; I'm good for it. But I'll never have to pay. Why does it stink so much? Haven't they cleaned the sand? Smells like someone burned."

"Quit complaining. We could be sitting up at the top like usual and you would complain you couldn't see the blood!"

"I'm not complaining! I just don't like the smell of burning flesh."

"Thank the gods it's not you burning."

"Yes, with Flavius it could be any one of us."

The blare of trumpets interrupted their conversation to announce the first armed match of the day.

Alexandros was excited, but much more nervous than he had expected to be as his time grew near. He wanted to talk to the Nightman, but the gladiator was nowhere to be found. Using two wooden swords, he had practiced in his cell to warm up. His apprehension increased considerably after he was brought to the arena gate. The last pair of praegenarii were finishing their match. His was the first real contest of the day. His opponent, the Bearman, stood beside him. They had walked side by side in the pompa earlier in the day, but Alexandros had barely noticed him in his excitement. This was his first opportunity to assess the man as an opponent

The Bearman's helmet rested on his right arm, and his long shield leaned against the corridor wall. His right arm was wrapped in thick cloth. A short plume decorated the crest of his helmet. Alexandros had admired the muscled gladiators in the training yard, but seeing the massive Bearman, who remained silent and unmoving, his admiration turned to loathing and fear.

He attempted, unsuccessfully, to prevent his knees from

shaking. His stomach was in knots, and he was having difficulty breathing. The Bearman was stoic in anticipation of an easy kill.

Trumpets sounded, the gate opened, and sunlight flooded the dim corridor. The arena was empty save the three armed guards who stood near the exit. Their job was to kill any winner who gave a performance that displeased the crowd and spur on anyone who lost their appetite for the match. The Greek and the Bearman were followed in the arena by a referee. They walked to the editor's box where a small table held their weapons—one straight sword for the Bearman and two for the Greek. As they examined their swords, the Greek's hands were shaking. The referee then checked the weapons and signaled his approval to the editor. Both gladiators grasped their weapons, saluted the editor and the crowd, and moved to opposite sides of the arena. Alexandros felt vulnerable in his loincloth as he watched the Bearman put on his helmet and grasp his shield, which covered him from neck to knees. Then he began to approach.

The Greek desperately tried to recall the Nightman's instructions—anything at all—but his mind went blank. In a few seconds, the Bearman was close, and the Greek began to retreat.

Think! Think! What did he say to do? The Greek cursed himself as no thoughts came forth.

He continued to back up but was careful not to get too close to the boards. Yes, that was something the Nightman had told him; don't get pinned against the boards. He moved to his left and circled the Bearman, who just kept coming. He wouldn't slow down and let the Greek think. Now the Greek began to run from his opponent. He heard whistles and shouts from the crowd. Some started throwing things at him.

"I do hope this isn't your featured bout," the senator said. "If this is what I can expect, you won't be leaving with much of my money!"

The Master was no longer smiling.

The Greek slowed a bit and, as the Bearman neared, he half-heartedly swiped at the gladiator with his swords. The crowd began to laugh. The Bearman became concerned that this boy was making him look bad, which could be fatal. He advanced and tried to corner the Greek.

"I suppose I should treat you with my winnings." Actius laughed as he pointed at the Greek. "And you, the expert on gladiators, bet on this?"

"It's far from over. Don't spend your winnings too quick."

"Have you anything I can throw at him?"

"I'm not giving you something to throw at my man! Throw your sandals!"

"Then what would I wear?"

The Greek thrust his left sword while moving to his right. The combatants were close now, and the Greek attempted to land a blow with his right hand behind the Bearman's shield. The Bearman smashed his shield into the Greek's chest. He flew off his feet and hit the ground, everything went black, and then stars appeared in front of his eyes. The Greek now remembered the Nightman had warned him that the shield was used as a weapon. Through blurry eyes, he could see the Bearman's sword rushing at him, but the large gladiator had overestimated the weight of the Greek and hit him too hard. If he had he reached the prone opponent in two steps rather than three, the Greek would not have had time to roll out of the way of his deadly thrust.

"He's had it!" Actius shouted as he jumped to his feet. "As good as dead!"

Frontis had to admit, at least to himself, it was not going well for the Greek.

The Greek staggered to his feet. The edge of the shield had cut his left thigh, the pain was nearly unbearable in his chest when he inhaled, blood trickled down his face from a broken nose, and his left eye was quickly swelling shut. He bumped into the boards, not realizing how close he had been. The Greek turned to face his opponent. The Bearman pinned him against the wall with his shield and struck with his sword, but the Greek was able to parry the blow and slip out to his left. He had lost one of his swords.

"Finish him!" Actius yelled, joining the chorus.

The Greek limped as he circled his opponent and searched for his other sword. The Bearman attempted to cut him off but, even wounded, he was too fast. He latched onto the second sword and moved to the center of the arena. Through the excruciating pain, he thought of his family and home. Running away from this man was not going to work.

The Greek stood alone in the center of the vast arena and watched the Bearman approach. Then he began juggling his swords. It was the first time he had held real swords and was acutely aware of the consequences should he accidentally grab the razor-sharp blades. But he didn't.

"What's he doing?" Actius turned to his friend. "That can't be legal. Has anyone ever done that before?"

"Not out of it yet," Frontis, now standing, replied.

The Greek's actions with the swords seemed to confound the Bearman. He moved laterally to his left away from the shield as the Bearman thrust his sword and reciprocated blow for blow, first with one sword then the other, keeping the Bearman off balance. As he struck down with the right sword, he managed to draw the other across his opponent's right arm. The cloth wrappings absorbed nearly all of the blow, though it did draw blood. The Bearman was becoming cautious of his young opponent.

"You've got him!" Frontis shouted. Others began to join his support of the Greek.

Blood ran into the Greek's mouth from his nose, the gash on his leg burned like fire, and he had to take short, shallow breaths to decrease the intense pain in his chest. He twirled the swords and moved like a panther, trying to cut behind the Bearman, who would have none of it and continually moved the shield to protect himself. The Greek moved right, in front of the shield, but when the Bearman thrust it at him again, he was prepared. He took a step back, dropped to the ground as it passed harmlessly over his head, and then jabbed up and pierced the skin on the Bearman's left arm, cutting deep into the flesh. The Bearman attempted to hit the Greek with the shield, but his arm faltered. He stepped back and thrust the lower edge of the shield into the sand, his left arm now useless. The crowd came alive at the sight of blood spirting from the Bearman's arm.

"Finish him!" Frontis called to the Greek, who was standing directly in front of him. "The advantage is yours! Kill him!"

Actius looked concerned as a cheer of support for the young fighter rose like the north wind on a cold winter day. The Greek moved toward the Bearman, who still fought back, pounding the Greek with his superior strength. He remained cautious and watched for an opening. The Bearman thrust his sword at the Greek's belly, but he pushed it up with one of his swords and jabbed with the other. His sword pierced the right side of the Bearman, who faltered, stepped back, and stumbled. The Greek gave no ground.

The Bearman knelt on one knee and rested on the handle of his sword, the point stuck in the sand. He looked up, and their eyes met. The Greek stood over him, one sword near his helmet and the other poised in the air to strike, but he couldn't do it.

"Kill him!" Frontis screamed. He jumped with excitement, clutching Actius by the arm. "What did I tell you? I knew there was something about this one!"

Then, out of the corner of his eye, the Greek caught sight of one of the armed guards and remembered the Nightman's words, "You must kill if you win or you will die." He thought of his family and freedom. Staring into the Bearman's eyes, he drove the sword into his chest and felt his body tense at the blow, then slump. His weight pulled the flesh away from the iron. The Greek looked at the blood covering the sword and became aware of the roar of the crowd.

"*Graecus, Graecus!*" Frontis shouted along with a chorus of spectators. Even Actius, who would soon be twenty sesterces poorer, was caught up in the euphoria and joined in.

Though the Greek couldn't understand Latin, he knew they were cheering for him, and it felt good. He raised both swords high in the air, walked around the outside of the arena, and stopped in front of the editor's box. Everyone was on their feet, including the Master. The Greek stared directly at him and smiled. He was free. He collapsed onto the sand.

Two men with a stretcher ran into the arena and carefully placed the unconscious Greek onto it, then disappeared under the seats headed to the infirmary. At the same time, two others went over to the body of the Bearman, rolled him onto their stretcher, and headed to the *Porta Libitinensis*. Near the gate, a figure in a blue mask representing Charon approached the body and struck the Bearman in the head with a hammer to ensure his death. Later, after his armor had been removed, the Bearman's throat would be slit for good measure.

"A fine match, don't you think?" Frontis asked with a wide smile on his face.

"Tell me truthfully, you had inside information, didn't you? You knew he would win?"

"Simply my intuition. You would not have been so quick to condemn the new fellow if you followed gladiators as I do."

"You're so full of shit, Frontis, I'm surprised you don't smell worse than this arena! A lucky guess, that's all. Now, who's up next? Care to wager again on the next match? At least give me a chance to win back my money."

"Not to fear. We've a long afternoon ahead. Plenty of time for me to increase my winnings, but perhaps, if the gods take pity on you, you might break even against me!" Frontis added, laughing.

***

When the Greek awoke, he was lying on a wooden table. Several people were standing around him.

"I see you're awake," the one in charge said.

"Who are you?"

"The medicus."

"But you're Greek?"

"The best are. How do you feel?"

"My chest hurts."

"That's to be expected with several bruised ribs, and your nose is broken. We stopped the bleeding. The gash on your leg is nothing, but you won't be fighting again for a while."

The Greek could make out another figure in the room. He was having a difficult time focusing as his left eye was swollen shut. His vision in the other was blurry, but he knew who the figure was when he spoke to the medicus.

"Come closer where I can see you," the Greek said. "I won!"

"You look like you lost." The Nightman laughed. His hair was matted, and sweat dripped from his whiskers.

"And you?"

"Another victory. The medicus says you'll live, but the wagon ride home will be worse than walking on fire."

"It doesn't matter as long as I get home."

What the Greek didn't realize was that they were talking about two different places.

* * *

Lucanus and the Master were standing together outside the amphitheater. The Master had counted out the money, kept a small portion, and handed the remainder to Lucanus to take back to the villa.

"It's a lot of money for me to carry," Lucanus said in a worried tone.

"You'll be traveling with a troop of gladiators. What better bodyguards could you want?"

"How long before you return?"

"A few weeks. I was planning to go to Capua, but the Greek's performance today changes everything. Stories and rumors are spreading already, and I plan to hurry them along. The more outrageous the tale, the higher the price for his next bout."

"You don't believe it was just luck?"

"If his victory was luck, he must have Fortuna riding on his shoulder!"

"He took a hard beating. The medicus says it will be several weeks before he can resume training."

"I have heard the possibility of major games in Pompeii in three months. If the rumors are true, he should be ready by then. That would give us enough to survive a while longer. Then, with some luck, Tiberius will have crossed the Styx!"

"Watch your tongue!" Lucanus cautioned the Master, his glance darting from side to side. "What if the wrong man should hear you say such a thing?"

"Relax, Lucanus. I fear there are many who feel the same."

They both turned toward the sound of an approaching horse.

"What of the contract with Maecenas?"

"The Nightman took care of that problem with his sword. He mentioned nothing of a family. There is no other name on the contract, so burn it when you get back. Never speak of him again. The senator can dispose of the body."

"Anything else?"

"Take care of my money!" the Master called as he mounted the horse and rode away.

***

It seemed to the Greek that there were thrice the holes and ruts in the road on the return journey. Though his ribs were tightly bandaged, the pain was nearly unbearable. He clenched his teeth and grasped the bars. The thought of returning home helped to take his mind off his anguish. It would soon be the harvest, and his father would need his help. He wondered what had happened to those goats he had been taking to market. Perhaps the dogs had driven them back to the farm. And the stories he would have to tell around the supper table after he returned!

When they eventually arrived at the school, the Greek was placed in the infirmary. His body was bruised and swollen, and it was nearly a week before he attempted to get out of bed. He was stiff and sore, but he was young and healthy and progressed faster than anyone had anticipated. On the second day back, he began asking to see the Master but was told he hadn't returned with the troop. He assumed that the man was making arrangements for his return home.

As each day passed, the Greek became stronger. He was excited and anxious and constantly asked after the Master's return. The Nightman came to visit regularly. He and the Greek were becoming closer. Now that the Greek had fought and won, they had more in common.

The Nightman had been the son of a wealthy Athenian merchant who owned cargo ships. When most of the fleet sank in a gale on a voyage to Rome, his father and all the cargo were lost. He was seized and sold into slavery to help pay the debt. Lucanus spotted him at the market and urged the Master to purchase him, thus he had ended up at the school. All this had occurred nearly six years ago, and since then he had fought eleven bouts and won all of them.

By the fifth week, the Greek had been sent back to his cell and began training again as a way to pass the time. He became agitated when he learned the Master had returned several days prior, but no one had told him. He was healed and ready for the trip home, but he did hope there was a land route back to Greece. He hated the thought of another sea voyage.

***

On his first day back, the Master stood at his familiar spot in the tower and watched his men train. He was especially pleased to see the Greek in the yard again.

"What does the medicus say of the Greek?" the Master asked Lucanus.

"He is healing well. Some light training to begin and then back to normal in a couple weeks."

"I purchased a trainer specifically for him. He's old but he was a good dimachaerus in his time. And he speaks Greek."

"The Nightman will be relieved. He didn't like training him. The Greek has been asking to see you."

"About what?"

"I don't know," Lucanus lied. "How was the trip? Are we going to Pompeii?"

"No. Those wealthy pigs don't believe we have anyone of

quality without the Giant. We might go to Paestum in two months, but we have to wait another week for an answer."

"Big or small?"

"Ten pair, if we go."

"And what about the Greek? What are they saying?"

"Most think he's a one-winner and will soon be slaughtered by a good opponent. Some think him a joke. We will find out if he is real when he fights in Paestrum."

A few days later, the Master was in the yard and noticed the Greek sparing with the Nightman. As he approached, the Greek spied him and hurried over in excited anticipation.

"I've been waiting for you. When can I leave? I'm good to travel now."

"Travel where? What do you mean?" the Master asked, perplexed.

"Thessaly."

"What about Thessaly?"

"It's my home. You told me if I won, you would give me an escort to Thessaly. I won!"

The Master burst out laughing but stopped when he saw the Greek glaring at him. "Men fight fifteen, twenty matches over many years before being given their freedom, if ever, and you expect to be set free after one? I expected you to die, but you may be of value to me. You are very stupid if you think you're going to Thessaly."

"No, you promised! You told me I would be free if I won!"

"Keep that tongue, boy, or I'll have it cut out!" The Master noticed men staring at them. He was getting angry at the nerve of this young slave. How dare he confront his owner. He turned and started to walk away when the Greek grabbed his arm and spun him back around.

But for the speed of the Greek's reflexes, he would have been dead. The Master's dagger sliced air and just nicked the Greek's throat. Lucanus stepped in front of the Master to prevent a second thrust that most likely would have reached its mark.

"He's a stupid boy! He doesn't know what he says. Spare him!" Lucanus pleaded.

Two men grabbed the Greek and pulled him away as the Master tried to push Lucanus out of his way.

"Spare him, I beg you!"

"No one touches me! You belong to me! I will do what I want with you! You will never be free! You'll die in the arena! I will see your blood, boy!"

"He doesn't know better. Spare him!" Lucanus had rarely seen the Master this angry.

"Whip him!"

"But Master—"

"Whip him! Do it, or you'll join him!"

Two guards seized the Greek and pushed him to the ground, and a third brought a length of rope. His hands were bound, and he was dragged to one of the practice poles and tied with his arms stretched high in the air so that his feet barely touched the ground. The Master and Lucanus had left the yard when the punishment began.

At first, the Greek was so angry he hardly noticed the leather as it bit into his flesh. But when the pain intensified, he screamed out his father's name, then his mother's, then he just cried. Everyone in the yard went back to their own business and ignored what was happening. The whip raised welts on his back that began to bleed. Finally, he lost consciousness. When the beating stopped, he was left hanging.

Well after dark, when the yard was deserted and the cells locked, a lone figure appeared with a dagger and trudged across the sand to the unmoving body. He reached up, cut the rope, and let the body fall to the ground. Then he picked up the Greek and carried him to the infirmary where the medicus was waiting.

The Nightman looked away as he laid the Greek on the table on his stomach. The marks on his back only served to remind him of his own scars. He gave the dagger to the medicus and left without a word.

It was late the next morning before the Greek regained consciousness. He was in pain, but it wasn't as bad as the beating he had taken in the arena. The Nightman visited him that afternoon, but the Greek remained silent. He wouldn't look at anyone. Within a few days, he was on his feet again, but the Nightman noticed a change in him. He was quiet, sullen, and there was an emptiness in his eyes. The Nightman knew that look. Everyone who faced the realization that this was their life had that look. Some never lost it; they usually didn't live. Others accepted their fate and became determined to survive, whatever it took. But one element was universal—no one was ever the same.

CHAPTER IV

WORD HAD COME TO THE MASTER THAT THEY WOULD FIGHT IN Paestum and the Greek was to participate. This was a large and prestigious venue, and much was expected of the Master's troop, so he would have to plan something special to showcase the Greek's abilities.

The young gladiator's body recovered from the beating, but when he began training again, there was an aggressiveness to it. No more juggling or comic antics to entertain the others. The look in his eyes caused even the veterans to stay clear.

After a week of training on his own, Lucanus appeared in the yard with an old gray-haired man who was tall and slim to the point of being skinny. His skin was wrinkled, and he walked slowly as if he had problems seeing. He had a long, thin face with a shock of white hair on top. They went directly to the Greek.

"Greek, this is your new trainer. He will be working with you from now on," Lucanus advised him.

"My name Urbicus. I train you."

The Greek stared at him. The man reminded him of his father, and the thought burned in his mind as he wondered if he would ever see him again.

"Where are you from?"

"I'm from Dacia, but mother from Athens. That where I learn Greek."

After Lucanus left, the old man continued. "Please, my Greek not good. At my other place, they were throw me out, too old. I have nothing, no home, no money. I starve in street. Please, do not tell Master. Eyes not good. Slow now, but once great. Can train you. Please, let me train. No tell anyone or I die in street." Tears streamed down his cheeks.

"I will not tell anyone. You will be my trainer," the Greek replied.

Urbicus smiled at the prospect of a new home and a future, at least for as long as he could keep the Greek alive.

The Greek noticed a difference immediately when he started training with Urbicus. He couldn't see well and was slow, but he knew the techniques of the dimachaerus. As the days passed, the Greek's anger was somewhat tempered, and he grew fond of Urbicus. The Greek had never heard of Dacia, but Urbicus was glad to tell stories any chance he had to help alleviate his terrible loneliness.

He explained that Dacia was north of Greece and his father had a small farm. When he was around eight years old, they were forced off the land by a war and became refugees. His father had been unable to feed his large family, nine brothers and sisters, so some, including Urbicus, were sold into slavery. He ended up a house boy to a wealthy couple in Rome.

As he grew older, a friend of this family, who was a lanista, noticed how athletic he was and bought him. Urbicus had fought his first bout at seventeen and quickly rose through the ranks to become a good draw, though he was never a star. He retired at thirty-two and became a trainer. Now with his health deteriorating, his last owner had thrown him out. Then the Master arrived looking for a dimachaerus who spoke Greek, and he became Urbicus' savior.

The Greek enjoyed listening to Urbicus' stories, though he doubted the truth of most. The trainer knew every trick and move there was for fighting with two swords, and the Greek was a sponge soaking up all his information. The Greek was much more cheerful now that Urbicus had arrived, but at times there were flashes that struck fear into those around him.

One day Urbicus was shuffling across the yard when another gladiator accidentally backed into him and knocked him to the ground. When the Greek saw this, he attacked the man. Fortunately for him, the Greek only had a wooden sword, or he would have perished. But even so, he beat the man severely before being pulled off. The Master had him confined to his cell for several days for the infraction, an action that angered the Greek even more. Those close to him could see the pain and hatred he carried. So much hatred for someone so young.

***

The time drew near for the Greek's next bout. The Master was excited at the prospect of a large payday and had a special event planned for him which would either enhance his reputation or kill him.

It was a long six-day journey southwest to Paestum, a town south of Campania, the region that contained one of largest concentrations of gladiators in Italy. Many stars of the arena had been made in this region that was rivaled only by Rome, but, under Emperor Tiberius, Rome had fallen out of favor. Paestum wasn't as prestigious as Pompeii or Capua, but it was still one of the premier venues for gladiators, and the Master knew that he could make the reputation of the Greek there. He was taking a chance by not bringing any other star. He had decided to rest the Nightman, and with the Bearman dead at the hands of the Greek, his reputation was suffering. It had been humiliating for him to have to beg the editor to include him in these games. The outcome would determine his future.

***

The Greek enjoyed the pompa. The crowd was enthusiastic and strained to see the wild boy from Greece. They wondered who he would fight. The first day was dedicated to the animal hunts, followed by some executions by beasts, and then a local troop of gladiators would entertain. The second day consisted of a repeat, except the Master's gladiators would be pitted against members of a Capua school in the afternoon. He would have preferred pairing his own men but had no choice in the decision. He had managed, however, to get the match he wanted for the Greek.

The Greek sat alone in his cell, waiting impatiently for his bout. He had hoped Urbicus would be with him, but the trip was too much for the old man. Urbicus was nervous, more so than the Greek, as he awaited news from Paestum. Their futures were now one and the same.

The crowd erupted when a Thracian, a local young man named Callistus who had a promising future in the arena, entered. He was tall, well-muscled, handsome, and had fought five bouts, all victories. He was well on his way to becoming a star. He knew how to handle a crowd. Callistus strutted around the arena carrying his helmet on his right arm and waving his shield in the air to the appreciation of the people.

Then the Greek entered. He had a scar on his leg, the marks of the whipping on his back, a crooked nose, and unkempt shoulder-length hair. Whistles and shouts greeted him. It was fortunate he couldn't understand Latin.

They were given their weapons, saluted the editor, and turned to face one another. Callistus immediately charged at the Greek, who sidestepped him. He hadn't fought anyone this nimble. Before he could get set, the Thracian was on him again. The Greek moved backward, but could barely stay ahead of his opponent. He didn't like the curved sword the Thracian used, and his small shield was more dangerous than the large ones he had faced before.

The Greek struck at the shield and knocked down the rapid thrusts of the Thracian's sword, but he was quickly winded, and his legs were tiring. The mid-afternoon sun bore down on the Greek, causing streams of sweat to run down his cheeks. Nerves had knotted his stomach at the beginning, but he was starting to calm down and remember Urbicus' words. As they went around the arena, he began looking for a weakness in Callistus. The Greek noticed that he thrust his sword out and up, which exposed his lower right side, but the back stroke was also dangerous.

The Greek had been focused on the Thracian's right side when he slipped in the sand. Off balance, the Greek jabbed his left sword in the ground to keep from falling. The Thracian moved in for the kill.

Unfortunately, Callistus' deadly blow missed the right side of the Greek's exposed neck, but it did draw a bit of blood. The Greek spun around in a flash; Callistus had never seen anything like it. He regained his balance and smashed a blow down on the Thracian's shield, the viciousness of which caught him off guard and rattled him. A second strike landed on his helmet and made the metal ring. He swayed backward and exposed his chest slightly, but it was all the Greek needed.

He plunged his sword into the Thracian's stomach just below the ribs. The sword did not penetrate too deep, and the blow certainly wasn't fatal, but Callistus knew he could no longer fight.

The referee moved closer to the combatants as Callistus staggered back one step. He was about to drop his shield and sword in surrender when the Greek landed a second blow that wasn't superficial. An unexpected amount of anger was behind the thrust. His sword went into the left side of the Thracian's rib-cage, pierced his heart, severed his spine, and emerged out his back. The Greek withdrew the sword as rapidly as he had plunged it in. Callistus was dead before he hit the sand.

The Greek walked to the center of the arena and thrust his swords into the air. Blood dripped down the lethal one onto his shoulder. The Greek lowered his swords and stared back at the people. He won! They should be cheering him! He dropped the swords and walked back toward the exit gate. He was exhausted and just wanted to lie down in the cool of his cell.

The editor glared at the Master sitting next to him. "My Thracian was surrendering when your boy murdered him!"

"I saw the blow strike before the Thracian dropped his weapons or raised a finger, and the referee hadn't stepped in. It was a legitimate kill! And besides, we had a deal. You still have a chance to get even."

The editor's face was red with anger, but he bit his lip. The Master was right; this wasn't over.

The Greek stood by the exit gate, but it did not open. Two men came in and dragged the body of Callistus out of the arena through the *Porta Libitinensis*. A young slave ran in, picked up the Greek's swords, dropped them in the sand in front of him, and scampered out as a mouse flees for the cover of darkness when a lamp is lit. The Greek didn't understand why they had brought his swords back, but then another Thracian walked into the arena.

Amandus was tall, heavyset, muscular, and had a definite swagger as he strolled around the arena.

He strutted up to the Greek and motioned to the swords. "Pick them up, Greek."

"You're Greek?"

"They can put that on your gravestone. Pick up your swords."

"I already fought. I refuse!"

Amandus moved closer. "Listen to the people. If you don't pick up the swords, I will kill you and be a hero." He raised his shield and sword, and the arena shook from the noise.

Streams of sweat ran down his cheeks, and he could hardly swallow, his mouth was so dry. The muscles in his legs twitched from exhaustion as he reached down and retrieved his swords. The Thracian jumped at him, but the Greek avoided the blow.

The Greek shifted to his right away from Amandus as he tried to regain some strength. The short break helped, but the swords seemed to have doubled in weight. He wanted to slow the pace, but this Thracian was much more experienced than Callistus and a far better gladiator.

The Greek continued to retreat as Amandus attempted to strike. He defended himself against the blows, but his arms were getting weary from the tremendous pressure exerted by the stronger opponent. Then he remembered Urbicus' words: everyone has a weakness.

Amandus never gave ground and was precise with his strikes. The Greek didn't know how much longer he could go on. The curved sword of the Thracian whizzed by the Greek's face time after time. He was having more difficulty intercepting the thrusts.

Suddenly, he noticed something. In the instant before the Thracian struck with his shield, he dropped it ever so slightly. It wasn't much, but it was all he had. The Greek felt as though he would collapse anytime and believed the crowd would call for his death. The thought of a possible kill invigorated him. He began twirling his swords, which seemed to confuse the Thracian.

The Thracian became cautious, which was more than the Greek had hoped for as it gave him a chance to recuperate. They came together again, and the Greek began to move right, trying to draw a thrust from the shield. Now he understood why Urbicus had him strike at a small target he had held in his hand. Occasionally, the Greek would strike true, but almost as often, he hit Urbicus' hand with the tip of the wooden sword. The old trainer never winced or complained. He had practiced this over and over and had often complained that it was useless.

Several times Amandus struck at the Greek with his shield as he continued to move right. The Greek managed to avoid each blow, but he must strike soon, and he would have to move into the blow to reach his target. The hit from the shield would surely knock him to the ground. And if he missed...

Then the Greek saw it! A slight flash of flesh under the rim of the Thracian's helmet. The Greek struck with a hard, straight thrust of his right sword. The Thracian's shield caught the Greek's arm and pushed it into the air. He turned his head to deflect the blow but still took a hard hit to the chest. The Greek tumbled to the ground, rolled, and was back on his feet, but the Thracian was right there trying to cut the Greek's legs.

The Greek retreated again as Amandus pushed forward. The Thracian stopped and stood stock still, staring at his younger opponent. The Greek thought it a trap and jumped back, but the Thracian didn't move. When the shield fell from his hand the Greek could see why: a stream of blood was flowing down Amandus' left side. The Greek hadn't been able to see it with the shield in place, but his blow had hit its target. The artery on the left side of the

Thracian's neck was severed; he was bleeding to death. The crowd fell silent as the Thracian toppled to the ground and his lifeblood turned the sand red.

The swords slipped from the Greek's hands as he staggered toward the exit gate. If he had to face another opponent, he wouldn't pick them up again. He had nothing left and would gladly welcome death. He stood staring at the closed door for what seemed an eternity before it opened. He walked through and collapsed on the floor of the tunnel.

The Master couldn't help but gloat, though he wanted to be a gracious winner. He would need these men in the future, and after the Greek's performance today, that future looked much brighter.

"You need to be careful with what you've created," the editor said.

"Perhaps you would be interested in purchasing him?" the Master asked.

"You should give him to me as compensation for my two dead Thracians."

"All part of the game, wouldn't you say? It could have gone the other way, and you wouldn't have heard me complaining."

"Yes, well, apparently you are a much better man than I," the editor said.

"You knew his reputation when you asked for him."

"Reputation? Lies and rumors spread by you. You were a cheat and a liar when in the arena, and you still are. You bring disgrace to the honorable profession of gladiator."

"Honorable profession? We train pigs for their slaughter to entertain the masses. There is nothing honorable about this."

"Those Thracians were honorable men! They meant something to the people!"

"Did they? Their bodies are still warm and their 'fans' chant my Greek's name. A gladiator's memory soaks into the sand with his blood!"

"You should watch your back, Master."

As the Greek lay on the floor, he could hear the crowd chanting *"Graecus."* He wished he could have reappeared in the arena to see the faces of those who had condemned him, but his body wouldn't move. Though uninjured, close to an hour in the arena had left him severely dehydrated.

The Master had sent word for the medicus to stay with the Greek and that he should be sent home in the middle of the night. As well, he ordered an armed guard, not for the Greek's protection, but to protect his property from the possibility of kidnap. There would be many lanistae who wanted a rising star like the Greek.

The Greek was feeling better when he finally arrived back at the school. Urbicus hobbled to him and hugged the Greek while tears streamed down his face. He had heard of the outcome, but he still begged for all the details of the victory. Very few men had won two consecutive bouts, Urbicus told him, so he was now in an elite class. He broke down in tears again when the Greek told him he had won because of his training. As news of the victory spread through the school, it brought a newfound respect for the Greek and a veil of fear among the other gladiators. Everyone wondered who would have to face him in the arena next, a fate that seemed certain death.

Two days after their return, the Master had the Greek moved from his tiny cell that faced the training yard to one of the larger rooms behind the baths that had small windows looking out over the countryside. The Nightman lived in this section; the Greek was moved next to him. The beds were bigger and there were two chairs, but most of all the Greek enjoyed gazing out the window.

The Greek had resumed training a week after his return, and at that time the Master announced they would be fighting in Beneventum. A match at Pompeii continued to elude him, but Beneventum was an acceptable substitute. The Greek would be the featured performer at the games in three months. The Master had arranged for him to fight a hoplomachus, a heavily armored gladiator named after the Greek hoplite warrior. The Master told the editor the Greek was Athenian and the hoplomachus would appear in Spartan armor, thus they would recreate the spectacle of the Peloponnesian War.

Training had been going well, but then Urbicus became ill. He developed a hacking cough which the medicus attributed to pneumonia and was moved into the infirmary. Urbicus protested the move. He believed that if he didn't prove himself useful, he would be dismissed. But the Greek had more influence than he realized, so Urbicus remained safe. The Greek visited Urbicus every chance he had and sometimes sat with him late into the night, but the medicus was evasive when the Greek questioned him about Urbicus' condition. He told the Master the truth; it was only a matter of days, maybe a week, before Urbicus would succumb to his disease.

Four days later, the Greek was sparing in the yard when Lucanus approached him. The medicus had requested his presence in the infirmary. The Greek hurried to Urbicus' side and was sitting next to him that afternoon when he died. The Greek returned to his cell and wept. He refused the call to dinner. The next day, Urbicus was buried in the gladiator's cemetery outside the walls of the compound with all the honors due someone who had fallen in the arena.

His death pushed the Greek into a bout of depression. He refused to train, bathe, or eat for several days. The Nightman was finally able to persuade him to return to his routine, but he trained with much less enthusiasm than before. Not for the first time, the Master wondered whether placing all of his hopes on the Greek's shoulders was a good idea.

***

It was less than six weeks to Beneventum. The Master sent a messenger to Capua with the funds to hire a new trainer for the Greek. He had received an inquiry from a man a few weeks prior, but he didn't speak Greek, and at that time there was no need for his services. The Master decided to take Lucanus and make the two-day trip to the slave market in Brundisium in hopes of finding someone cheap who was bilingual.

The slave markets were not as full as usual due to the relative calm in the Empire; wars and invasions always replenished the stalls. Anything could be had here, for the right price, whether one needed a domestic or common laborer, a skilled worker, or a sex toy. The vendors called out with bargains as they walked along the row of shops, but the Master went directly to a gentleman he had dealt with in the past.

"Master," the fellow greeted them as they approached. "I have many specials for you today, my friend."

"Special high prices, Mercatus."

"You hurt me. I always give you the best deals. What are you looking for? I'm afraid I have nothing for your school. Peace is difficult for an honest merchant."

"There isn't an honest merchant within an arrow's shot of me. Any one of you would cheat your own fathers or sell your mothers."

"We only try to make a living, just as you."

"No gladiators today. Do you have anyone who speaks Greek as well as Latin?"

"Yes, of course...maybe. I will send my boy to see," he replied. A young boy who was sitting nearby jumped up when the merchant called him. After instructing him with the Master's wants, the boy disappeared into the large shop. "Business is good?" he continued.

"Terrible. Tiberius offers no games. The senators do not want to appear free-spending, so my gladiators do not fight but continue to eat. Tough times."

"Yes, Tiberius makes it difficult for everyone."

The boy returned leading a woman. She was short and slim, had long matted hair, and she wore a filthy tunic. She had never been pretty. Her face was creased with wrinkles, though she was probably no more than twenty-five years old. Even from a distance, they could smell her foul odor. She stood silently staring at the ground.

"What's this?" Mercatus slapped the boy hard with the back of his hand. "You bring us this piece of shit! She is only good to feed to the beasts! I apologize, Master. This boy is stupid. I sell quality merchandise."

The Master ignored him and walked over to the woman. "You speak Greek?" he asked her in Greek.

"Yes," she whispered.

"Where are you from?"

"I was in Tarentum," she answered so softly he couldn't hear.

"Speak up, slave."

"I was in Tarentum," she repeated more forcibly.

"Where did you learn Greek?"

"Crete."

"Is that where you are from?"

"Yes."

"You also speak Latin?" he asked, switching back to Latin.

"Yes," she responded.

Turning to Mercatus, the Master asked, "What do you want for her?"

"For her? Very valuable. Speaks Greek and Latin. Very expensive. Difficult to find a woman like this. Top quality."

"How much?"

"One hundred."

"Sesterces?!"

"Yes, one hundred sesterces. A bargain."

"You were going to feed her to the beasts a moment ago. Ten."

"Ten! The governor will give me twenty to throw her to the lions!"

"Fifteen, last offer."

"Fifty."

"Lucanus, let's go. We'll see that other seller you mentioned," he said as they started to walk away.

"Okay, yes, twenty, but no lower."

Without turning back, the Master said, "Fifteen."

"Yes, good, for you, fifteen."

After the Master paid, they led the woman away to their cart and began the long journey back to the school. She sat in the back staring at the floor. It was late in the evening when they reached the tiny inn where they would stay the night. The inn was one building that was mostly stable. The top floor consisted of three rooms. A small dining room and bar were squeezed in one corner of the lower floor. Lucanus unhitched the mules and led them into the stable, where he fed and watered them, then returned out into the cold, damp night to retrieve the woman and chained her to a post behind the animals. The Master had entered the dining room and was eating porridge and dark bread when Lucanus came in.

"No slaves!" the owner yelled at him.

"He's mine," the Master responded. "Mind your tongue, or you'll lose it! Bring more food for him."

The innkeeper mumbled to himself, but the Master was too big a man to confront.

"Is the woman safe?"

"Chained up with the mules."

"Take her some bread and water. We don't want her to die. Then we'd have to go back for another. You can eat in the room."

The innkeeper's wife, a short, fat, grumpy woman, set a bowl and some bread before Lucanus."Bring me some more bread and a jug of water," Lucanus ordered the woman. She growled under her breath about the nerve of a slave to give her orders but shuffled away.

When she returned, she threw the bread on the table and set the jug down hard, splashing out some of the water.

"I don't know why we have to stay here every time we go to Brundisium," Lucanus complained. "There's a better inn a few miles back."

"This place is cheap. If you want to pay, we'll stay there next time. Now go, take care of the woman."

Lucanus picked up the food and water and headed for the stable. Afterwards, he went to their room, ate his supper, and curled up on the floor next to the bed.

The Master finished eating and ordered a jug of wine. Two men entered the bar and sat at a corner table. One had a patch on his left eye, and the other limped. As soon as they were comfortable, the Master went over to their table.

"I've a jug of wine to share with my own kind," the Master said.

"And what kind would that be?" Eyepatch asked in an unfriendly manner.

"The kind of sand and blood."

Both men looked up at him, and a wave of recognition spread over them.

"Always glad to share wine with the Master." Eyepatch motioned to an empty chair. "Join us."

"You know me?"

"I fought against your men years ago in Capua. I am Fabius, a Thracian, and this fine gentleman is Artorius, one of the best retiarius to have ever walked the sand."

"I remember you. What happened? Were you freed?"

"Abandoned, more like it. I lost my eye while training. Caught the point of a wooden sword. Artorius here, he got the back of his lower leg sliced and can't fight no more. We both got kicked out by our lanista and ended up living on the street. How'd you get into it, on your own or forced?"

"I was a lawyer in Athens. An Athenian was accused of getting into a fight with a Roman soldier and beating him to death. They charged the Athenian and put him on trial. No one would help, so I volunteered to defend him. When the trial began, they added charges that he was a Christian and refused to sacrifice to the emperor. Then they accused me of the same thing. I was found guilty and sentenced to die in the arena at Rome.

"When they brought me in, I was determined to take that gladiator to Hades with me. So when they gave me a sword and shield, I overwhelmed him and sliced him to pieces. That was in front of Augustus. He immediately converted my sentence from death to being a gladiator for ten years. Seven years later I returned to fight in Rome in front of Augustus, who remembered me and was so impressed with my victory that he freed me on the spot."

"Fortuna rides with you. I can see that, Master. For us, not so. A few years after we had been on the street, we met again in Tarentum and decided to go into business together."

"What kind of business?" the Master inquired.

The men hesitated, then Fabius said, "Bodyguards, sometimes, but mostly we take care of problems for people...people with money who want to eliminate a problem permanently. If you should ever need our services, just ask the innkeeper. He knows how to get hold of us."

"I'll remember that. More wine!" the Master called to the innkeeper when he noticed their jug was empty.

The three drank long into the night before the Master finally stumbled up the stairs to his room and collapsed onto the bed. They had planned to leave early, but Lucanus couldn't rouse the Master. The mules were prepared and the cart loaded by the time the Master showed up. They arrived back at the villa late that evening. The Master instructed Lucanus to place the woman with the domestic slaves, who protested her presence and insisted she sleep with the pigs in the barn.

The following day, the woman was sent to the baths. Her hair was cut and she was given new clothes before Lucanus took her into the training yard to meet the Greek. Everyone stared at her. It was rare for a woman to be present while the men trained and, because of this fact, Lucanus had doubts as to the Master's plan. If she was to translate for the Greek and his new trainer, who hadn't arrived yet, she would be with him constantly and could distract the others. Given her appearance, even after the thorough cleaning, it shouldn't be too much of a problem. But she was female, and not all the men were given access to female companionship on a regular basis.

Lucanus explained to the woman that her role was to translate for the Greek. She would be given to him and housed in his cell. The Greek was sparing with the Nightman when they approached. "Tell the Greek what I just told you," he instructed the woman.

She began to speak in hushed tones.

"Speak up!" Lucanus shouted as the woman winced in anticipation of being struck. When no blow came, she continued telling the Greek her purpose.

"What is your name?" the Greek asked when she finished. He wasn't pleased with the prospect of this woman following him around like a puppy follows a boy who has become its new master.

"Murena."

Lucanus left them and explained to the other trainers the reason for the woman's presence. They were not happy with this show of preferential treatment. Even though the others realized his skill and potential, there was still jealousy among some of the more experienced gladiators. But, though they grumbled amongst themselves, they all knew better than to complain.

After Lucanus had left them, the Greek said, "I am the Greek and this is the Nightman. He is also Greek. Where are you from?"

"Crete," she replied.

"I'm from Thessaly and he is Athenian. Have you ever been to Thessaly?"

"No."

With that, the two gladiators returned to sparing as the woman stood staring at the ground, which the Greek found very distracting. His family could never afford a slave and he wasn't familiar with owning anyone.

That evening after their meal, Murena returned with the Greek to his cell and sat on the floor in a corner while he and the Nightman conversed.

He was becoming close to the older gladiator. He had begun thinking of the Nightman as the only family he had, and was surprised to learn the man had a wife and children on the outside. This, he had explained, was why he left for several days at a time when not training. The Greek couldn't understand why he returned, given he had a choice, but, in fact, he didn't have one. The Master had a long reach in southeastern Italy and would harm his family if they tried to escape, and there was the Master's brand on the left side of his neck. If anyone spied it, he would immediately be killed as a runaway slave. No, he would always return, but he did hope for freedom one day if he survived long enough.

The Greek was uncomfortable having Murena sleep on the floor, and by the fourth night invited her to share the bed. He had only meant that she sleep beside him, but she misinterpreted the gesture and before entering his bed, slipped out of her clothes in the dark and lay next to him. He felt her nakedness and became aroused as she caressed him. He was the kindest man she had ever known, and she wanted to show her appreciation. She pulled up his tunic and moved on top. Straddling him, she guided him into her and began rising up and down while softly moaning. It didn't take long before she felt his body tense and release into her, then she slid off him and quickly fell asleep. The Greek lay awake, staring into the darkness.

***

A week later, the new trainer arrived at the school. He was a small man, not much bigger than the Greek, but he was fast and agile. He had also fought with two swords. His name was Cassius Victorinus, and he had lived up to his name with twenty-two wins, three draws, and no losses. The scars on his body read like a map of his career. The Greek marveled at his ears; he had never seen such large ones, though they had many pieces missing. And his nose had been broken like the Greek's. Cassius had a bad temper, was quick to anger, and didn't like having to depend on a woman to translate his instructions. However, he was an excellent teacher, and it wasn't long before the Greek began to improve.

Day after day the Master, who was becoming more confident about his impending match, stood in the tower and watched the Greek. The Master spread word that he was taking bets on the Greek's certain victory and offered long odds.

Cassius was a fine trainer, but he was arrogant. He disliked Greeks but knew the Greek could offer him a huge payday if he continued to win. His style was to show the Greek who was boss. He chastised him and sometimes struck him when he wasn't pleased with the results of his training. However, one morning he quickly, and violently, learned his place in the hierarchy when, unhappy with the Greek's efforts, Cassius decided to take out his frustrations on Murena. She was becoming bolder each day and stood next to Cassius calling out his instructions to the Greek. Cassius struck Murena a hard blow on the side of her head, knocking her to the ground. It was the first time she had been hit since being given to the Greek.

Cassius realized his mistake when he caught a glimpse of the anger in the Greek's eyes. He was still fast, but he was nowhere near as fast as the Greek. He attempted to defend himself from the blow, but the wooden sword smashed down and broke his left arm. The Greek then used his other sword against Cassius' right ear, a blow that would leave him deaf. Another strike hit him in the testicles, and as he doubled over in pain, a vicious blow landed on the top of his head that rendered Cassius unconscious before he struck the ground.

The Nightman, who had been training nearby, and two other gladiators, seized the Greek and pulled him away, as much to protect him from the retribution of the guards as to save Cassius.

The Master had observed all from the tower. "Lucanus!" he called.

"I saw, but remember—"

"Have the Greek thrown in a small cell alone, no food or water."

"For how long?" Lucanus asked.

"Until tomorrow morning. Send Cassius to the infirmary and call in the medicus. Send the woman back to the Greek's cell, and Lucanus, be sure nothing happens to her." The punishment was lenient. They were going to Beneventum in less than two weeks and the Greek was the main attraction. He was going to be a star and the Master had plans to regain his wealth on the blades of the Greek. He could ill afford to harm the young gladiator.

Cassius would recover from his wounds but he was never right in the head after that day. He would lose his balance when walking and became forgetful. The Greek, despite his young age, was no fool. He now understood the power he possessed.

CHAPTER V

FOR THE TRIP TO BENEVENTUM, THE GREEK AND MURENA RODE IN an open cart, though they were shackled to the floor. Murena was in high spirits and chatted along the way. For the first time in her life she felt happy. She had never attended gladiatorial games and was excited at the prospect and confident in the Greek's ability to win. She had been studying his opponent and advised him of the man's weaknesses. Slaves often sat in silence but developed keen powers of observation. Even though she didn't know a lot about the matches, she was a quick study. In the back of her mind, she knew her fate was forever tied to the Greek's.

What Murena didn't know was that the Master had, about a week before the Greek attacked Cassius, changed his opponent for the match in Beneventum. The original had been a young fighter with a promising future, but the new man was older, bigger, stronger, and had much more experience. He was known as the Boarman and was as vicious as his namesake. He would prove a tough opponent. If the Greek survived, the win would enhance his reputation significantly.

The Greek would fight last late in the afternoon. He relaxed alone in his cell and waited for the appointed time as Murena had wanted to see the events of the day. She found a place early in the morning and stood at the very top of the arena with other female slaves. She was thrilled with the events but found standing all day with little food and water difficult. The sun was scorching hot, but she was unwavering in her desire to see her man perform.

The Greek warmed up in his cell with the wooden swords, which felt natural in his hands now. When his time came, two guards appeared and asked for the swords because they wanted to be sure he was unarmed as they escorted him to the entrance gate. He was rapidly gaining a reputation as a dangerous man.

The Greek recognized the Boarman as they stood together waiting to enter the arena. He had seen him in the training yard but never paid him much heed other than to notice his large size. The Boarman stood in silence with a smile on his lips. He believed he had found the Greek's weakness and was confident in a victory.

The Greek planned to walk to the center of the arena and put on a show for the audience by juggling the swords while backing away from his opponent. Then he would strike like lightning. He would have the people crying his name again. The doors swung open and temporarily blinded them as they walked out of the dark tunnel toward the editor's box. The equipment of the hoplomachus was similar to a Thracian's, except that the hoplomachus used a thrusting spear as his main weapon and carried a dagger. They examined their weapons and turned to advance to the center of the arena when the Boarman caught the Greek's eye.

"I'm going to cut out your heart and feed it to that whore!" the Boarman snarled in Greek. "And then cut out her cunt and watch her bleed to death!"

For the first time, an opponent was taunting the young gladiator.

What did he say about a whore? Who is he talking about? Does he mean Murena? The Greek was rattled.

Out of the corner of his eye, the Greek saw the Boarman rushing at him. He turned, defended against the thrust of his spear, and moved out of the way. However, the strike had dislodged one of his swords, which fell onto the sand.

Everything happened so fast that the Greek had trouble concentrating. He kept thinking about the Boarman's words, but the Boarman knew exactly what he was doing. He rushed at the Greek as a bull mad from biting flies charges at an innocent passerby in his anger. The Greek searched desperately for his other sword. The Boarman realized his advantage and moved closer to where it lay on the sand.

The Greek became obsessed with regaining his sword and

continually moved toward it, but the Boarman remained steadfast and guarded the fallen sword as though it were life itself. The Greek would strike at his spear, but then the Boarman's shield was free to swing at him. One time it glanced off the top of his head. Though not serious, the blow caused it to bleed profusely.

High in the stands, Murena was shouting for the Greek and admiring his skill. She did not realize the danger he was in. She loved being part of the crowd, and when a chorus of *Graecus* spread around the structure, she attempted to inform the women around her that the Greek was her man. She had never been proud of anyone before that moment.

As the Greek attempted to retrieve the sword, he had to repeatedly dodge the point of the Boarman's spear and was cut several times on his arms and torso. His head continued to bleed. He darted from side to side but could find no weakness in the Boarman. The sword in the sand became his point of focus, but the Boarman knew exactly where it was and never moved far away. The Boarman would take two steps, just enough that the Greek thought he had a chance and would lunge for it, then cut him off with another thrust of the spear.

From the editor's box, the Master also knew the Greek was in trouble, but he wasn't too concerned. If the Greek won, he would receive a substantial prize from the editor, which, in fact, belonged to the Greek, but the Master had no intention of ever relinquishing any of it. And he didn't care if the Greek lost. He had pushed up the odds and had several of his men bet against him, so either way was assured of a huge payout. Had this been any other gladiator, the Greek would have dropped his other sword, knelt, and surrendered and, given his popularity with the crowd, they most likely would spare his life. But it was not in his nature to surrender.

The Greek was pommeled yet again as the Boarman used his spear as a club and knocked him to the ground, but he immediately sprang up and away from certain death. Loyalties shifted from the Greek to the Boarman and back depending on which one seemed to be ahead at any given point. By the time the Greek had regained his footing, the Boarman had his spear and shield raised high in triumph. The Greek stared at his naked chest and ached to plunge his sword into it, but it seemed impossible to get close enough. Then it hit him.

The Greek stood tall and began to play with his sword, twirling it on one hand, slicing the air, and shifting it from hand to hand as he mocked the Boarman. He moved closer, and the Boarman charged once again. The Greek feigned right but moved left, slipped in the sand, caught himself, and just missed another blow by the Boarman who stepped back and raised his hands in triumph. The Greek straightened up and in one motion flipped the sword so that he grasped the tip of the blade, drew back, and threw it at the exposed chest of the Boarman.

His shield dropped back in place and obscured the Greek's view. The young gladiator now stood helpless in the middle of the arena, not knowing if he had struck the Boarman.

The crowd gasped. No one had ever done such a thing for as long as gladiators had fought. This was what they had come for— the new and unexpected. A deafening roar rose from the onlookers, and another chorus of *Graecus* surrounded the combatants. People who attended the games on a regular basis realized the plight of the Greek as they could see no better than him if the sword had indeed reached its mark. It seemed no one knew except the Boarman.

The Boarman couldn't believe that he had a sword dangling out of his belly. He covered the sword with his shield and attempted to pull it out with his other hand. It had struck on the right side just below the navel and above his protective leather belt. It had pierced the skin, but no vital organs. With his attention momentarily distracted, he felt a tremendous force against his shield. The Greek had thrown himself at it and knocked the Boarman backward. Before he could regain his balance, the Greek grasped the sword lying on the sand and stepped back.

When the Boarman came to rest, the sword had bounced enough

that it fell out by its own weight. He had endured worse wounds. His attention was diverted back to the Greek, who struck at him once more, but he counterattacked and pushed the Greek away. When the Boarman glanced down, he saw that part of his intestines were slipping out of the gash in his belly. He placed his left arm over the wound and held the shield tight to his body.

Sweat and blood obliterated the Greek's face, and he was more frustrated than ever. The Boarman continued to press him and throw insults that flustered the Greek, who was allowing his anger to push him to recklessness. He drove at the Boarman and repeatedly ducked back out to avoid the thrust of the shield.

Then he noticed the Boarman's shield wasn't moving. Perhaps it was a ploy to lure him in, but the Boarman seemed to move slower. The Greek attempted to maneuver to where he could see behind the shield but found it impossible. He sensed an advantage and ignored the other sword lying on the ground and attacked his opponent.

As the Greek struck over and over at the Boarman's spear, his shield remained tight against his body. The older gladiator realized what the Greek was doing and knew he must counteract it. When the Greek moved in again, he swung out his shield and struck him. It was a much weaker blow than before. Momentarily caught in the rush against the Greek, he had failed to notice a length of his intestines that were now hanging down from the gash.

The Greek pressed the Boarman, who had to retreat as he scrambled to prevent more of his intestines from coming out. He could feel himself weakening. Finally, the Greek pushed the Boarman back far enough to retrieve his second sword. The Boarman's words no longer bothered him as the Greek planned his slow, painful death. He walked to the center of the arena, twirling and juggling his swords, and the crowd went wild.

Murena was caught up in the euphoria. She jumped and screamed until she began to lose her voice. The people were in a frenzy, worked up by the previous matches and pushed over the edge by the brutal combat before them in this final match.

And the best was yet to come. Everyone knew the Greek let no opponent surrender, so viewing a kill was a sure thing. Fights broke out in the stands between supporters of the Greek and those of the Boarman, and even the Master was caught up in the excitement and stood cheering on the Greek.

The Boarman knew he had to keep fighting. The Greek played with the older gladiator as a cat with a wounded mouse, preferring to torture before the ecstasy of the kill. He circled the Boarman, constantly swinging his swords. He would feign an attack, withdraw, and strike from behind before the Boarman could turn around. The Boarman's body was being cut to pieces. He had ten wounds for every one on the Greek.

The Greek felt rejuvenated. Gaining the upper hand had given him his second wind, and he took full advantage of it. The crowd was out of control. Patrons were being beaten—several would be found dead after the arena emptied—and many were no longer paying attention to the bout. The editor had ordered more guards into the arena before he and the Master discreetly removed themselves from their box to the safety of the bowels of the arena.

The Greek was in his own little world, oblivious to the violence erupting around him, and could only hear the chants of his name. The referee stood off to the side, quaking with fear. The Boarman was growing weaker and stumbling around when a crazed fan managed to jump into the arena and come to his support.

The fan placed himself between the two combatants. The Greek hesitated two heartbeats before driving his sword through the fan's chest. Gazing into the stands, he could see the people shaking their fists, fighting, and screaming, while others were scrambling over the railings in an attempt to enter the arena. The Greek stepped over the body and began to realize the danger should more make it onto the sand, and decided to end the match. He pressed the Boarman, who finally fell to his knees. Unable to get up, he dropped his sword and shield and sat with his head down, but he managed to look up into the eyes of the Greek just before the fatal blow.

"Now I will cut out your heart!" the Greek said as his blade pierced the Boarman's chest.

Spectators swarmed him before he could reach the exit. He cut down two or three, which caused the others to halt and allowed him time to reach the gate. It closed behind him, even though he still held both swords. No one had dared ask for them. Once locked in his cell, a guard came to him and requested the surrender of the swords. He lay on the bed, exhausted, as the medicus came in to tend his wounds.

Though unhurt, it would be several hours before Murena could escape the violence and return to him. It had been the best day of her life.

On the return trip, the Greek and Murena were in the last cart and once more accompanied by several armed guards. The Master preferred Germans as the most loyal and fearsome guards and had purchased three more in Beneventum with some of the winnings from the Greek. His prizes were increasing in size exponentially. The Master continued to keep it all, but it was becoming more difficult as Murena could understand the talk amongst the other gladiators and had begun to realize that victors were paid. The Greek had asked Lucanus, but he pleaded ignorance and even the Nightman didn't want to become involved. Others, though, were glad to cause trouble if the opportunity presented itself and had urged the Greek to confront the Master about his missing funds. This proved impossible as the Master avoided him.

The Greek's wounds were not serious, but once they returned home, Murena became overly protective of him. News of his victory over the Boarman spread through the school and what had happened wasn't lost on the Greek. He and Murena acquired an air of superiority over the others, and some even thought the Greek considered himself the lanista. He no longer had a trainer, nor was the Master searching for one, and he was becoming lazy, trained little, and spent more time with Murena. They ignored the rules to the point of having sex in the baths. Other gladiators joked that the Master was the slave, comments that made their way back to the Master.

***

"What is it?" the Master demanded as Lucanus entered the tower.

"There's someone to see you. He says his name is Drusus Atius Longus, son of Lepidus of Brundisium."

"Drusus? Here?"

"You know him?"

"We've met. He fancies himself a gladiator. Perhaps he wants to join us!"

"The son of Lepidus a gladiator? Are you serious?"

"He acts as his father's secretary and enforcer and is prone to violence."

"Should I send him away?"

"What does he want?"

"He won't say, only that he wants to talk to you and it is worth your time to see him."

"Take him into the garden."

"He is waiting in the courtyard. I will tell him," Lucanus replied, turning to leave.

"And Lucanus, search him. Be sure he has no weapon."

Lucanus acknowledged his demand and continued out of the room.

The Master was concerned that Lepidus had sent his son all this way to meet with him, considering how it had ended after the games in Brundisium. Lepidus was powerful and seldom took a slight such as that without seeking revenge. At the bottom of the stairs, the Master turned right into a long passageway that ended by the garden. Drusus had already arrived, and the Master stopped to observe him for a few minutes before making his presence known.

"Welcome, Drusus."

"Master, it is good to see you again. I was sorry I missed you at the games, but my father had me away on business."

Business that no doubt cost some poor bastard his life, he thought. "May I offer you wine?"

"No, thank you. My father doesn't like me consuming wine when on a job. He says it is too distracting."

"Your father should know, considering his proficiency in finances. Sit," he motioned to a chair, "and tell me, what brings you all this way?"

"My father has a proposition for you. Easy money for little effort."

"You have my attention." The Master sat down a safe distance from his guest. Drusus was one of a few men who made the Master nervous.

"After some court proceedings in Brundisium, we find ourselves with thirty prisoners who were sentenced to die in the arena by gladiator. We have received a fairly large sum of money from the questor in this matter. Now we need to find some gladiators to carry out the sentences. There won't be any formal games, but we think it will draw a large crowd anyway. My father is willing to pay three times the going rate for five gladiators, if you include the Greek."

The Master sat up at the mention of the Greek. He was extremely suspicious of Lepidus, but he knew refusing wasn't going to be an option. He might be able to depend on Senator Flavius to protect him from Lepidus, but even that was no guarantee of his life.

"The Greek just fought in Beneventum and was wounded. It might be a while before he could perform again."

"He will not be required to fight a regular opponent. These prisoners will have a sword and shield, but no training. Easy kills. I would be happy to do it myself, but Father says it would look bad for the family."

I imagine you would like that, he thought. "Forgive me, Drusus, I mean no disrespect, but after the incident in Brundisium, which I'm sure you're aware of, I am a bit suspicious of your father's motives for bringing the Greek to the city."

"I understand, but this is business. My father has a chance to make a lot of money. He's offering 3,000 sesterces for the executioners instead of the standard 1,000. Plus, there is another reason."

Here it is, the real reason this prick is here.

"There are certain wealthy women around the region who have a great affection for gladiators and wish to show that affection in a physical way. They are willing to pay a small fortune for the opportunity. My father is in contact with three such ladies, who must remain anonymous, that will pay 5,000 sesterces each to meet privately with the Greek. And you would receive half the fee for your gladiator's service."

"Fifteen thousand sesterces to turn the Greek into a whore?"

"That's right. Half is yours to be paid in advance."

The Master was impressed. The fee was good, but not if something happened to the Greek. "Again, forgive my asking, but what assurances do I have no harm comes to the Greek or anyone of us going into your father's territory?"

"Me."

"You?"

"My father is a smart businessman. He thought you might be hesitant, so to assure you there will be no revenge on his part, I will stay here under your protective custody until everyone returns from Brundisium safely."

"You will stay as hostage?"

"Guest, Master. I will be your guest for the time it takes. The Greek must arrive three days before the executions to service the ladies. When all is finished and you return home, I will go back to Brundisium. Agreed? Oh, and one more thing, I have with me 10,000 sesterces as a deposit and a contract for the balance to be paid to you before the executions begin."

"So you're offering 15,000 for five gladiators—"

"Including the Greek."

"Including the Greek, plus 7,500 for the Greek's other service?"

"That's right. And we'll give you 10,000, nonrefundable no matter what happens, plus the entire balance before the executions."

The Master could hardly believe his good fortune—a bonus dropped in his lap. "I will need to read the contract first."

"Of course," Drusus replied. He pulled a document out from

under his cloak. "Take your time. I will enjoy your hospitality, and when you are ready, my servant will take the contract back to my father."

"When are the executions?"

"In fifteen days."

"Where will I take him? To your villa?"

"No, to the amphitheater. There is a cell that has access through a secure tunnel. These women must arrive and leave without being seen. Have the Greek there three days before and well rested. On the fourth day, he performs first in the executions."

"Very well. I will read the contract and let you know my answer soon."

"There is only one answer."

The Master acknowledged the threat. "While you're here, perhaps you would like to train with the gladiators?"

Drusus' face lit up at the suggestion. "It would be a privilege for me to train at your school."

"My assistant will arrange everything. For now, rest. Lucanus!"

He emerged from the shadows like an unwelcome guest. "Yes."

"Drusus is to be our guest and wishes to train with the men." The Master stood and approached Drusus. "I look forward to doing business with you and your family again."

The men grasped hands and then Lucanus lead Drusus away. The Master studied the contract. He knew he would sign it no matter the terms; no one refused Lepidus. But at least he felt a little better knowing Drusus would remain at the school until the safe return of the Greek.

***

Lucanus approached the Master, who had gone up to the tower to observe the gladiators in the training yard. "Something needs to be done about the Greek. He could lead a revolt if we're not careful. I believe the others would follow him, and he isn't even branded."

"You worry too much. I've plans for him. First, we are going to Brundisium to execute prisoners."

"You trust Drusus?"

"Lepidus does not offer choices."

"Why are you sending the Greek to an execution?"

"He was requested, and there is other business for him."

"The women."

"Watch your ears, Lucanus, and your mouth. No one is to know why we are taking the Greek early, understand?"

"But he will ask."

"Tell him it is for security reasons, but don't mention the women to anyone."

"What about his training? He is slacking without a trainer."

"Order the Nightman to train him again. Tell him he won't have to fight as long as he trains the Greek."

"I'm sure he'll accept, but what about the money? He has a family to support and without the purses from victories—"

"Tell him I'll pay the standard fees, and he can spend more time with his family. How many children does he have?"

"Three—his wife had another not long ago."

"The standard fee plus a percentage of the Greek's winnings, if he remains silent about it. And the woman stays here."

"They won't like that. When are we going?"

"In ten days. The Greek has healed enough for what he needs to do in Brundisium."

The Greek enjoyed the Nightman's company and having him as a trainer, but he was angry Murena couldn't go to Brundisium. The Master rode out several days in advance of the performance and left instructions for Lucanus concerning the travel arrangements. The Nightman and the Greek rode in their own cart surrounded by guards.

"These prisoners were sentenced to death," the Nightman told him concerning the executions.

"Like I was," the Greek said.

"No, you never committed any crime other than being a slave."

"But I was free before I was captured."

"Being captured made you a slave and it was legal to execute you in the arena. But these people committed terrible crimes against the empire, and that is why they must suffer a horrible death. It is your job to render that sentence and kill them in the worst possible way."

The Greek wasn't sure what he meant by "the worst possible way" but remembered, vividly, his first time in the arena and had an idea what was expected.

"Why are we going so early before the executions?"

"I know the Master has something planned for you, but not what it is."

***

The Master decided to pay a call of respect to Lepidus a few days before the executions to repair the damage from their previous dealings. He arrived late in the afternoon at the massive complex that sat on a hill overlooking the city. A slave welcomed him and led him through the entrance to an office where Lepidus waited. The house was full of statues plundered from Greece, and the walls were painted with scenes of gardens and temples.

"Master, so good of you to come. Wine?"

"Thank you, Lepidus."

"Be seated. I understand you have had some luck with that boy I brought from Greece?"

"He does well." *So that's what this is about—the boy. He probably wants to lay claim to him.*

"I'm glad I could be of such benefit to you. Here, drink." He offered a cup of wine to the Master. "I want you to know there are no hard feelings about the incident after the last games. The economy is poor, which I'm sure you're aware of, so every sesterce is important."

"It is forgotten."

"Good. And Drusus? He's well?"

"Yes. He is training with the men."

"My son would like to be a gladiator. Perhaps he wants to assert himself out from under his father and be more independent. I trust you understand my family's situation. You see, in these difficult times I must do things for money, things I normally wouldn't do, but such is life. I have many close female friends who follow the gladiatorial games and the individuals in them with great interest. These women are able to pay for certain indulgences of a sort not appreciated by those of good social standing."

"What are you getting at?"

"Some women are attracted to gladiators and wish to pursue that attraction on a physical level, and they have the means to do so. They only require someone who knows how to keep these 'business transactions' confidential. And, of course, they require a gladiator of high quality to fulfill the desire."

"In these tough times, we all must do that which is unpleasant. But you understand, given your influence, why I am hesitant."

"You flatter me. And it is true, possibly, in good times I might not let your little display go unpunished, but money is money. And besides, I know Senator Flavius holds your prick, and even I don't want to get on his bad side."

"The senator is a good friend, true, but I would rather be your ally than rely on him."

"You are doing me a favor, and we both make money. There is no reason not to forgive you. I appreciate you coming here to discuss the matter, and I respect you for that. Know that we separate friends." Lepidus stood and extended his hand.

"I am glad I came. I look forward to doing business with you in the future."

"You will, unless you kill my son up there." After a moment's hesitation, Lepidus burst out laughing.

"Rest easy, I left orders to keep him alive."

The two men grasped hands. The Master left with an uneasy feeling in his stomach.

***

When they arrived at the amphitheater, the Nightman and the

Greek were separated. The Greek was led down a long hall to a cell at the very end. The many cells under the arena were deserted. The prisoners would be brought in either the night before, or morning of, their execution. He laid down on the bed and soon fell asleep.

He was awakened by a slave bringing him food and water. The slave appeared terrified of him, a fact that the Greek found bewildering and upsetting. He paced around the cell after he ate, his unease growing. He called out to the Nightman, but the entire section appeared to be empty save for him. Not long after that, two sets of approaching footsteps could be heard—one heavy, the other lighter.

The Greek saw the guard first, the one who had brought him to the cell, and then a short distance behind him, a veiled woman. He sat on the edge of the bed as the guard spoke to him and then unlocked the cell door, allowing the woman to enter. He locked the door behind her. After the guard was out of sight, she removed her head covering and pulled a pin from her hair. A wave of long dark hair cascaded down her back.

"So you're the famous Greek. I saw you fight in Beneventum against the Boarman; it was an unbelievable performance. You had me squirming on my cushion. I knew I had to meet you in the flesh," she cooed, though he did not understand a word. "I was told you don't speak Latin, but that is fine. I didn't come here tonight to talk."

The Greek was standing by the side of the bed. She moved forward, pushed herself against him, and ran her hands along his arms, which were developing into those of a man. She grabbed his shoulders and pushed him back onto the bed, then slowly unfastened the pins on her gown.

"Let's see if you're worth 10,000 sesterces, shall we," she said softly, pushing up his tunic to expose his genitals.

She was the most beautiful woman he had ever seen. Her skin was as white as milk, and her breasts were round and firm. He tried to think of Murena, but could only focus on the woman sitting on his chest. She bent down and gave him a long lingering kiss as she took his hand and guided it between her legs. She slid back and forth on his fingers while reaching around and grasping his penis, which had become erect. After stroking it for a few moments, she pushed back and guided him into her, then sat down, fully engulfing his erection.

She screamed with delight as he penetrated her and began thrusting her loins up and down at a furious rate. She reached out, grabbed his long hair, and pulled until he complained of the pain, then bent down and bit him on the shoulder. She held onto his arms. Her many rings and bracelets cut into his skin, but his continued protests fueled her passion. She pounded him harder and harder moaning, screaming, and yelling. He just wanted it to be over.

Finally, he came, filling her with his seed, but it did not slow her. In fact, she thrust faster, even as he became flaccid and slipped out of her. She reached down with her hand between her legs and vigorously rubbed herself while continuing to ride him. She swung her other hand, striking his face and chest more violently as her orgasm intensified. Then she let out a piercing scream and collapsed in sweaty exhaustion on his chest.

She continued to moan and breathe hard for a long time as the Greek stared at the ceiling. Eventually, she sat up, wiped herself on his tunic, and slipped off the bed. She smiled and spoke as she was dressing, then called to the guard, who returned and released her.

The next night saw a repeat performance, though with a different woman. She was a bit older and heavier, but as enthusiastic, though without the biting and hitting. The third night, another was lead to his cell. She wasn't pretty or thin and liked it even rougher than the first. The Greek was left bruised and sore. He hoped she was the last.

But the Master didn't care who they were, what they looked like, or their reasons as long as they were willing to pay. This, combined with the prize money the Greek had won, including a nice payday for the executions, would help the Master survive financially. And, if he could find enough women who wanted to fuck the Greek, the young gladiator might never have to fight again!

CHAPTER VI

MARCELLUS OWNED THE LARGEST BAKERY IN BRUNDISIUM. HE WAS a prominent client of Lepidus and faithfully arrived at his villa early each morning as a show of support. In return, Marcellus had a monopoly on the bread supply in the city. Lepidus knew how much he and his friends loved watching the gladiators and had given him four tickets to the event. Even though this spectacle only involved the execution of prisoners, the Greek would be participating. Marcellus and his friends had been in this very arena the day he had killed the Giant, so there was great anticipation at seeing him perform.

Priscus, a fuller, was a bigger fan of the gladiatorial games than Marcellus, but he lacked the political connections. He was grateful of his friend's ability to acquire tickets. In fact, Priscus had traveled all the way to Beneventum to see the Greek fight in his last match and was ecstatic that the gladiator was in Brundisium. His best friend, Cuspius the carpenter, was the lowest class of the four, but keen to advance his status. He also loved the games. His one claim to fame that made the others jealous was having a distant cousin who had become a gladiator, though he had never seen him fight or even met him. The goldsmith Trebius was the fourth member of their group and nearly as wealthy as Marcellus. He detested Lepidus and would never approach him as a client, but was glad to take part in his games.

Because of the influence of Marcellus, the four had seats among the upper classes, a few rows from the arena. They were close enough to see the wounds and blood and, they hoped, to draw the attention and acknowledgment of the Greek. The executions would last through the afternoon, so they had brought light snacks and water, as well as cushions to sit on.

The Greek stood behind the entrance gate and wondered what this was going to be like. He remembered how the Giant had worked the crowd until he made a mistake—a fatal mistake. The Greek wouldn't be so careless. He stepped into the arena to the shouts of the audience; he was why they had come. He sauntered in front of the editor, Lepidus, and saw the Master sitting behind him. They exchanged glances before the Greek picked up his swords and calmly walked to the center of the arena where he began to juggle them. At once, he had the audience in his control. He walked around the outside near the people and cast glances into the crowd. Some reached over and tried to touch him.

The entrance gate opened and a slim, naked man was pushed into the arena. He stumbled and nearly fell, but caught himself. He gazed around at the scene as though awakening from a nightmare, though, in fact, he had just walked into one. One slave handed him a small round shield, and another gave him a sword, which he held awkwardly. He was an accountant for a local wealthy individual and had never had any reason to wield a weapon. He was convicted when money disappeared from the books, even though it was the owner's young wife who had stolen it to purchase clothes for her lover. She remained silent, and he was condemned to death by gladiator.

The Greek approached twirling and swinging his swords. When the man finally noticed him, his situation became clear. He looked for a route of escape but, like a rat trapped in a corner, he had no options. As the man stood trembling, the Greek felt pity for him but, remembering his own plight that first time in this arena, his pity evaporated. He rushed at the man, who dropped his weapons, turned, and ran to the closed gate. The man pounded on it and screamed, but the only way out for him was through the gate of death.

The Greek stopped. How could he make this entertaining if the man didn't put up some resistance? Then he had an idea. He picked up the discarded sword of the man, who continued to bang on the gate, turned it over in his hand, and threw it to the right of the man's head.

The man momentarily froze as the sound of the sword striking the wooden gate sent a chill down his spine. With a trembling hand, he pulled the sword from the gate and turned to face the Greek.

The Greek smiled at him, the man vomited, and the crowd laughed. He approached the man again, who made an effort by thrusting his sword at the Greek. He was rewarded with a shallow cut down the left side of his chest and screamed as a tiny ribbon of blood appeared in the trail of the blade. The man's fear and desperation grew. He continued to back away, but the Greek was relentless. He turned and ran. Chasing the man seemed fruitless because there was no place to corner him. When the man briefly stopped, the Greek threw one of his swords. It glanced off his side and left a small wound. Whenever the man stopped to catch his breath, the Greek would hurl another sword. The injuries inflicted were minor, though they did draw blood.

The victim grew weak from his efforts and the wounds and collapsed on the sand. A sword flew from the hand of the Greek and struck the man in the throat. He grasped at the wound, managed to stand, and fell again. He crawled to the wall, pulled himself up, and attempted to flee. Blood ran down his chest and sand was caked to his body. He leaned heavily on the wall as his plight worsened. As the man staggered, the Greek drove a sword into his lower back, which caused him to drop to his knees.

With a quick swipe of his sword, the Greek severed the man's left ear. He screamed in pain and grasped the side of his head as he struggled to get away. The Greek picked up the appendage, examined it, and then casually tossed it into the stands.

The action was taking place in front of Priscus, who could not believe what had just happened. He reached out to grab for the ear and was about to catch it when, at the last possible moment, a man from another group directly in front of him snatched it from the air. The man held the trophy high, but his joy was short lived.

Cuspius jumped into the lower seats and kicked the man hard in the genitals. This was not enough for him to surrender the precious prize, but when Trebius bit the man's hand, he had to let it go. It fell amongst the bleachers and caused a frenzy, but Cuspius, the largest and strongest of the four, fought off the competition and was finally able to secure the ear, which he promptly handed to Priscus. He would dry the ear and keep it as a prized possession for many years to come.

The Greek again pursued the helpless man as he looked for another appendage to remove. At last, he settled on the other ear. His aim was a bit off and it removed part of the man's scalp. The Greek retrieved it and again threw it into the crowd. Several men grabbed for it, but everyone missed, and it fell onto the seats. This caused another small riot. After the events were over for the day and the amphitheater vacated, two bodies would be found in this area.

The Greek lost interest in the man, who was helpless and bleeding heavily but still had no mortal wounds. He returned to the center of the arena and began once more to entertain the crowd with his swords. Two attendants were sent in with large hooks, which they jabbed into the man's lower legs, and dragged him to the exit. There was still enough life in him to squirm and scream. When they neared the gate, a man representing Charon delivered a tremendous blow to the side of the man's head and drove the life from him. The attendants dragged the body out of the arena.

When the crowd broke out in laughter, the Greek's attention was diverted to the entrance. An extremely fat man, also naked, had entered the arena. The man struggled with his weapon and dropped the sword from his pudgy hand. The Greek drove both his swords into the sand then walked over to the man, picked up his sword, and handed it to him. He took two steps back, smiled, knelt down on one knee, and raised one finger into the air, the signal of surrender for a defeated gladiator. The crowd roared with laughter again, and even Lepidus was overcome with a fit of uncontrollable mirth. The Master managed to grin.

The man thought he saw an opportunity and thrust his sword at the unarmed Greek, who dodged the blade with little effort. The man nearly stumbled and fell over, but it made the Greek angry. As he retrieved his swords, he remembered his father telling him of wealthy, fat men who preyed upon peasants and took their land. The man's rolls of fat disgusted the Greek.

Death was too easy for this man. The Greek wanted to humiliate him. As he approached, the man tried to back away but stumbled and fell again. The Greek stopped, dropped his swords, and walked up to his victim. He dodged another blow from the man, then stepped close, slapped him hard on the face, and retreated.

The man's cheek turned red from the blow as he tried to regain his senses. Another blow struck the same spot on his left cheek, followed in quick succession by several body blows, which, while not serious, created a lot of noise. The victim turned and attempted to flee, a comical sight in itself, but the Greek added to the hilarity by kicking him in the buttocks. Some people were laughing so hard they fell out of their seats, but the Master was not amused. What he didn't need was to see another star killed in this arena for the sake of the show.

The boredom of the crowd, as well as his own, meant it was time to change tactics. Spectators began to throw objects at the fat man, and when a chamber pot struck his head and opened a large gash exposing the first blood, people shouted their approval. The Greek took the hint and returned to his swords. He retrieved them and turned toward the man, who was trying to catch his breath.

He had long abandoned the shield, and the sword hung limply from his hand. He turned pale as the Greek neared. Instead of his hands, the Greek slapped the man with the flat side of the blade which opened a gash on his right cheek and knocked him to the ground. He began to carve shallow marks on his back that caused the man to scream in pain and crawl away from his tormentor.

The Greek had the attention of the audience once more. The unarmed man regained his footing and faced the Greek. With a rapid left to right motion, the young gladiator's sword sliced through the man's belly and exposed his intestines. They spilled out of him like an upturned pitcher of water. The man squealed and grasped at his falling insides, trying to push them back into place, but the tide was too strong. He collapsed onto the ground moaning and crying, all the while cradling his innards. He rocked back and forth on the sand, shaking violently.

The Greek gave up on the man and instead approached one of the guards stationed around the interior of the arena. He was heavily armed and wore a helmet, breastplate, and greaves. The guard stood motionless as the Greek neared and gestured at his sword to indicate he wanted him to fight. The guard slowly lowered the point of his spear, which came to rest a few inches from the Greek's naked chest. He toyed with it in a mock battle. The guard glanced at the editor, who had a stern look on his face, and raised his spear. The Greek tried to get his attention, but, much to his disappointment, the guard ignored him.

A commotion in the arena drew the Greek's attention. Two attendants, their hooks sunk into the fat man's legs, were struggling to pull the unconscious man and failing miserably. They called for two more men, who came to join their colleagues and drove their hooks into the man's arms. The four of them were able to slowly move the mass until one accidentally stepped on the man's protruding intestines, slipped, and fell on top of the heap. He sprang up and frantically attempted to brush off the blood, slime, and sand that covered him. This victim was certainly giving the people their money's worth.

The Greek turned back to baiting the guard. The Master didn't know if he was playing or attempting to draw the guard into combat. Either way, he was disgusted by the action. The crowd loved it. Another chorus of *Graecus* echoed through the arena as the Greek danced in front of the guard.

From the corner of his eye, the Greek saw the next victim enter the arena. The prisoner held a sword and shield, but wore a dirty tunic. A mass of tangled hair obscured the person's face. The Greek started toward the figure but stopped, turned, and went to the center of the arena. He threw down his swords and continued to the front of the editor's box.

He looked directly at the Master. "I will not kill a woman!"

Half rising from his seat, the Master yelled, "Kill her or die!"

"No!"

The Master turned to Lepidus and gestured. Only the editor had control over the guards' actions. With the Master's consent, he raised his arm. The guards lowered their spears and began to advance, but the Greek was unmoved. Another gesture and the guards stopped.

"Kill her or die!"

The Greek glared at the Master, turned, retrieved his swords, and strode toward the woman. The first blow was aimed at her shield, but when she raised it to ward off the strike, the Greek thrust his other sword into her chest and through her heart. He withdrew the blade as she fell, dead before she hit the sand.

The Greek, seething with anger, spun around and stormed back toward the editor's box.   When he neared the side of the arena, he viciously threw one sword then the other. Before anyone could react, the swords struck point first into the wooden wall directly below the Master. Lepidus turned pale with fear.

"Kill him!" the Master yelled.

The guards awaited his signal. Lepidus had never heard such a reaction from the crowd. The structure shook from the yelling and vibration of stomping feet. *Graecus* drowned out all other sounds. Lepidus feared the spectators would riot and destroy the amphitheater, with him in it, if he ordered the guards to kill the Greek. He gestured for them to stand down.

The Greek thrust his arms into the air and the noise increased. This was his greatest moment. If only Murena could see him. If only his family could see him. They would never believe the story when he told them how much these people loved him. The common people—not the wealthy, not the owners of slaves, not the ones who preyed on the poor. He was one of them, and his message was clear to all. He turned slowly in the center of the arena and absorbed the adulation. No one was better than him.

Finally, he lowered his arms and walked to the exit gate. He glanced back at the Master and Lepidus, then the gate opened, and he left the arena.

***

The Nightman knew immediately that it wasn't good. He had a bad feeling even before arriving on the scene. As he and Lucanus were talking with the owner of the inn, they heard shouts from the stable at the back of the building. They rushed toward the noise. It was worse than he had wanted to believe. One of the three guards lay on the floor near the horses with part of his head missing. The other two were uninjured, but shaken and scared. They explained in stutters that, while transferring the five gladiators from their respective carriages to the leg chains attached to support posts, one had grabbed an axe and struck down the first guard. He had then threatened those around him with death if they tried to prevent his escape. They had quivered in fear. One gladiator had stepped forward and asked to accompany the axe-wielding man. He refused, but another followed as he ran out of the barn.

Lucanus' first action upon returning to the school was to confine all the gladiators to the barracks. Two missing was bad enough; they did not need a whole-scale riot. Next, he sent a message to Senator Flavius asking that he spread the word throughout the region and help search for the runaways. Bassus was branded, but the Greek was not, nor did he wear a collar or have any identifying marks that indicated he was a slave.

The senator responded that he would do everything in his power to assist in the recapture of the slaves though, in fact, he did nothing. He was in no mood to offer assistance after the financial soaking the Master had given him at his son's funeral games.

***

The Greek could not understand why he had grabbed that axe and killed the guard. He ran from the inn into the night. He didn't know where he was going, but he ran. The moonlight guided him. He fell often and became tangled in grape vines more than once, but he continued to run until it felt as though his beating heart would burst his chest. When his legs refused to go any farther, he crawled until he collapsed from exhaustion.

It was daylight when he awoke to the muffled sounds of voices. He observed a small group standing by a mound of dirt and decided to investigate. It was a burial. A child's body was wrapped in a stained white cloth. After the body was lowered into a shallow grave, three men covered it with dirt and packed the ground until little evidence of the event remained.

The people walked away from the grave and headed toward the Greek. When they spotted him, there was a collective moment of hesitation as they peered at the dirty, long-haired individual who stood before them. One of the men moved forward and spoke.

"That was Hilarus." He motioned toward the grave. "Run over by a team of horses. Only seven years old, he was."

The Greek stood in silence, staring at the man.

"Where you from? Looks like you been through some hard times. You from around here?"

"What's he saying?" another called from behind.

"Nothing. Don't say nothing."

"Maybe he don't speak our language."

"Someone speak any other language?"

"I speak some Greek. I was born there. But it's been a while," an older stout lady said as she moved toward them.

"Try it."

"Who are you?" she asked in Greek.

"They call me the..." He hesitated.

"They call you what?"

"Miltiades," the Greek replied.

"Miltiades? A fine name. Where are you from, Miltiades?"

"Thessaly."

"I was born near Olympia. What are you doing here?"

"I am on my way home, back to Thessaly."

"You're a long ways from Thessaly, and you look hungry. Come with us for some lunch. I am Blandina, and this is Fabius, Rufinus, Paulus, and Martinus. We belong to the villa over there." She indicated several buildings by the foot of a hill. "Are you a freedman?"

"I am free."

She turned and translated their conversation for the others, then turned back to the Greek. "We are bringing in the harvest. If you can work, the master will pay for extra hands, especially those of a free man."

"Do you know where Thessaly is?"

"It is east."

"Is it possible to walk to Thessaly?"

The woman once again asked the others. One man produced an animated reply.

"He says it is possible, but it would take many months, maybe even a year. It is much faster by sea—less than two days from Italy to Thessaly."

The Greek hadn't thought of working, but if he had money, maybe he could buy passage on a ship to Thessaly. "I can work. I was born on a farm."

"Good. I am the cook. Come with us. We will eat and then you can work."

The Greek felt a sense of relief.

***

The Master didn't return with Lucanus and the others but was off again in search of another venue for the Greek. The demand for him to perform grew. Rumors about Tiberius' imminent death were circulating again. He must keep the Greek alive. A victory in the Imperial games could set the Master for life.

It was late in the evening when rapid knocking woke the Master.

"What is it?" he bellowed, exhausted from a long day's ride.

"A message has arrived for you. It is urgent."

The Master was traveling west and had stopped for the night at the villa of a good friend.

"Enter!"

The door swung open, and two men with lamps stepped into the room. The Master was sitting up, covered by a thin sheet, while a young naked boy lay next to him.

"What is so important you disturb me?"

The second man moved closer. "I'm sent by Lucanus. There was an incident at the inn last night when they stopped on their way home from Brundisium. He said it was important to get to you as soon as possible."

"What is the message, fool? Tell me!"

"Two gladiators escaped."

"Two? Which two?"

"One was Bassus."

"And the other? Come on, out with it!"

"The Greek."

The Master cried out in anger. He kicked the boy, who yelped in pain as he hit the floor and ran from the room.

"Prepare horses. We return immediately!"

"We should wait 'til first light, Master."

"No! The moon illuminates the road. We leave tonight!"

Bassus had been caught within a day. The brand on his neck exposed him as a slave, and under questioning from some passing centurions, he gave up the story. The Master arrived at the inn mid-afternoon to find Bassus chained in the stable and badly beaten, which caused him to fear that he might die before they would be able to crucify him.

The Master hired a wagon and guard to accompany Bassus home, but he remained to search for the Greek, who was far too valuable to die on a cross or remain free. He shuddered at how close his violent temper had come to having the Greek killed. His best guess was that the Greek would head east to the coast and attempt to gain passage to Thessaly, but that would be difficult without funds. His only option would be to stow away, but that was a dangerous proposition. If he was caught, the penalty was being thrown overboard. Word spread like wildfire of the run-a-way gladiator and stories of his viciousness in the arena caused fear among the people, stories embellished by the Master in hopes it would speed his recapture. The Master, in his haste to arrive at the inn, had ridden within viewing distance of the villa where the Greek had been taken in by kindly servants.

Everyone got on well with the strong young man. He was a good worker, knew the job, and kept to himself to avoid any questions. But some were suspicious of the scars and cuts that adorned his body.

A week after his arrival, the Greek spotted a small group of men approaching the workers. He fled into nearby brush until they passed. This action, along with the rumors that were circulating the countryside, was a cause for grumbling amongst some of the crew. It could be dangerous to be so close to the stranger who wielded the curved scythe with such precision, and there might be a reward.

The Greek grew more paranoid as the days passed and he continually looked over his shoulder, not only for the guards he suspected were searching for him but also at his fellow workers. His fear increased when three new men were hired—large, muscular men who took an immediate dislike to the Greek. His ragged appearance and small size made him a target of taunts and ridicule, more so when they discovered he could not speak Latin. One of the new arrivals seemed to see the darkness in the Greek's eyes and stayed clear, but the other two continually harassed him.

***

He half expected it as he sat stoically, his head in his hands. The blade of the sword pressed against his neck caused him to lean back in the chair.

"If you're going to do it, make it quick," Drusus said. "But know one thing. My father had nothing to do with the Greek's escape. Why would he? He only wants money and prestige, and this would add neither. Even kidnapping the Greek would be pointless because everyone knows you own him. And if my father wanted to buy the Greek, he has ways to persuade you into selling. I'm sure you are well aware of that."

The Master slowly pulled back the sword. Drusus made a good point. Lepidus had nothing to gain in the Greek's escape except the possible humiliation of the Master.

"I wanted to be sure you weren't involved. You are free to leave anytime. Your father kept his part of the contract; now I keep mine."

"Your generosity is appreciated. My father will hear of it. Perhaps he will allow me to be in the arena after the training I received, for which I thank you, but I must return, or my father will think me idle and lazy."

"You and your family are always welcome. I will have my servant saddle your horse. Safe journey."

"One last point." Drusus stopped on his way out. "We would be happy to extend our services to search for the Greek."

"The offer is welcome, but I am capable of finding him."

"Very well. I will be off."

The Master had returned to the school in a terrible mood, and his encounter with Drusus hadn't helped to improve it. Bassus had been returned to a reasonable state of health, which allowed his execution on the cross in the courtyard by the gate. The three other gladiators were questioned under torture until the Master was satisfied they had nothing to do with the Greek's escape. It seemed the attempt was spontaneous and unexplained, though he did suspect that it was connected to what had occurred in Brundisium. But it was part of the game. An exercise to toughen the young man and remove any hesitation he had at killing an opponent.

Life had become unbearable for Murena. The Master had her moved out of the Greek's cell and placed with the domestic slaves, but her ever-growing arrogance was a cause of their hatred toward her. They would not accept her into the household and forced her to sleep on the dirt floor of the stable. They pushed and struck her at every opportunity. Reduced to the lowest jobs, such as cleaning the latrines, she was despondent.

From where Murena slept, she could see the rotting corpse of Bassus on the cross and wondered if she would hang there beside the Greek after he was caught. What would happen to her if he wasn't captured? It didn't matter. She prayed to the gods that he would be free.

The search continued. Senator Flavius had finally supplied some men to assist in the hunt, for a hefty fee. The senator had delighted in seeing the Master plead for his help, an action that made the Master feel ill. Word was sent to the ports along the coast and spies moved among the docks, but not a single report had come in. The Master's hope was beginning to wain when an obscure rumor reached the school; two workers on a large villa to the west had been killed in a grisly attack by a fellow worker. A chill had run down the Master's spine. It did not make sense for the Greek to go west away from the coast and home. Nevertheless, the rumor bore checking, so the Master and several guards headed out to the location of the alleged incident.

It took a day and a half to arrive at the villa. The Master was met by the manager, who was still in a state of shock.

"The youth was hired on two weeks ago. I found him to be a fine worker, though he appeared nervous. Several days ago, I hired three new men. Two of them began to harass the youth."

"What was he called?" the Master asked.

"Miltiades."

"Continue."

"Three days ago, my field foreman came screaming to me, 'Something terrible's happenin'! Come quick!' So I ran with him as fast as I could, but it was over when we arrived."

"What was over? What happened?"

"The workers that saw it say these two new men were pushing Miltiades around trying to get him to fight. Then one strikes at him with a scythe, but he moved away. They never seen anyone so fast.

When the other fellow attacked, everything changed. His expression got different, and there was something about his eyes that put fear in the ones around. But before the two could get away, the youth struck them with his scythe. Clean cut off one of them's hand! Then, so fast the others could barely tell what happened, he cut their throats. Both of them! They was dead before they hit the ground!"

"Where is he now, Miltiades?"

"Dropped the scythe and ran off. But not before..."

"Not before what?"

"When we ran down to the field, he must have come up here. He found where I keep the money for pay—they were supposed to be paid that night—and he ran off with it."

"How much did he take?"

"Over a hundred sesterces."

"Any idea where he was heading?"

"Some said Thessaly by ship. Must be heading to the coast. You think it's your man?"

"Sounds possible."

"What about the money and those two workers we lost? The owner's gonna be mad at me. You gonna repay the money?"

"I don't have money on me, but I'll send it back after I return home. I'm good for it."

"Where did you say you was from?"

The Master ignored the question. "I'll send the money," he called out as he was leaving.

Why had the Greek gone west? he asked himself. *It just doesn't make sense.*

From the description of the killings, the Master believed it had to be the Greek, and after learning about the money, he became much more concerned about losing him. It would not be difficult for the fugitive to find someone to take him to Thessaly with that amount of cash.

***

Even though no one asked, and the Greek never ventured the truth, most suspected he was an escaped slave. When reports arrived of a runaway gladiator, his identity became clear. He and Rufinus, the oldest of the group, had become close. Rufinus had traveled to the coast many times and knew the countryside well. The largest port was at Brundisium but, he had warned, many would be watching for him. It would be best to go farther north, though the two-day journey on foot to Barium would bring him perilously close to the school.

Rufinus knew of a small sheltered harbor where a smuggler operated and could be had, for a price. Several of the slaves secretly hoped for his success, even after the killings, as it gave them the feeling that a small piece of themselves would also be free if he made it home.

It was slow traveling northeast toward Barium as the Greek could not follow the main roads. Instead, he traveled through forests and fields. Occasionally, he would buy food at a market in the small towns that dotted the landscape, but more often he stole what he needed. Five days passed before he arrived at the east coast and turned north.

According to Rufinus' directions, the smuggler was less than a half day's ride south of Barium and lived in a ramshackle farmhouse a short distance inland. The Greek hid in the brush each night, dreaming of his homecoming. He was worried as to how his family had been since his departure, especially his father. He didn't even know how long he had been gone.

The Greek came upon some buildings that seemed to match the description of the smuggler's home. But he was afraid of being captured should it be the wrong place and decided to hide in some bushes. His attempt to conceal his appearance was thwarted by several large and angry dogs that barked ferociously when they caught his scent. When the dogs got closer, he feared for his safety and called out. A short scruffy man in dirty clothes appeared at the door.

"Who approaches," he called out in Latin.

"I am sent by Rufinus of the villa Vinicius Flaminius," the Greek replied.

"You're Greek?" the man replied in perfect Greek. "What do you seek?"

"Passage to Thessaly."

"Go to the port in Barium. Many ships sail east."

"I need private transport. I will pay."

The man waved for the Greek to enter the house and called off the dogs.

"A man can't be too careful in these times," he told the Greek as they entered the house. "Is someone after you?"

"How much to Thessaly?"

"A normal passage is a few sesterces but, under your circumstances, 80 sesterces."

"And you will take me to the shores of Thessaly?"

"I don't take you nowhere. Someone else does that. But yes, on the shores of Thessaly."

"What kind of ship?" he asked, as though knowledgeable of water craft.

"Cargo. Someone will take you out to it in a small rowboat and load you onto the ship. When you approach Greece, the captain will put you in another small boat to the coast. You land rough on the beach, wherever the pilot can find a safe location. Then you're on your own."

"When will I go?"

"I have to check when the next ship is leaving. I'll need to find a ship with a 'friendly' captain, but don't worry, there are many like that. Probably two or three days. I have a place to hide you until you can leave. You'll go at night, and you must pay in advance."

"Half now. The rest when I'm in Greece."

"No deal, boy. All now. That's the only way."

"Half or I find someone else."

"Go then. Good luck, gladiator."

The Greek glared at the man.

"I'm not stupid. I hear the stories, though looking at you it's hard to believe you're much of a gladiator. There's a reward for you. I could make more turning you in than sending you to Greece. I'm taking a risk. You see, there's a certain senator very interested in your return. I could end up a slave myself if anyone found out I helped you. Go on. Walk out that door. Find somebody else. You'll be hanging from a cross by tomorrow."

"Why would you help me?"

"My parents were Greek, and I don't like it when these Romans make slaves of us. Eighty sesterces cash, now, or no deal."

The Greek didn't trust him, or believe his story of being Greek, but the man knew his identity. It appeared he had no other choice.

"Where will I stay?" the Greek asked after handing him the money.

"I got another place, a shack, about a mile south right on the coast. It's hidden in some trees. No one goes there. You'll be safe. I'll give you some bread and water. Wait until I send someone for you."

"How will I know you sent him?"

"When someone calls out the word 'Thessaly,' you'll know I sent him to take you to the boat. Good?"

The Greek stood in silence. The man collected some old bread and cheese and a jug of water, placed them in a sack, and handed it to him.

"Walk to the shore, then head right until you see a grove of trees. The shack's hidden in them. The gods be with you. Safe journey."

The Greek tried to remain calm, but could not help but feel overjoyed at the prospect of going home.

***

This time the Master had come to the gate to meet Senator Flavius personally, but a feeling of dread engulfed him as he watched the senator's carriage approach.

"Senator, my dear friend," he said while offering his hand.

"Master," the senator responded.

The Master kissed the senator's large ring and stood back to allow him to step down.

"Come into the shade, and welcome. I am having some wine brought."

Together they entered the villa and continued through to the back garden. After indulging in some wine, the senator leaned back in his chair and stared at the Master. It was high time someone taught this man a lesson in appropriate social standings. Today he would be master in name only.

"Master," the senator began, "it has come to my attention from one of my many, many sources that your gladiator, the so-called Greek, is, as we speak, sitting in a shack by the sea awaiting passage to Thessaly. Within two days he will be on a ship heading to Greece. It would be but a small matter for me to send word that he be captured and returned to his rightful owner."

On the one hand, the Master was elated the Greek had been located but, on the other hand, it was this despicable piece of shit sitting before him that would be the one to return him. For this, he would owe a massive favor. The senator drained his wine cup and set it noisily on the table to his right where it was refilled by a slave.

"Have you met my nephew, Catalus Paulus from Tarentum?"

"I've never had the privilege."

"He's an up and coming young man in the political world who would benefit from some well-timed assistance. I propose a small, but impressive games would gain the attention of the local people and increase his support, and I believe you are such a man to produce these games. I would never impose on someone such as yourself the entire burden of staging games, only of supplying the entertainment and a few miscellaneous expenses."

The Master's face grew red with anger. Even in good times, the financial burden would be overwhelming. Now it might well bankrupt him.

"Surely you can't expect someone of my modest means to supply my gladiators for free and assume part of the cost for the games?"

"You're quite right." After a short pause, the senator leaned toward the Master. "Only those of the 'highest' status can afford such an undertaking. And don't worry about the costs, I am more than glad to lend you any short-comings at a reasonable rate of interest if your school is offered in collateral."

It was all the Master could do to restrain himself from slitting the senator's throat.

"The entertainment will be enough for your contribution. Say, fifteen pair. And it won't even be *sine missione,* so your losers might survive. My nephew will be a kind editor. Of course, I can't speak for the will of the spectators. And one final point. Should you decide to spare the Greek's life, he fights."

"I haven't decided his fate yet, but he won't be in any shape to fight."

"I will give you two months. That should be plenty of time for him to heal from whatever punishment you have planned. Do we have a deal? And remember, in two days he will be in Greece and out of my reach."

The Master rose abruptly, startling the senator. "Do I have a choice?"

"So you agree?"

"Yes. Bring the Greek back to me unharmed."

The senator stood and headed for the door. "I wish I could stay longer, but I must send word immediately." He stopped and turned back to face the Master. "There is a fee required for the gentleman who supplied this information to me. Plus, of course, my expenses to return him. Ten thousand sesterces should cover it. Do you wish to pay me now or should I add it to your account?"

"I don't have that kind of money here!"

"I'll put it on your account. There are few men I would trust with such a debt, but, for you, think nothing of it." The senator walked to his waiting carriage and from the seat stared down on the Master, a look of satisfaction on his face, and motioned for his driver to leave.

"Has he found the Greek?" Lucanus asked after the senator's carriage disappeared through the gate.

"He's near Barium waiting for a ship to Thessaly."

"Are we going after him?"

"No. The senator's men will return him."

"What is that going to cost us?"

"The fat pig owns us." With that, he stormed back inside.

***

"Thessaly!" someone shouted in the fading daylight.

Never had the Greek's homeland sounded as sweet. It had been three days since he arrived at the shack and, nearly out of food and water, he had begun to doubt that man's word when the call came. It wouldn't be long before he was on Greek soil once more.

A lone figure walked toward the shack and surveyed the area. The Greek stepped out the door.

"Thessaly," the man called again.

"Yes," the Greek waved and pointed at himself.

The man motioned with his hand to follow, and the two began walking to the south along the coast.

"How far to the boat?" the Greek asked, but the man indicated he didn't understand.

The Greek and his guide came to a narrow path that led to a long stretch of beach. The Greek could see several people standing near a boat. They seemed unaware of his arrival. When the man accompanying the Greek began to speak to the others, they grabbed the Greek by his arms and legs and pushed him onto the sand where they bound him with ropes. As the Greek struggled, he became aware of a cart moving toward him. He was dragged into the cage on the cart and shackled hand and foot to the floor. He raged against the chains, but he knew it was over. The Nightman had been right; he would never leave this place. He would never be free. Once a gladiator, always a gladiator.

***

Rufinus was sobbing in the corner of his room when Blandina came in with some food.

"Oh Rufinus, don't blame yourself. Any one of us would have

given them the information under torture. You held out much longer than most could have. And besides, it was a nice dream to believe the young man would return home. But that's all it was. This is our lot in life. He will never be free, and neither will we."

Rufinus knew she was right, but he felt for the young man as if he were his own son. He had betrayed his son. No one was surprised when the body of Rufinus was found hanging in the stable the next morning.

CHAPTER VII

IT WAS TENSE AT THE SCHOOL. THE TRAINERS HAD ATTEMPTED TO resume regular workouts, but it was difficult. The body of Bassus had hung from the cross until it rotted and finally fell to the ground. The Master refused him burial in the cemetery and had the remains thrown into the river. The gladiators had seen escapees crucified before, but something was different this time. The Master was neglecting the school. He had become obsessed with recapturing the Greek and left the decisions to Lucanus, who continued to fear a revolt among the gladiators and kept most in their cells. The Nightman was spending more time with his family and did not know if he would have to fight again.

Rumor on her wings flew repeatedly amongst the men: the Greek had returned to Thessaly. He was dead. He had been captured. Every day there was something new. The speculation enhanced the Greek's standing, which had become that of myth. Before his escape, some were beginning to believe he was not human but one of the immortal gods, or at the least the descendant of a god. Perhaps his mother had lain with Mercury, who had wings on his feet. That would explain his speed in the arena. Others believed he couldn't be killed by ordinary arms and that it would require a weapon fashioned by the gods to bring him down.

The Master stood in the tower and watched the slow progression of the wagon into the deserted yard. Several heavily armed guards, courtesy of the senator, surrounded the cart. The Greek was released from his shackles and led into one of the small cells. He dragged his feet and his head hung low. He had the appearance of defeat.

"What do you plan for him?" Lucanus asked the Master after a long silence.

"Is he hurt?"

"He doesn't appear to be. I can have the medicus examine him if you like."

"Give him food and water. Send for the Nightman."

"He's with his family so it will be a while."

The Master continued to stare out the window. Lucanus had never seen him in such a state before. Even the death of the Giant hadn't affected him as much.

Many had hoped the Greek would make it home, but most knew that was only a dream. Since word of his recapture reached the school, the servants had become fearful their treatment of Murena would cause them harm should the Greek regain his status. His return was cause for great agitation and sadness.

The next day, the Nightman returned to the school and climbed the stairs to the tower. He could not see anything ending well for the Greek.

"Enter," the Master called at his knock.

"You wanted to see me?"

"You know he's back?"

"Yes."

"What would you do?"

The Nightman stood in silence. Of all the scenarios he thought might occur, this had never crossed his mind.

"I don't understand."

"If you were in my place, what would you do? Crucify him? Pretend nothing happened? How can I trust him again?"

"How can you trust any of us?"

The Master turned to face him and began to laugh. The Nightman stared in disbelief. He had never seen the Master laugh.

He grew quiet and looked out the window again. "To be master of the most dangerous men that exist and have no trust. Why do you return?"

"You would hunt me down and kill my family," he replied in a brief moment of honesty.

"You believe that?"

"Yes."

"You're right. I would. I can't have trust or loyalty, so I choose fear. Is that wrong?"

"It's just our life. We're entertainment. Accept it or die."

"Entertainment. Pigs to the slaughter." The Master was talking as much to himself as to the Nightman. "There is something about him. I've never seen it before, only heard tales. He can be an exceptional gladiator, a star fighting in Rome in the Imperial games. I don't know what it is but he is destined for greatness. Perhaps he is descended from the gods. You will begin training the Greek again," he continued, turning to the Nightman. "I will find another dimachaerus to work with you, but stay with him. Go talk to him. Tell him if he wants to live, he fights. If not, I crucify him."

As the Nightman began to leave, the Master asked him, "Do you think he's descended from a god?"

Without looking back, he replied, "No!"

The Greek looked toward the light as the door opened and the Nightman entered. He sat on the only chair in the darkened cell.

"I prayed to the gods you would make it to Thessaly."

"So did I."

"Now what? Do you return to the arena? If not, the Master will crucify you like Bassus."

"Bassus shouldn't have followed me."

"What will you do?"

"Is there anything left for me other than death?"

"You might gain your freedom, given your skill and popularity." He could see the Greek looking at him in the dim light. "No, there isn't anything else," he replied solemnly. "Fighting will prolong your life, and where there's life, there's hope."

"You told me hope is for fools."

"Perhaps I was wrong."

"Do you want me to fight?"

"I want you to live."

"Where's Murena?"

"She was moved to the stables."

"Will I get her back if I fight?"

"I don't know."

"Send her to me."

"Will you fight if she comes?"

"Yes."

The Nightman called for the guard and returned to the Master with the message. As shadows grew long across the courtyard, the Greek heard someone outside. The window slid open, but he could not make out the face peering in.

"Murena?" the Greek called out.

"What is it about you?"

The Greek recognized the Master's voice. "I was free! I would be in Thessaly now if you had let me go."

"You have a gift. Men become free in the arena, as I did, and I offer you a chance at that freedom. Life could be good for you. Tiberius won't live forever. The Imperial games will return, but even if they don't, some generous editor might grant you freedom."

"What do you mean?"

"You and the woman, you could both be free if you continue to win. But, if you escape again, I will find you and you will die on a cross next to Murena."

The Greek stood and walked to the small opening. He could barely see the Master's features, but it was enough; if only he had a sword.

"I will never be free until your blood soaks into the sand!"

***

The Master had managed to find and hire another trainer for the Greek, but it wasn't easy. He had extended his funds to their limit and owed the senator a great debt and, with only the senator's nephew's games planned, for which he would receive nothing, the future looked bleak. And all for the sake of the Greek. The one bright spot was that the escape had seemed to enhance his reputation, though some editors were reluctant to bring the Greek into their venue for fear he would attempt it again. Finding another match was difficult.

Jantinus was a young Celt who had fought as a dimachaerus with a bright future until he made a mistake and was stabbed in the thigh. Now in search of work, any work, as few would hire ex-gladiators, he found his way to the school of the Master. He was unable to speak Greek, so the Nightman worked with him as they began preparing the Greek to fight in Tarentum.

The Greek soon regained his fighting form and seemed to retain the killing spirit he would need in the arena. If anything, he was even more aggressive. Murena had returned to him the second night, but their movements were restricted. They remained in the cramped cell. The Greek was only allowed out to train, eat, and bathe. Murena was confined to the cell at all times except for an occasional trip to the baths with other slaves. She became fearful for her future as rumors flew that the Master had a terrible fate planned for the Greek in his next bout.

***

The journey to Tarentum was fraught with apprehension. It was the first time the Greek had been taken out of the security of the school since his escape. An armed guard, supplied by the senator for a large fee, accompanied the wagons. The Greek rode in a cage chained hand and foot and there were strict orders he not be released until they reached the arena. He was even forced him to sleep in the cart. Murena was not allowed to accompany him.

Catalus Paulus, nephew of Senator Flavius, was a piece of humanity the world could have lived without. A big man, he was completely devoid of intelligence, humility, morals, or looks, and considered himself a gladiator, much to the embarrassment and humiliation of his family. Catalus spent most of his time drinking and chasing young women and showed no inclination to pursue any occupation in life. The senator owed a debt to Catalus' father, thus he was attempting to make a politician of him. It appeared an impossible task. If any bright spot was apparent to the Master, it was that Catalus would surely cause a scene at some point.

Once the Greek had been secured safely in his cell, Catalus appeared. He laughed and mocked the young gladiator, then challenged the Greek to a bout and insisted the Master allow it. The senator himself had to intervene to remove his nephew from the cells. The Master missed this event, though he certainly would have enjoyed pairing the young man with his Greek. He even contemplated offering a bet with the senator on the outcome, but thought better of it considering his financial situation.

The Greek was the featured performer. The Master had kept his opponent a secret other than the fact it was to be a murmillo. As the Greek walked to the entrance gate, a strange feeling came over him, a feeling that this was right, this was what was supposed to be, the path the gods had prepared for him. The Nightman was correct; he would always be a gladiator.

The murmillo was waiting by the gate as the Greek approached. A helmet rested on his right arm while his shield leaned against the wall. He was nearly as big as the Giant, but the Greek was extremely confident. Light flooded the tunnel as the gate flew open and the two walked to the center of the arena, turned left, and approached the editor's box. Catalus, seated next to the senator, immediately began to hurl insults at the Greek as the senator attempted to silence him.

After the gladiators examined and secured their respective weapons, the murmillo put on his helmet and they moved to the center of the arena. Already, cries of *Graecus* surrounded them. The Greek began to put on a show with his swords, and as he listened to the people, it was confirmed in his mind; he truly loved the adoration of the fans.

His opponent, a young, unskilled, and poorly trained man, was already overwhelmed before a single sword thrust. The Greek started to advance, but his opponent was moving in the opposite direction. He tried to engage him, but the murmillo continued to elude combat.

The cheers of *Graecus* evaporated to whistles and boos. Objects were thrown into the arena as the Greek chased his opponent. He came to rest in the center once more and listened to the reaction of the crowd. The Greek realized what the Master had done to him— he was being humiliated. He decided to try juggling his swords again, but the crowd laughed.

A guard came into the arena carrying a long metal rod that glowed red at one end. The murmillo leaned against the boards and cowered behind his shield as the guard walked up to him and pushed the rod onto the man's thigh. The murmillo screamed in agony and fled toward the Greek, who swiped at him, but missed. The anger of the crowd grew and fights broke out.

As the Greek watched the attendant with the rod leave the arena, he was struck with an idea. He walked over to the gate, sat down, and folded his arms. Shouts grew louder. The patrons were on the verge of a riot when the senator gave a sign to the guards. The gate opened again and the same man returned with another hot poker and headed straight for the Greek. Just before he could singe him, the Greek sprang up and attacked the man.

The rod rang out with each strike of the Greek's swords. A silence crept over the audience as they watched in disbelief. It was against the rules of civilized combat for a gladiator to attack a guard. He struggled to fend off the Greek while he backed toward the gate. One of the three armed guards ran to his assistance.

The Greek slashed at the rod and then the guard's spear, breaking it midway. Before the guard could unsheathe his sword, the Greek cut him down and resumed his attack on the first man. He finally knocked the rod from the attendant's hands and stabbed him. The Greek now swung around to face the other two guards, who ran at him with spears lowered. He struck at both and deflected their blows, though one grazed his right shoulder and caused a superficial wound. They abandoned their spears and drew swords.

They attacked the Greek, who fought like a madman, striking and deflecting their blows, stabbing, and moving rapidly from side to side. The crowd was on its feet screaming and calling for more blood. They had never seen anything like this and lapped it up like wild beasts at a feeding frenzy. With all that was going on, everyone had forgotten the murmillo. He stood leaning on the boards and watched the events unfold, oblivious to his own fate.

The Greek continued to battle the two guards. They were showing signs of weakening in their attempt to kill the wayward gladiator. The Greek was finding it difficult to discover an opening in their armor, but finally managed to slash the arm of one, which caused him to drop his sword. With one swoop, the Greek slit his throat and nearly sliced off his head in the process. The other, now rendered helpless against the Greek, battled on, but was quickly overwhelmed and killed.

The murmillo realized his peril and ran past him, but the Greek moved fast, cut off his escape, and slashed the back of his legs. He collapsed onto the sand, screaming in pain. The Greek thrust his sword into the man's belly, twisted it, and slowly pulled it out.

Catalus had been leaning over the edge of the wall and screaming at the Greek, when, in the frenzy of the moment, arms swinging wildly, he lost his balance and plunged down into the arena. A cloud of dust rose around him as he shook his head and tried to stand. The crowd began calling for his blood.

The Greek stepped in front of him, flipped one of his swords, and extended the handle to Catalus. The senator was screaming for his nephew to run as he called for more guards. The crowd was out of control. They yelled for the Greek to slit the throat of this detested rat of a man. The Greek couldn't understand them, but he knew what they wanted. Catalus shook his head in refusal. He was trembling with fear. In a flash, the Greek grazed Catalus' neck with his other sword. It was enough to draw a thin line of blood. He backed away and raised his swords high in the air.

As if it was a signal, the crowd went wild. Sandals, food, pieces of the seats, and anything people could find were thrown in all directions. People were jumping, and being thrown, into the arena and Catalus was running in panicked circles. He attempted to climb out, but the smooth walls allowed no grip.

Senator Flavius was winding his way through the bowels of the structure, headed for a secret passageway to safety, but Catalus would not be as fortunate. His remains would be discovered the next day below the editor's box. The Greek, swords in hand, made his way to the exit gate where the Nightman was waiting to hurry him through the tunnels and out of the arena. This was going to be expensive for someone.

***

The Master left before dawn for the half day's journey to the senator's villa where his presence had been "requested." He believed the senator was going to blame the riot on him. No one could possibly have expected the Greek's reaction. The situation was bad enough with the 10,000 sesterces that he owed for his share of the games, as well as his own expenses and the ire of the gladiators who received nothing for their performances. He might have to sell some of his charges before this was over but their value would have diminished. The Greek was beginning to cost more than he was worth.

Senator Flavius owned one of the largest estates in southeastern Italy and his arrogance and spending ways had, unfortunately, caught the attention of the Emperor's entourage. Not only had the amphitheater been severely damaged in the melee, but the madness had moved into Tarentum and erupted in looting and burning. Part of the city lay in ruins and, with Catalus dead, the blame was extended directly to the senator.

Senator Flavius was in a terrible and fearful mood when the Master arrived, but as a man of high standing descended from one of the more prominent aristocratic families in Italy, he hid his feelings well. The senator was in the middle of discussing the situation with his closest associates and left the Master to wait for nearly two hours without so much as an offer of food or drink. When he finally sent word for him to be brought in, the Master was seething with anger. The senator was seated in the atrium of the massive villa, a room where only the lowest were welcomed.

"Senator," the Master said as he bent to kiss Flavius' ring. "My deepest sympathies on the loss of your highly-respected nephew. He was a shining example of manhood."

"He was a boil on my ass and the world is better off without him. But no matter. His death, and more so the riot that followed, have resulted in grave consequences for myself and, by extension, for you."

"But surely you can't blame me for the riot? I have no control over what happens in the arena. It is obvious more guards should..." He trailed off as the senator glared at him.

"It is only our mutual respect that prevents me from sending an official complaint to Rome blaming you for the entire matter."

That, and the fact no one would believe you, you fat shit, the Master thought as the senator continued.

"I am not the kind of man to blame others, but that still leaves us in an unfortunate situation. As I'm sure you've heard, there has been a rumor that my life might be in peril."

A bit of good news.

"And, given your status in life and your reputation, I thought you might be of assistance to me in such a matter."

"What do you mean by that?"

"I mean no disrespect, but you are a former slave freed by your blade. It is not as though you gained freedom from any type of 'achievement.'"

The Master wondered if he could will the death of the senator.

"I still don't see how I could possibly be of any help in this situation."

"Oh, but that is where you are wrong. I owe an enormous favor to a certain senator. He is a close associate of Gaius, surely soon to be emperor, who owns several gladiators at Capua. Gaius is most desirous of matching one against your Greek. The match would be *sine missione*. Gaius' man is one of the best in Italy. Of course, given the view of his uncle, Gaius must keep his ownership of gladiators a secret so you cannot repeat anything that passes today."

"You want me to offer the Greek as a sacrifice to save your ass from the emperor's assassins? That is what you request of me?"

"He could win. It is not a sure loss."

"The Greek is not an ordinary gladiator, but his competition has been far from the quality you're talking about. I know Gaius' stable by reputation, and there are few the Greek would stand a chance against, especially if you mean to pair him against Beryllus."

"I have guarantees it wouldn't be Beryllus. The Greek will fight his second man, Maximianus Aureus."

"Maximianus? He's as good as Beryllus! It's a sacrifice!"

"You know of this Maximianus?"

"He is a secutor from central Italy. A dirty and cruel fighter who must have fought twenty-five or thirty bouts and never lost. The Greek has not met an opponent of his caliber. This is a sacrifice!"

"You may refuse."

"And if I do?"

"I will seize your school for what is owed, have you banished from Italy, and send the Greek to fight Maximianus."

"You wouldn't dare!" the Master exclaimed, rising from his seat.

"In a heartbeat."

"If I agree, my debt is paid?"

"I will forgive the money you owe me if the Greek fights Maximianus. The prize money will cover the debt."

"If Gaius is sponsoring the match the award must be excessive."

"25,000 sesterces."

"That's more than I owe you!"

"Think of it as payment for my goodwill."

This bout would most likely mean losing the Greek, but at least he would no longer be held in debt to this goat sitting across from him. He offered his hand to the senator.

"We have a deal?" the senator asked while rising to clasp the Master's hand.

"When is the match?"

"Two months, in Capua. I will send a guard to accompany the Greek to the site, no charge to you."

"Two months," the Master replied, pulling away from the senator's grasp. "I must be off if I am to return before dark. As always, a pleasure." The Master's words dripped with sarcasm as he walked across the atrium to the door.

"One final point," the senator called after him.

The Master stopped just outside the doorway but did not look back.

"If the Greek loses, the debt remains."

"What? Do you—" The door slammed in his face, ending the conversation.

***

The results of what had happened in Tarentum had become known among the gladiators, and many were resentful toward the Greek for putting them under the thumb of the senator. They knew the school would be broken up and everyone sold if he foreclosed. Lucanus had been waiting for the Master's return, but he brushed past him without a word and retired to the private area of the house. It was late the next morning when he called for Lucanus to join him in the tower.

"What is Jantinus like? Is he a capable trainer for the Greek?" the Master inquired.

"Not of the quality of Urbicus, but sufficient. He was a better gladiator than a teacher. Why do you ask?"

"Send for him and the Nightman. I want to speak to all three of you."

Lucanus headed for the training yard and returned with both. Jantinus was amazed at being in the tower. He went to the window and stared across the courtyard until the Master yelled at him.

"The Greek fights in two months at Capua against a secutor, Maximianus Aureus."

"From the stable of Caligula?" the Nightman asked in surprise.

"Yes."

"Maximianus is one of the best in the empire. Why would you pit him against someone like that?"

"Necessity! Never question my decisions! And he will win! You two will make sure of that. Your fate is his fate."

Jantinus grew pale. He wanted to say something, but dared not. The Master looked directly at him.

"Have you seen Maximianus fight?"

"No," he responded, barely above a whisper.

"No matter. You and the Nightman will train the Greek. He must win. Whatever it takes, he wins. Get to work!"

The two returned to the yard, leaving Lucanus and the Master alone.

"How bad is it?" Lucanus asked after gaining the courage to speak.

"If the Greek wins, we're clear. If he loses, I still owe Senator Pig 20,000 sesterces and the Greek will be dead. We could never make that kind of money without him. Even the Nightman can only make 1,500 on a bout. If we keep everything, it will take years to pay him."

***

The Master rode out without informing anyone of his intentions before the sun had risen the next day. It was late in the afternoon when he arrived at the inn on the road to Brundisium. He pulled the innkeeper aside and spoke in hushed tones. After a dinner of porridge and bread, the Master sat in a corner with a jug of wine.

Two figures entered the bar and walked over to the Master's table.

"Don't sit. We'll go outside to talk. Too many ears in here." The Master motioned at the innkeeper's wife.

The two men followed him silently out the door and along the road a short distance before stopping.

"I've a job for you. Pays good."

Fabius glanced at his partner, Artorius. "What kinda job?"

"I need a problem eliminated."

"Anyone we know?"

"Senator Flavius."

"A senator! Are you out of your fuckin' mind? Even if we could get close enough, it would be suicide. His guards would get us before we could escape. No one is stupid enough to go after a senator, except the emperor!"

"I will pay double the rate," the Master said.

"Double? With what? Word is you're broke and about to sell the school. The senator owns you."

"No one owns me! If you two are cowards, I'll find someone who has the balls to do it!"

"Good luck! You won't find anyone to take out a senator. You best cozy up to Tiberius, get him to do it," Fabius said.

"Yeah, I heard he likes little boys, but maybe he could go for a washed-up gladiator," Artorius added. They walked away laughing.

The Master was furious, but they were right. No one would assassinate a senator. And who was he kidding? He had no money, not even enough for a deposit. He went to his room dejected.

***

The Greek got on well with Jantinus, who was young and had much in common with him. Even though they were unable to understand one another, they learned to communicate. Jantinus had been a rising star when injured and recognized the caliber of the Greek's abilities. But he had heard about Maximianus. It would be extremely difficult to defeat him.

The Greek realized something was different this time. They pushed him to train harder than for any of the previous bouts. All he knew was the name: Maximianus. Jantinus warned him to be ready for anything and described some of the dirty tricks that Maximianus used on opponents. It would be the first time he fought a secutor, so the Nightman arranged for him to spar with a fully armed individual.

After three weeks of training, the Master had the Greek moved back to the large cell near the Nightman. Murena remained forbidden to enter the training yard. Everyone, especially Murena, noticed a change in the Greek after his return. He was serious and sullen in demeanor as though he had aged decades. The Nightman hoped this would help him win.

Two weeks before Capua, the senator arrived to assess the Greek. "Only in the best interests of the school," he told the Master. But the Master believed the senator planned to bet heavily on the match. And not on the Greek. He huffed and puffed his way up the steep staircase to the tower and stood next to the Master where they could view the training yard. The Greek was fighting a secutor.

He appeared slow and unprepared as he was pushed around by the other gladiator. He was constantly on the defensive and cautious to the point the senator thought him afraid. The senator shifted from one foot to the other and grew red with anger; he suspected the Master of instigating a ruse to humiliate him. He swore an oath under his breath to further punish the Master and see that he was put in his rightful place in the social order.

"Must be an off day," the Master said, grinning widely as the senator stormed out of the tower.

It would take four long days to travel from the school to Capua, and the Master was nervous, not only about the match but the trip itself. It appeared the senator had misgivings as well; he sent several armed guards to accompany them. They avoided inns and stayed with trusted friends. Senator Flavius wasn't about to take any chances; his life depended on this match. Gaius had a lot of influence with his uncle. If anyone could get him off the hook with Tiberius, it was him.

The amphitheater at Capua was much larger than any the Greek had fought in previously, and he was in awe during the pompa. The crowd was loud and rambunctious in anticipation of the featured match between their man, Maximianus, and the Greek, whose reputation preceded him.

The Greek was calm as he lay in the cool of the cell awaiting his bout. He had attempted to see Maximianus, who entered first during the pompa, but had been placed far back in the line behind the novices as a gesture of disrespect by the editor. He didn't understand why everyone seemed so concerned for him. He was experienced now; he had fought and defeated two gladiators in sequence.

When his call came, he rose and stood stoically, waiting for the cell door to open. Two guards accompanied him to the gate. Still no Maximianus. He wondered if there had been a change. The gate opened and the Greek stepped into the arena.

A lone figure stood by the editor's box. He wore a helmet that completely obscured his face except for two tiny eye holes. He wore a greave on his left shin, armor on his right arm, and heavy leather wrappings on his shield arm and around his waist. He was big, but not massive like the Giant. He held a single straight sword in his right hand.

The Greek approached as the crowd whistled and booed him. He stood by the small table and began examining his swords. Suddenly, there was movement to his left. Before the Greek could react, Maximianus' sword sliced through his neck. He stepped back and fell to the ground. He couldn't breathe. Blood gurgled in his throat. His lifeblood poured into the sand. The people began cheering and chanting his name. *"Graecus, Graecus."*

"Graecus!" the guard called.

The Greek was startled awake by the voice. He was covered in sweat, and his limbs trembled. What had the dream meant? His mother had told him all dreams foretell. Would he die today?

The Greek followed the lone guard to the gate. In the dim light, he could see a figure standing to the left wearing a helmet and carrying a long shield on the right arm. A metal greave covered his right leg and his left arm was sheathed in thick leather wrappings; he was left handed. But the Greek had dreamed him right handed. Was the dream false? The Greek was deep in thought when the gate opened and they stepped into the arena. The crowd erupted in a chorus of *Parvus Aureus*, a nickname for their favorite.

Maximianus strode around the arena, arms raised, while the Greek went directly to the table in front of the editor's box. He watched Maximianus, distrustful, as he completed the rounds. The older gladiator walked behind the Greek, then thrust the lower edge of his shield and struck the back of the Greek's calf. Maximianus stepped back and stood staring at the Greek. The helmet he wore was pierced by two tiny eye sockets; the Greek could see neither features nor eyes, which dismayed him.

The two warriors moved cautiously to the center of the arena. Maximianus attacked the Greek, who was limping, but even with his injury, the Greek proved far too agile. The blows struck air. The sight of the Greek wounded caused jubilation amongst the crowd as they spurred on their star.

Maximianus pressed the Greek, who realized how strong this man was as metal crashed against metal. The Greek studied his opponent, but failed to notice any weakness; his skill with the weapons was superb, his size and strength superior to that of the Greek, and he was almost as quick and agile. The Greek moved first left then right. He was confounded by the fact that Maximianus was left handed.

Suddenly, while moving laterally, the Greek was blinded in a hail of sand thrown up by the lower edge of Maximianus' shield, which was specially designed with a narrow lip along the bottom. The Greek retreated and struggled to open his eyes enough to see the shadow of his opponent rushing at him.

He flayed blindly with both swords and struck the shield, but felt a stinging sensation on his right arm then a thin ribbon of blood trickled down. He tried to rub the sand out of his eyes, but Maximianus would have none of it and pushed his advantage. Just as the Greek managed to regain some sight, another cloud of sand engulfed him.

The Greek fell back. Maximianus was relentless in his charge and never gave ground, intent on the kill. But for his speed, he would soon have fallen. He fought back blow for blow. Maximianus turned his shield horizontally and thrust it violently into the chest of the

Greek as he sliced at his legs in an attempt to render the Greek helpless, but he made a mistake. As Maximianus lowered himself onto one knee, shield held above his head, he slipped ever so slightly and had to twist the shield to keep from falling forward. He had perfected this move and rendered many opponents helpless, but never had he faced one as fast or astute as the Greek.

The Greek spied the massive back of his opponent exposed and propelled himself over the shield, spun around, and plunged a sword into Maximianus. Maximianus pulled away enough to lessen the damage of the blow. It wasn't a fatal blow, but it was serious and placed him in deadly peril against an opponent with the Greek's skill. Maximianus had gained some respect for the Greek; this was not going to be an easy kill. Their maneuvers brought the crowd to their feet screaming for their champion, though some were shifting their allegiance to the Greek.

Now the Greek attacked viciously, his swords a blur, slicing and thrusting in a never-ending assault. It didn't take long for the wound and the heat to begin to wear down Maximianus. He began to think he might lose without drastic measures. The Greek moved in close when he caught the glint as the sun glanced off metal and he turned his body, but the dagger, which Maximianus had concealed in the wrappings of his right arm, had pierced his right side.

The Greek pulled the blade out and dropped it, but Maximianus was on him again. He was struck with the shield and knocked off balance. The Greek attempted to stretch back as far as possible without falling over as the tip of sword nicked the lower part of his neck and drew blood. The people sensed victory was near for Maximianus. When the Greek thought about how near he had been to freedom, and home, his anger grew.

The anger transferred to his swords. Blow after blow rained down on Maximianus, who was beginning to weaken. The Greek's swords found their mark on the body of his opponent; blood ran freely from the wound on Maximianus' back. He no longer attacked the Greek but was backing away from the ever-increasing number of blows. A small chorus of *Graecus* began to rise in the stands. Blood and sand caked the naked skin of the Greek, his long hair was matted with sweat and dirt, and he fought with a viciousness seldom witnessed.

Unable to fight, Maximianus leaned his weight on the shield and stood like a wounded deer awaiting the final thrust of the spear from the hunter. The Greek stepped back, moved to the center of the arena, and began juggling the swords. Maximianus dropped onto one knee. The Greek returned to Maximianus and motioned for him to remove his helmet with his sword, but he refused. He attempted to stand, but his legs wouldn't hold his bulk.

The Greek moved in for the kill. Maximianus sprang up as a tiger springs from the bush onto an unsuspecting antelope and thrust his dagger into the Greek's right side again. With one last bit of strength, the Greek plunged his sword into Maximianus' chest, whose arm jerked back and pulled the dagger out. He stiffened and collapsed onto the sand. The audience was stunned at the death of their champion. He had fought for nearly ten years in Capua and was loved and respected by the people, and now he was dead.

The Greek staggered to the center of the arena, his right hand pressed against the wound to staunch the flow of blood, and raised his sword into the air. The silence continued for a few seconds before the people erupted into shouts of *Graecus*. The Greek turned, soaking in the sights and sounds, then collapsed onto the sand.

***

She peered out the window day after day waiting for him, for a sign, for anything. But nothing. No one came. The baby screamed while the older children vied for her attention. She could never get used to being alone. His time spent at home had increased of late but it would never be enough.

And then he appeared. He walked slowly. His head hung low as though bearing bad news, but it didn't matter. He was home. She wiped her tears as her husband stopped and stared at her.

"He won," Miltiades began, "but he was seriously wounded. I don't know if he will fight again or live. He remains in Capua; he was too fragile to move. I stayed two days with him and he had not awakened. The Master sent me home."

She knew all too well their fate was tied to the Greek. If he continued to fight and win, the Nightman would remain a trainer, but if not, he would be forced back into the arena. Every time the Nightman left her, she feared that he wouldn't return.

Her name was Decima. She was a slave sold into the local brothel that supplied the school. The Nightman had been taken with her beauty and demeanor the first moment he saw her, but at the time, he had been an unknown prospect who had fought only three bouts. He had requested the Master purchase her as his wife. On the advice of Lucanus, and believing that the Nightman would be a star, the Master had agreed and even set them up in a small house near the school. As the Nightman grew in prominence and his winnings increased, they were able to purchase a bit of land on which sat a house that was a two-hour walk from the school. Happy with her new life, Decima gave birth to a son, now five, and then a daughter, four, and recently another boy.

Her oldest boy, Marcus, was beginning to understand what his father did and would, on occasion, grasp a stick, brandish it like a sword, and proclaim he was a gladiator. Whatever the gods held in store for his children, the Nightman prayed every day none would claim that fate. The Nightman was proud of his family, though at times he longed for his other wife, the one left behind in Athens, and their two children. After so many years, he had given up any hope of returning. Even if he did go back, she would have remarried, and his children would have no memories of him.

A week after the Greek's match with Maximianus, a sullenness had settled over the school. The young gladiator remained in the infirmary at Capua with the medicus by his side day and night, as ordered by the Master, who was gravely concerned for his well-being. It was still not known if he would survive. The dagger had breached a lung and caused severe bleeding. The victory had erased the Master's debt to the senator and enhanced the reputation of the Greek, but if he died, it would be for nothing.

The Nightman was playing with his children when the noise of an approaching carriage echoed through the small house. He watched Lucanus descend and limp up the walkway to where he stood in the open doorway.

"The Master sends me. The Greek is awake. The medicus says he can travel and you're to go get him in Capua."

"What's his condition?"

"I don't know. The Master fears for his safety in Capua. You need to come back with me."

"Do I go alone?"

"No, I'm to accompany you with an armed guard."

"From the senator's greedy fingers?"

"You've not heard the news? Senator Flavius is in hiding. He fears the death squads of Caligula."

"Has Tiberius crossed the Styx?"

"No, but Caligula practically runs the empire."

"What about the Greek? Does Caligula seek revenge on him?"

"Not to worry. The death squads were created from the mind of the Master, nothing but rumors to scare the fat pig. If anything, Caligula wishes to purchase the Greek, not harm him. Come, it is a long journey to Capua."

The Nightman gathered a few clothes and departed without a word to either Decima or the children. The trip was long and tiring, and both men were apprehensive as to what they would discover upon arrival. It had been three weeks since the match. They found the Greek pale, thin, and barely able to stand on his own, but the medicus was cautiously optimistic.

Due to his fragile condition, it took seven days to return to the school. When the Greek finally saw the compound, a wave of joy came over him, the joy of being home again. But it was tinged with sadness at the fact he was beginning to accept the school as home. Though he thought of them less and less, he still longed to be in Thessaly once more with his family.

Murena was ecstatic at his return and took over his care. They were again in the large cell, and the Master had relaxed the restrictions, which allowed her to accompany him everywhere in the compound. Now it caused less friction with the other gladiators and trainers for, after his defeat of Maximianus, the Greek was considered an elite gladiator, a status few achieved. Some of the gladiators had even gone so far as to make offerings at the shrine of Hera where the Greek sacrificed every day to ask for her divine protection.

The Greek never spoke of his bout with Maximianus to Murena, though she heard the stories circulating. She believed he was sent from a god and her divine protector. Within a month of his return, the Greek was training again. No one was happier about this than Jantinus. No new match was set, but requests were coming to the Master for the Greek's appearance. Everything appeared to be going well: the senator remained in hiding, the Master's debts had been paid, and the Greek was healing. Now the Master began plotting his rise to stardom and a match in the Imperial games at Rome. If only Tiberius would die.

CHAPTER VIII

IT WASN'T OFTEN THAT THE MASTER REQUESTED THE NIGHTMAN come up to the tower. He entered without knocking and stood next to the Master in silence.

"We're going to Venusia in two months. Will the Greek be ready?"

"He's training. There doesn't seem to be any permanent damage. I think two months will be enough time. What's planned for him?"

"A special event. You and he are going to fight two opponents, together, as a team."

"You said I don't have to fight any more if I train him!"

"Circumstances change. This is a good payday, and it will be your last match."

"What does it pay?"

"800 sesterces. Plus, 200 more from the Greek's share, if you're quiet."

"What kind of match? What do you mean we'll be fighting together?"

"You and the Greek against two opponents. Everyone fights at the same time. Train with him and develop some new techniques together. I want a flashy show. Don't worry about your opponents. They'll be soft, but put on a show and make it look difficult. Maybe you could try some of the juggling the Greek does. Give them something new."

The Nightman was suspicious. It wasn't like the Master to set up the Greek with a sure win. That wouldn't help his reputation. But it was good pay, and it might be interesting to fight with the Greek. He left without accepting because an answer was irrelevant.

"What did he want?" the Greek asked upon the Nightman's return to the yard.

"You and I are going to fight as a team against two opponents."

"Together? Have you ever done this?"

"No, but I did see a match where gladiators fought as teams once. Sometimes they even put several on each team, but the lanista doesn't like that. Too many could be killed at once."

"How long?"

"Two months. Will you be ready by then?"

"I'm ready now!"

The Nightman could remember being young and cocky, but age had taught him a bit of wisdom, the wisdom to know how dangerous it was in the arena even against a soft opponent.

The Master wouldn't divulge their opponents, but Jantinus seemed unconcerned and rose to this new challenge. The old trainer, Pinna, who taught the Nightman, had seen several such bouts.

They performed most of their training in the yard, but Pinna had requested the use of the villa's front courtyard that would be free of other gladiators to allow them to work on new maneuvers. The Master obliged them but increased the guards on the main gate and forbade anyone to enter or exit while they were training. The Master had told Pinna to concentrate especially on the Nightman's performance.

The trainers would pit the Nightman and Greek against two opponents to develop methods and signals for them to use to communicate while engaged in battle. They found it difficult to work together without bumping into one another or slicing into the other with a sword, a possibly fatal mistake in the arena. The Greek had regained his strength and seemed to improve his skills every day with the assistance of Jantinus. He was resolved to his fate as a gladiator and believed the gods had not abandoned him but were propelling him in this new direction.

***

Venusia was a long day's journey from the school. Only the Greek and the Nightman went, accompanied by Jantinus and several guards. The Master didn't believe in the Greek's newfound appreciation of the sport and remained skeptical as to his loyalty.

Lucanus had insisted that they brand the Greek on the neck but the Master refused. He preferred the young gladiator retain the appearance of a free man.

The Nightman and the Greek were placed in separate cells at the arena across from one another. They were to fight last in the featured match. When their time arrived, they followed the guard to the entrance gate where their opponents were already waiting. The Greek wasn't aware at first, but the Nightman recognized them; one was a Thracian and the other a dimachaerus. It was rare for gladiators of the same style to fight as opponents. The Nightman's heart stuttered with anticipation.

When they entered the arena, it became clear who the people had come to see. A wave of *Graecus* flowed through the crowd. People were already standing, calling to him, and stamping their feet with excitement. Everyone was here to see the son of a god, the mere boy who had defeated one of the best gladiators in the empire and would soon spill blood in their arena.

Their opponents went directly to the front of the editor's box, but the Greek and Nightman walked around the exterior of the arena with their arms raised in triumph and soaked in the adulation. The Nightman knew it wasn't for him, but the Greek didn't mind sharing with his friend, his brother of sand and blood.

They arrived before the editor, saluted him, inspected and grasped their weapons, and strode to the center of the arena. The Greek put on a show for the crowd while their opponents stood near the wall and watched in amusement, but they knew this wouldn't remain amusing for long. Both were experienced gladiators with winning records and much more dangerous than the Master had let on; they had the ability to not only put on a good show but to win.

When the crowd grew tired of the Greek's antics, the two gladiators motioned to one another and stepped forward. The four men engaged in combat near the center of the arena. They were all cautious. They tested one another to determine ability and, most importantly, find a weakness. This initial sparring looked impressive, but it was not dangerous.

The Greek tried to isolate the Thracian, but he would have none of it and left the dimachaerus to fight with the young gladiator. The curved swords of his opponent and the fact he had no shield confounded the Greek, whose every blow was countered. The Nightman was having better luck; he was far superior to his rival.

Without warning, the two opponents broke off combat and moved together, back to back. The Greek and the Nightman stared briefly at each other and exchanged hand signals. They stood shoulder to shoulder and moved forward, but, just as their opponents turned to face them, the Greek and the Nightman split apart, made a small circle, and rushed in from each side. The speed of their attack rattled their opponents and, together with the viciousness of the Greek, turned the match in their favor.

The Greek pounded the swords of his opponent, and the sound rang through the arena. The dimachaerus was bigger and stronger than him, but not as skilled, and soon backed away. A few nicks to his body drew blood that enticed the crowd to new heights of ecstasy. The Greek was so engrossed in his own world, he hadn't noticed the plight of the Nightman.

Perhaps his long absence from the arena, his age, cockiness, or all of these combined had driven the Nightman against the wall of the arena. His left side and arm were bleeding, and his shield was nearly useless. The Greek believed the roar of the crowd was for him. Out of the corner of his eye, he spotted the Nightman about to surrender. The Greek knew that this Thracian would take no heed.

He pushed back his adversary and knocked him off balance, turned, and sent one of his swords hurtling at the Thracian's naked back just as he was about to plunge his sword into the Nightman's chest. The wounded Thracian spun around and dropped his weapon as he tried in vain to pull the metal from his flesh, but it was too late. He staggered sideways and the Nightman, seeing his advantage, drove his sword into the man's side. The gladiator collapsed onto the ground, his lifeblood sinking into the sand.

The Master was intently watching the match from high in the

stands; he had not been invited into the editor's box. The fact the Nightman was in peril was of great concern for him. Losing such a gladiator would have dire consequences on his financial situation.

As the Greek regained his balance and assessed the situation, his opponent realized his advantage and attacked ferociously. The Greek reacted in the nick of time as the blade sliced dangerously close. He managed to move enough to deflect the force of the blow, which left a thin cut on his arm and a trail of blood. Both swords were slashing the air a hair's breadth from the Greek's skin, who defended as best he could with his one remaining weapon.

Backing away, the Greek noticed a movement to his right and nearly struck at the Nightman before he realized who it was. Another blow just missed the Greek's neck and caused him to move away from the Nightman, who was attempting to hand the Greek his curved sword, but the Greek's opponent would have none of it. The man knew the Nightman couldn't fight and, if he could get to the Greek before he grasped that second sword, he might win.

The Greek ran toward the edge of the arena in hopes of drawing the dimachaerus away, but instead of following him, the man turned and rushed at the Nightman. Distracted with what he believed to be a certain victory, he had not realized the speed of the Greek nor the anger behind his blows. The man was poised to inflict a fatal blow on the Nightman when the Greek ran behind his opponent and, with one swift strike, severed his head. It flew to the left, hit the sand, and rolled several feet away. The man's body slumped to the ground.

The Nightman looked up at the Greek and came to the realization that he was no ordinary man. The Greek smiled and raised his sword high. The crowd went wild. The Nightman motioned to the head of their fallen opponent. The Greek drove his sword into the severed neck and raised it into the air. Spectators were beckoning the Greek toward them and pointing to the head. In one swift gesture, he flung it into the stands.

The Greek helped the Nightman to his feet, and they hurried to the exit gate and out of the arena. The echoes of *Graecus* could be heard above the thunder of pounding feet as they wound their way through the passageways. A guard met them and hurried them out a door where a waiting carriage sped away with them safely inside. They traveled for several miles before arriving at a villa on the outskirts of town where the medicus was waiting.

***

The Master had expected to be in a better mood, but given the result of the bout in Venusia, his situation was about to become dire. As much as he loathed Senator Flavius, his hatred paled in comparison to his feelings he had for the man who would soon be standing next to him.

Scelestus Nothus was a lanista with a school located near Venusia. He was the reason the Greek and the Nightman had fought there a week before. Never a gladiator himself, he was the ultimate exploiter of them and always called for bouts to be *sine missione*. He matched poorly trained men in the arena, men who he picked at random from the slave markets, to be thrown to their deaths against experienced fighters. Scelestus had no regard for the mechanics of the game; to him, it was simply butchery. But these were hard times that required a man to do things he never would have contemplated under normal circumstances. Approaching footsteps on the stairs alerted the Master to Scelestus' arrival.

"Master, still standing around pissing up the wall, I see."

"Scelestus, I hope all is well."

"As long as there is blood to spill on the sand, what could be better?"

"Wine?"

"Only to clean the dust out of my throat."

"Of course." The Master motioned to a nearby slave.

"I see your extra prick still dangles from your neck," he said, casting a glance towards Lucanus, who had led him up the stairs.

The Master motioned for Lucanus to depart. "How was your trip?"

"Pounded my balls on Tiberius' rat-ass roads. How do you think I am?"

"My hospitality is extended if you require a bed for the night."

"A bed with an ass? Or your preference, a prick."

"Either can be arranged."

"I'll pass. I'm staying with a cousin not far from here, and he always brings in the nicest ass for my visits. So, let's get this business settled."

"As you wish. My offer remains. 30,000 sesterces and he's yours."

Scelestus burst into a fit of laughter. "After that performance?" he asked, attempting to control himself.

"An off day. He hadn't trained for a while, but it won't take much to put him back in shape."

Suddenly serious, Scelestus stared at the Master. "Sell me the other. I'll give you 40,000, cash, by tomorrow."

"He isn't for sale. He's headed for Rome."

"Rome? He will be retired, or dead, long before there are any games in Rome. Tiberius grows younger sucking the juice from those young pricks. He's going to live forever. Gaius will be killed before Tiberius allows him to rule. You'll never make anything with him. 45,000."

"If he's worthless, why do you offer so much?"

"Because I have the connections to make money with him. No one will deal with a slave! Owning this place doesn't make you any better. Now me, I was born free, and remain so. I've never soiled my hands with blood for the people. I can make him a star. The other? He's past his prime. I couldn't give you more than 10,000."

"Ten thousand!"

"Easy, friend," Scelestus cautioned, touching his belt, under which a dagger was concealed. "You aren't the only one prepared."

The Master stepped back and took a deep breath. "25,000."

"Word is, you're sinking in debt. The good senator took you for a ride and that mess in Tarentum." He shook his head. "Of course, considering where you came from, it doesn't surprise me. I'm doing you a favor by being here. No one else will buy your shit. The only thing you have of value is the Greek. 50,000."

The Master stood dumbfounded. Was he hearing correctly? This piece of human garbage was offering 50,000 sesterces for the Greek? He could run the school for two years on that even without any bouts. "20,000 for the Nightman, final offer. That's all you're going to get here today."

"18,000, final offer if you won't sell the Greek."

"You'll pay in cash on delivery?"

"If he heals. I don't buy damaged goods."

"That might be a few months."

"I can wait. And he trains. I want him in shape."

"It will be taken care of. I need a deposit."

"You don't trust me?" Scelestus grinned broadly.

"Not as far as I can spit."

"Perhaps I underestimated you, Master. Maybe you're not as stupid as I used to think. No, I think you are," he sneered, handing the Master a bag of coins. "Ten percent, return fifteen if he isn't delivered. Agreed?"

"Agreed. 18,000 for the Nightman, when he's healed."

"Agreed. Now, as much as I hate to leave your company, ass awaits. Must take care of this problem," he said, pointing at his crotch.

I should kick this piece of shit down the stairs, the Master thought as Scelestus departed.

Lucanus returned shortly. "So, did you do it?"

"18,000 for him."

"What about his woman and children?"

"That's up to Scelestus and no concern of mine."

"He isn't going to take this well. When does he leave?"

"Three months, if he's healed. I could have doubled that if he had fought better in Venusia."

"If not for the Greek, he'd be dead. At least we got something for him. And eighteen isn't bad, considering his age. He's only got maybe five more years left in him."

"He offered me 50,000 for the Greek. You think I should have taken it?"

"Not if you want to fight in Rome. We've no other prospect."

The Master returned to the window and watched the Greek sparing in the yard. "Is the Nightman still in the infirmary?"

"Yes. The medicus says he should be walking around again in a few days. Are you going to tell him?"

Silence greeted Lucanus' question.

"What about the Greek? Jantinus doesn't speak Greek," he continued.

"The woman can translate, and by now they should be able to work without words. He'll be fine."

"Until you sell him."

"Leave me!"

***

The Nightman was sitting at the edge of the yard watching the Greek spar. There was a bond between them that hadn't existed before Venusia because he knew the Greek had put his own life in jeopardy to save him. No one had ever done such a thing. When you entered the arena, all that mattered was self-preservation. The Greek had broken that rule. There was no one like him, and perhaps there never had been. He jumped when Lucanus touched his shoulder.

"Come to the villa with me," he said.

The gladiator rose slowly, favoring his left side, and followed Lucanus.

The Master was in the central garden. He seldom met with gladiators in the garden. He offered the Nightman a chair and sat opposite him.

"You have been good for this school," the Master began, "but now I have a way for you to better serve me."

"I don't understand."

"I have sold you. You'll be going to Venusia."

"With Scelestus? You can't be serious! Why would you sell me to that pig?"

"Scelestus will help your career in ways I can't. He has connections, even in Rome. Wouldn't you like to fight in Rome?

You can gain your freedom there."

"How much?"

"How much?"

"What did he pay? I have some savings. I could buy my freedom. How much?"

"18,000."

The Nightman slumped back in the chair. "What if I offered you all my winnings?"

"The deal is done."

"How long before I leave?"

"Three months, maybe longer. You must heal and train, and don't think of doing anything stupid. Harm yourself and I'll sell you and that whore to the beast master."

"What about my family? What happens to them?"

"Don't worry. Scelestus will take care of everything. He's moving your family to Venusia. It'll be better than here. You'll be closer. This is best for everyone."

"And what about the Greek? Who'll train him?"

"He will be fine. And besides, that woman can translate for Jantinus. That's what she's for."

The Nightman looked dejectedly at the floor. Everything was supposed to be good. He would train the Greek and make enough to support his family, and it wouldn't have mattered how long he continued to work. At least there would be no more fighting. But this. Scelestus had the reputation of being the worse lanista in the empire. The Nightman stared at the floor, shaking his head.

It would be another week before the Nightman told the Greek of the deal. No one was prepared for his reaction. Everything the Greek had was taken away: his family, his freedom, his dignity, and now they were taking the only friend he had. His new family was being ripped from him. He brandished wooden swords and screamed for the Master to enter the yard. Everyone stayed clear of him until, exhausted from the anger and tears, he collapsed in a heap where he was left for the night.

Within a week, at the persuasion of the Nightman, the Greek was training again. Both knew these would be their last days together; they might never see one another again. It was difficult, but the Greek had become resigned to his fate. The Master had arranged for another bout in Capua. He had agreed to allow the Nightman to train the Greek if the gladiator got himself back into shape. They attempted to put the impending separation out of their minds as best they could so the Greek, Murena, and the Nightman could enjoy their time together.

Everything had been going well, so well, in fact, that the Master made a rare appearance inside the yard. He was distracted momentarily while speaking to Lucanus, but a moment was all the Greek needed. When he saw the man, anger flashed red before his eyes. Instantly, he was beside the Master with swords striking. The Master didn't have any chance to grasp his dagger. It was lucky that guards were close by and able to secure the Greek before he inflicted any serious damage, though the Master was bleeding, and everyone in the yard had witnessed the attack. The Master's leadership had been questioned before, but now he lost all credibility.

The Greek was confined to a small cell alone. However, it was eleven weeks before Capua, and the Master's fortunes depended on this bout. He hoped this would be the pathway to Rome, so there was nothing he could do to lessen those chances. Suppressing his rage, the Master agreed to let the Greek resume training the next day. But he would not be caught unawares in the yard again. The Greek would be made to pay for his indiscretion.

***

The Master headed to Capua to confirm arrangements for the special bout, a bout he was positive would propel the Greek into the Imperial games. While the Master was away, Lucanus observed the growing disrespect of the Greek and Murena. The Greek trained shorter hours than everyone else, had longer, and private, access to the baths accompanied by Murena, and demanded better food.

Even though Lucanus was the authority when the Master was absent, his words meant little to the Greek. He hated having to rely on

Murena to translate and suspected her of telling the Greek what she wanted him to hear. Lucanus tried to use the Nightman, but he refused to become involved, and the messages that he sent to the Master remained unanswered.

Probus was a German soldier who had become a prisoner of war and was bought by the Master several years before the Greek had arrived at the school. He had a nasty disposition that belied his name and a particular hatred of Greeks. But as much as his hatred made him desire a match against the Greek, he knew better than attempt anything in the training yard as the Greek had a large following of supporters.

The Nightman cautioned the Greek that his arrogant ways were drawing the ire of his fellow gladiators. Though it was not good to befriend these men, it was even worse to make them his enemies. Even the trainers and slaves were beginning to despise him. He needed to draw less attention to himself and save the performances for the arena.

The Master arrived back at the school after he had managed to secure the details of the match in Capua, the site of the largest gladiator school outside of Rome. The Greek would be the featured performer again, but he didn't know anything about the match except that he would be fighting a Thracian. Lucanus had a bad feeling about it, but he didn't dare question the Master. It was bad enough he had to inform him of the Greek's antics during his absence. The news did not seem to distress the Master in the least, which made Lucanus suspicious. In fact, the Master made no attempt to discipline the Greek, or even speak to him.

The Nightman put the young gladiator on a rigorous training routine, much to the chagrin of the Greek, though he complied out of their mutual friendship. With the Nightman training him, Murena had little to do. She spent most of her time lounging about in the courtyard or relaxing in their cell, which was left open during the day. She was allowed to wander the grounds and the main house until she began to order the household slaves around. There were

too many complaints about her for the Master to ignore, so he had
to confine her to the enclosed areas where the gladiators roamed.
She complained to the Greek about her treatment, but he was busy
training again and, while sympathetic to her plight, only half-
heartedly passed her grievance on to Lucanus.

Few would volunteer to spare with the Greek due to his
aggressiveness and temper. Several opponents were severely
wounded before the Nightman made him switch to fighting against
the stuffed practice dummies.

One hot afternoon, Murena left to lie in the coolness of their cell.
Many had departed early from training, but the Greek continued
working in the nearly deserted yard. The feel of the practice swords
in his hands comforted him, though he preferred the real ones. He
was about to leave and collect Murena for their jaunt to the baths
when a young gladiator, a recent arrival the Master had purchased
cheap with some of the Greek's winnings, approached him. This
fellow was also training as a dimachaerus, and the Greek seldom
had the opportunity to work with such a fighter. The young man was
nervous as he indicated his desire to spar. He didn't speak Greek,
and the Nightman had also departed, but the Greek understood and
agreed, suggesting he would go easy on him.

The young man was fast and agile but lacked the natural skill
with the swords that the Greek possessed. In spite of his
inexperience, he was a good match for the Greek. The Greek could
appreciate the abilities of his opponents, though he had little respect
for any of them. He knew that in a real bout against this young man,
he would soon kill him. The Greek was nearly clipped on the ear as
he lost his concentration daydreaming about screaming crowds, but
he quickly recovered and taught the young man a hard lesson. With
several consecutive blows, he disarmed the young opponent,
knocked him to the ground, and stood poised for the kill. He smiled,
offered his hand, and helped the young man to his feet.

The Greek was sweating from the workout as he walked back to
his cell. The yard was deserted, and he anticipated the cool of his

cell and the bath to follow. Murena would probably be asleep and well rested, which meant she would keep him awake most of the night talking and making love. He felt good.

The door in the far corner of the yard that led to his cell was locked, which was unusual. He called for a guard and waited. Muffled sounds came from down the hall, but he didn't think anything of it. Fights between gladiators were a regular occurrence.

A guard appeared and opened the door. The shaded hallway felt refreshing as he walked toward his room. By the third step, he heard a scream. The hair stood on the back of his neck as he bolted to the end of the hall, turned right, and saw three guards standing outside his cell. Another scream.

"Murena!" he shouted. Probus stood inside the Greek's cell. He had Murena by the neck and was slapping her repeatedly. He grasped her hair in his left hand and slammed her face into the table each time she shouted. With his right hand, he struck her on the back, sides, and about the head.

The Greek grabbed the cell door but it was locked. He tried desperately to reach Probus through the bars of the cell, then turned to the guards and shouted at them to open the door. They didn't move. When he lunged for the keys, one guard grabbed the Greek around the neck while two others held his arms down. The Greek screamed and fought, but it was useless. The guards only tightened their grasp on him. He would have sliced them to pieces if he had a sword, but the guards never carried weapons.

He continued to struggle as Probus released his grasp on Murena. She fell limply onto the floor. He turned to the Greek and laughed. The fourth guard opened the cell door, and Probus nonchalantly passed by them. The guards pushed the Greek into the cell and locked the door behind him. He rushed to Murena, who was unconscious. She was bleeding about her face and had several welts on her back and sides. He picked her up and placed her on the bed, cradling her in his arms.

"Get the medicus!" he screamed at the guards. "Hurry, get the medicus!"

The guards turned and walked away. He sat holding her and rocked back and forth while tears streamed down his cheeks.

Murena never regained consciousness. She died during the night. The Greek never let her go.

***

The next day, late in the morning, the Nightman approached his cell with two other gladiators. The Greek had not moved all night.

"We are going to bury her in the cemetery outside the walls. I will see that she has the proper rites, but you can't be there. You must stay in your cell. Do you understand? I will take good care of her, but you must let us in to take her."

The Greek slowly looked up at him. His eyes were red and puffy; Murena's blood stained his hands and face. He turned his gaze to Murena one last time and then nodded his approval. The door opened, and the three men stepped into the cell. They wrapped a cloth around Murena's body and carried her away.

CHAPTER IX

FOR THE NEXT SEVERAL DAYS, THE GREEK LAY ON HIS BED unmoving and would take neither food nor water. The Nightman sat by his bedside talking, but the Greek wasn't in the cell anymore. In his mind, he was back home in Thessaly and could see everything as clear as day. He and Murena were running the farm; it had been a good year. Plenty of rain had produced a bumper crop, and the animals were healthy and grew fatter every day. They had a growing family—a boy and a girl with another on the way. Murena was so happy with her protruding belly, which he would rub upon returning from a hard day's toil in the fields. Even his father had regained his health with his return from Italy. The Greek would sit by the fire in the evening and recount his adventures in Italy with Murena by his side and the children at his feet. His father was proud of him. Tears would run down the side of his face as he imagined the life that he would never live.

By the fourth day, the Nightman began to fear for the Greek's life. Desperate, he leaned close and whispered in the Greek's ear.

"The man who did this is named Probus. He's going to be in Capua. He is retiring, it's his last fight, and he is to appear in a special match right after you. If you stall in the arena and hold your swords, I can arrange for him to enter before you leave. He will not have a weapon."

The Greek turned his head toward the Nightman. "You promise I will be able to kill him if I go to Capua?"

"I will find a way for you to kill him. But silence. Only we can know this."

The Greek sat up on the edge of the bed. "Why did this happen? She didn't deserve this. Why didn't he kill me?"

The Nightman had difficulty holding back his tears. He knew the reason Probus had attacked Murena, but could never divulge the truth for fear of what would happen to his family. It was six weeks until Capua.

The Greek worked hard and regained his fighting form, and now he was filled with an even greater rage and hatred. All he could see before him was blood and pain, and he wanted to inflict as much as possible. He possessed the blood lust the Master had once felt he lacked.

As the Greek trained, he searched the yard for Probus, but the Master had moved him to another location. The Greek pointed out the young dimachaerus to the Nightman. He was hesitant when the Nightman requested he spar with the Greek again but reluctantly agreed.

The Greek was nonchalant as he approached. The young man began apprehensively. He realized the Greek seemed to be enjoying himself and relaxed. This was a good opportunity for him to learn from a master gladiator, especially one the young man admired.

But suddenly everything changed. The gladiator's blows came fast and hard. He began to fear for his safety, but before he could retreat, the Greek brought a hard blow to the young man's genitals. As he buckled and fell toward the ground, the Greek hit the young man's head twice in quick succession with the flat of his sword, splitting it open. The Greek then grabbed one of his swords and beat him viciously on the head before being pulled off by the Nightman and several others who had gathered to watch.

After the incident with the young dimachaerus, the Master forbade the Greek from sparing with anyone. The guards who had assisted in the attack on Murena were insistent that they be placed somewhere safe, away from the Greek. The Master had to threaten them with whipping before they would go anywhere near him.

Most of the guards who worked at the school were former gladiators who, upon retiring, suddenly found themselves with no means of support. They were freedmen but had few prospects, and even though a few had been stars in their time and adored by fans, the social stigma they carried caused them to be shunned by the outside world. They worked as guards in the school and were little more than household slaves. In these circumstances, they worked cheap. Most got along well with the gladiators, but they all knew how dangerous the Greek was, and the fact that he was much more valuable to the Master than any of them.

Vitalis was one of the oldest guards in the Master's employ, and it was he who had unlocked the outside door for the Greek on that fateful day. He had wanted nothing to do with the incident but was coerced by the others. The Greek had not looked him in the eye since that day. Vitalis' hands shook every time he saw the Greek; the gladiator could hear the jingle of his keys as he locked the cell door each night.

About a week after the Greek had begun to train again, he was late coming to his cell. Vitalis nervously paced in the hall. The Greek walked into his cell, stopped just inside the door, and stood silently with his back to Vitalis as he struggled to lock the door. The Greek liked the fear he instilled in the guards. Vitalis had been momentarily distracted by his keys as he stood near the bars of the Greek's cell when he caught a movement out of the corner of his eye.

The Greek reached through the bars and pushed a narrow length of cloth around Vitalis' neck with one hand, then grasped the other end and pulled it toward the bars. The keys fell from Vitalis' hands as he tore at the cloth. He tried to scream, but the cloth bit deep into his throat. It wasn't long before his struggle ceased.

The Greek held the cloth until his fingers grew numb. When he released it, the lifeless body of Vitalis slipped to the floor. The Greek reached through the bars, picked up the keys and opened his door. He pulled the body to the end of the hall, dropped the keys on the guard's chest, and returned to his cell. Several other gladiators witnessed the scene from the safety of their cells, but no one seemed to recall seeing anything by the next day. The Greek was no longer one of them. They had turned him into something very different. No one knew what that was, but everyone feared him.

The day after the death of Vitalis, one of the three remaining guards decided it was safer on the outside, even if it meant having to live on the streets. No one ever saw him again. Another thought it would be a good idea to carry a concealed dagger, even though it meant a whipping if he was caught. He considered that punishment better than facing the Greek unarmed. He was found dead in the baths with the dagger sticking out of his belly four days later. It was three weeks to Capua.

***

The Master stood in the tower watching the Greek spar half-heartedly against a dummy. He hated him because for the first time since becoming a gladiator all those years ago, he was afraid of someone; he feared the Greek. But patience was necessary for the large payday that awaited him if the Greek stayed alive. The bout in Capua would provide for the school financially for almost a year, whether the Greek lived or died. It would be a challenge even for the Greek, but if he won, a match in Pompeii was guaranteed and, after that, if there was a new emperor, it would be on to the Imperial games. The Master just needed to be patient and cautious.

***

The Greek and the Nightman rode together in a cart to Capua. The Nightman had tried to get information on the Greek's opponent, but the details were sketchy. He did find out the man was one of the best from the Capua school.

The Greek was transferred to his cell upon arrival and told he would remain there until his bout the next afternoon. He would miss the dinner for the gladiators that evening and the pompa the next morning. He was uneasy with the wait, not so much because of the upcoming match, but at the prospect of meeting Probus.

The Greek found that time passed slowly. He stretched out on the bed or paced around his small cell. The guards brought him dinner, which killed a little time. He was unable to sleep and could only think of revenge. His match was of little concern to him.

He couldn't eat breakfast the next morning; butterflies roamed his stomach as they had not done for a long time. He would have to impress the crowd so that he could stay in the arena and bask in their shouts long enough for Probus to enter.

A guard opened the cell and pointed in the direction of the entrance gate. The Greek was anxious for blood and the adrenalin rush it gave him. He would be ready for Probus when the time came.

The Greek walked through the torch-lit corridors until he could see the streams of daylight coming in through the cracks in the gate, but there was no opponent. He looked back; the hall was deserted and silent. When the gate opened, he strode confidently into the arena, which exploded with sound.

He walked around the entire stadium and stopped in the very center before noticing the editor's box and the men standing in front of it. The assistants were there with the weapons, and a gladiator stood on either side of them. The Greek wondered which one was his opponent, though it mattered not. He went to the table, picked up his swords one at a time, examined each, and returned to the center where he proceeded to put on a show for the spectators. The two gladiators, both Thracians, secured their swords, saluted the editor, and turned to face the Greek. Their movement caught his eye. He ceased juggling his swords and stood motionless.

As the two approached, they separated and walked to the left and right of the Greek. The Greek remembered Urbicus' story of how he had once fought two opponents at the same time. He had dismissed it as another tall tale. What had Urbicus told him about winning such a bout? His mind returned to the present as the two Thracians attacked. One was taller and faster than the other, who had large muscles and a powerful build.

The Greek retreated against the onslaught. They were attempting to surround him, but the Greek was too fast. He would strike at one and retreat before the other could get close enough for even a glancing blow. The Thracians pulled back out of frustration and conversed. The Greek saw them retreating and thrust his swords high in the air to a tumultuous reaction from the crowd.

The Thracians approached again, side by side, and advanced as fast as they could. They were nearly as nimble as the Greek, but each blow received a swift counter blow. Then the Greek remembered that Urbicus had told him: no two men are equal. Pick the weakest and kill him first. The Greek studied their movements and determined the shorter, muscular fellow should be eliminated before the other.

When they came at him again, the shorter one was to his left, so the Greek stepped left and attacked him. He struck a few blows and drew blood; the man began to panic. The Greek continued to attack the weaker man, who tried to retreat behind his partner, an action that brought whistles from the crowd. The Greek attacked the other Thracian, who was left to face him alone.

The young gladiator would strike, retreat, move around his opponents, and attack again with blurring speed. His opponents separated to each side again and forced the Greek to the wall of the arena, but it was impossible to corner him. As the Greek moved away from the wall, he attacked the weaker man and slashed down behind his shield. His blade cut through the man's protective wrapping into muscle and bone and caused him to shout in pain and drop the shield. A blow from the Greek's other sword pierced the man's side.

The man stumbled back and grasped at his wound while the Greek turned on his other opponent and began to attack. He smashed one sword down on the shield and thrust with the second, but the taller Thracian was more experienced than his partner. Sweat ran down the Greek's face, stinging his eyes, and his wet palms made grasping the sword handles difficult. He went after the wounded, shield-less man, but the other Thracian guarded him.

And then the Greek saw a vision of Murena. She stood behind his opponents; he knew that these two were between him and his revenge. He lowered his swords and began to move around the two Thracians. He sidestepped their blows, a mocking grin on his face, and dared them to stab him. The tall man was becoming angry and lunged at him as the Greek back-peddled and circled. What the Thracian hadn't noticed was the fact that he had left his wounded partner exposed, and once he did realize the situation, it was too late.

When the Greek believed he had enough time, he turned his attention to the wounded man and attacked. Overwhelmed, the man attempted to retreat, but the Greek plunged both swords the man's body. Neither was fatal, but the attack rendered him defenseless and lying on the ground.

The Greek turned to face the other Thracian, who was fast approaching, and engaged him in a ferocious battle. He fought with an abandonment and savage brutality that few at the arena that day had ever witnessed. The roar was deafening as the Greek pursued his opponent, who at this point was only fighting for survival. He wanted to throw down his weapons and surrender but knew the Greek would kill him, armed or not. Exhausted, cut on his arms, chest, and side, and bleeding profusely, he stumbled back onto the ground. The Greek thrust his sword one last time, driving it through the man's throat. Blood spurted in the air like a fountain come to life, though this flowing stream meant death.

The Greek then went to the other Thracian who was crawling along in the sand and drove his sword into the man's heart. As he leaned over the body, he noticed something protruding from the wrapping on the man's arm near the point of the first wound. It was a dagger. No one in attendance had ever seen a gladiator fight and defeat two opponents at once. They were ecstatic at the performance, no one more so than the Master.

For a moment, the Greek was caught up in the jubilation of the spectators as they called his name and reached out over the arena walls in a vain attempt to touch him. He noticed a face in the crowd that reminded him of Murena. The sight thrust him back to reality. He had come to Capua for a reason. As he swaggered around the arena, he watched the entrance gate. His arms were beginning to grow weary when the gate started to open. He moved toward it as a young man entered the realm of death. The Greek thought that this must be the victim for Probus's farewell performance and readied himself for the man to enter, but no one followed.

The assistants were after the Greek; they motioned for him to surrender his swords. He ignored them. Some guards joined them, but none dared come too close to the armed Greek. The gate remained ajar, but no one else entered. *Where is Probus? The Nightman had promised he would be here,* he thought.

Then the Greek saw more guards approaching from the opposite end of the arena and knew he had to do something. He stood in the bright sun and could see only black through the open gate, the black of Hades. Maybe Probus was standing in the shadows laughing at him.

The Greek threw one then the other sword high into the arena wall past the back side of the gate. The fans went wild, and several leaned perilously over the edge trying to grasp the weapons. The assistants and guards were in a panic. The swords were stuck in too high for anyone to reach from the ground, though one spectator was being lowered toward it from the top by two compatriots.

With everyone's attention diverted to the weapons, the Greek rushed to the prone body of his opponent, grabbed the dagger, and slipped through the open gate into the corridor. He stood motionless inside the hall in the dim lamp light and listened, but the only sounds were from the commotion outside. His heart was pounding as he fondled the dagger in his hand and slowly advanced down the corridor. With his eyes adjusted to the light, he could see that the hall was empty. Probus had to enter this way if he was going to fight, so the Greek continued down the corridor until he heard someone approaching. He pressed back against the wall and held the dagger close to his body.

Probus rounded a corner. He carried his shield in his left hand and balanced his helmet on his right arm. He paid no attention to the small figure against the wall until nearly upon the Greek. Probus looked directly at him and spit. The liquid struck the Greek below the left eye. He took one step past Probus, turned, and reached his arm around the front of the man, a difficult feat as Probus was considerably taller. With one quick motion, the Greek slit his throat from ear to ear. Probus dropped the shield and stumbled against the wall as his helmet clanged to the floor. He grasped his throat with both hands and sank to his knees.

The Greek moved around in front of Probus. He could hear the gurgling sounds of the man's last breaths as they locked eyes. He wanted Probus to carry the image of his smiling face forever in the next life. A long moment stretched between the two gladiators, and then Probus slumped back onto the floor.

The Greek cut open Probus' loincloth, grabbed his genitals in one hand, sliced them off, and placed them in the dead man's mouth. Next, he cut off his nose and ears and threw them along the hall, then gouged out his eyes. He sliced open his stomach, allowing the intestines to spill out, then opened Probus' chest and ripped out his heart, which he tossed in the opposite direction. The Greek stood up, admired his handy-work, dropped the dagger on Probus' chest, and continued down the corridor, content with the deed.

The young gladiator wandered around the labyrinthine hallways under the amphitheater until he met a startled guard. The Greek was covered in blood. The guard's hands were shaking as he motioned for the Greek to follow him. Without a word, they walked along the corridors to a large cell at the end of one of the passages. The guard stood by the cell, motioned him in, and locked the door behind him. He sighed with relief and departed.

The Greek fell unto the bed, exhausted. As he lay in the silence, he admired his blood-covered hands, turning them from side to side as he thought of Murena. Suddenly, she was standing by the door. She approached and sat on the edge of the bed as she had often done. She was pleased with his revenge; the mutilation of Probus' body would prevent him from being admitted to the underworld. The boatman wouldn't ferry anyone across the river Styx to Hades unless the body was able to carry the shade. She had feared Probus would haunt her in the underworld. Now his shade would drift between this world and the lower realm and be tormented for all eternity. Murena hugged him and softly kissed his lips, then she was gone. He woke up calling her name, tears streaming down his cheeks.

The Greek rose from the bed, went to the table, and poured some water into a bowl. He scrubbed his hands but the blood had dried and wouldn't come off. He didn't know how much time had passed, but he was hungry. The ever-present lamp light gave no indication of whether it was day or night. No reply came when he shouted for a guard. He sat on the edge of the bed and gently ran his hand over the place Murena had been sitting; it felt warm. He paced the floor, checked the door to see if it was open, lay on the bed tossing and turning, and paced some more.

He was dreaming about his family when voices in the distance roused him. Five men appeared outside his cell door. The first man was well groomed with short hair and a handsome beardless face. A gold necklace hung around his neck and several rings adorned his fingers. He was of average height and a bit portly. He stood staring at the Greek for what seemed a long time before speaking.

"At last I see the mighty Greek in person. I must admit you appeared much larger in the arena. I have never seen such a performance as you put on yesterday."

The Greek stood motionless in the middle of the cell.

"How rude of me. Allow me to introduce myself. I am Julius Tullius Pontus from the family of Senator Pontus of Capua. I own the school here in Capua, and now I own you."

The Greek remained silent.

"Do you understand? The Master told me you only speak Greek and, although Roman through and through, I was educated in Greece and have been complemented on my Greek speech and pronunciation. Perhaps someone such as yourself from the backwaters of Greece cannot appreciate my way of communicating."

"When am I going home? Where is the Master? I want to see him."

"The Master has left. The school is connected to the arena by a tunnel. You will be home shortly."

"This isn't my home. Where is the Master? Where is the Nightman?"

"You don't seem to understand. I purchased you from the Master. You belong to me."

"I belong to no one! I am not a slave! I am a gladiator!"

"One and the same, boy. One and the same. You will fight for me from now on, and you will win. I have never paid 60,000 sesterces for a gladiator before, but you are not just any gladiator, are you? Do you know how much 60,000 sesterces is?"

"No. When am I going home?"

"Poor ignorant boy. 60,000 sesterces is more than you will ever possess. It is enough for you to live on for the rest of your life, if your life is long. Are you wounded?"

"No."

"Yesterday a gladiator was found near the entrance to the arena. He had been mutilated, a terrible event as he was about to retire. Do you know anything about that? You seem to have a lot of blood on you and I don't recall seeing you leave through the exit gate yesterday. And with all the confusion around the entrance, I thought perhaps—"

"I know nothing about this."

"I thought not. You would be fed to the beasts, were you not so valuable. Though I doubt the beasts would stand a chance against you! You are going to fight at Pompeii next in a special bout contracted for as a condition of your sale, and then Rome in the Imperial games. Do you know who Gaius is?"

"No."

"Someone as ignorant as you wouldn't. He is a great and generous man who will soon be emperor. He is a friend to gladiators. The taller Thracian you fought yesterday, he was good?"

"Not as good as me."

"He belonged to Caligula. I thought he might be angry when he heard the news that you had killed yet another of his gladiators, but he was only disappointed at not being able to purchase you for himself. He has plans for you in the future. A bright future after Tiberius is dead!"

"Is the Nightman staying in Capua with me? He trains me. Did you buy him also?"

"No. I have the best trainers. You will have your own. You will be a star in Rome. But first, you must advance past Pompeii."

"When is Pompeii?" he asked.

"In the spring, in March. You will be the main bout. It won't be easy, but you'll be ready. Do you want anything?"

"Is it still night?"

"No, it's mid-morning."

"Food. I want some food and the baths."

"I'll send you to the baths first. You will begin training in a few days, rest for now. These guards will take you to the baths and then your new cell. It has a nice view. I think you'll enjoy it. Anything else you want? A woman?"

"Only food and the baths."

"You will like it here, Greek. You'll like it."

Julius turned to the guards and gave them instructions in Latin, adding a word of caution when handling the Greek.

"Take off your loincloth before they open the door. They will take you to the baths naked. It is not far," Julius ordered the Greek.

He slipped the blood-stained cloth to the floor and stood by the door waiting, but they didn't open it until Julius was safely away.

***

The Master sent the Nightman directly from Capua to Scelestus in Venusia. Upon his arrival at the school, a much larger facility than the Master's, he was led into a spacious cell that had several windows; it was reserved for the star in the ranks. Scelestus had never owned a fighter of the Nightman's caliber and planned to push him to the top, at the same time squeezing out any of the Master's men from the arena at Rome. Rumors flew on swift wings that the much-anticipated demise of Tiberius was near and there was only one way to guarantee the Greek never made it to Rome.

Scelestus peered in at the sleeping Nightman, who suddenly jolted awake.

"Are you finding the surroundings to your liking?" Scelestus asked.

"What have you planned for me?"

"Ah, right to business, I like that in a man. You will be in a special bout. Think of it as a warmup for the main event."

"What are you talking about?"

"Rome. In short time, Tiberius will cross the Styx and the Imperial games shall flourish once more. The first are likely to be in celebration of the death and deification of the glorious grand shit Tiberius given, of course, by the noble Caligula. And you will be there. Think of it. Win, and you're free, with a huge purse to go along with it. You'll be set for life. No more games. Just freedom. I have the connections. Why, not three months ago, I sat at dinner with Caligula himself. I would not have purchased you, and for much more than your worth, if I were not certain of the future. You will take me to the arena in Rome and fame on your blade."

"What of my family? When are you bringing them to Venusia?"

"Your family? What family? The Master never spoke of any family."

"He told me you were bringing my wife and children to live near the school. I spend a lot time with them. You can trust me to return."

"Is your wife beautiful? And the children, what ages?"

"Six, five, and one. Two boys and a girl. When are you bringing them?"

"Give me some time to make the arrangements and everything shall be as you wish. Just tell me where they are."

The Nightman was relieved Scelestus would honor his request. He had thought the man was a scoundrel, but the Master was the true rogue. Perhaps this wouldn't be too bad. All he had to do was win one match and then fight in Rome for his freedom. Decima wouldn't have to be afraid for his life anymore. They could buy a small farm and retire. They would no longer be slaves to the will of others, but able to live in freedom.

CHAPTER X

SENATOR FLAVIUS WAS IN A FOUL MOOD. HE HAD SPENT TWO months in hiding, traveling by night, and living in constant fear of Caligula's men, only to learn it was all a rumor perpetuated by that disgusting piece of human vermin, the Master. And now the news that he had sold both the Nightman and the Greek for nearly 80,000 sesterces. Add in several minor gladiators, and it brought the figure to more than 100,000 sesterces, enough for the Master to live well for the rest of his life. The thought made the senator ill. It was obvious that the Master was planning to flee, abandoning the school and the remainder of his gladiators. Or perhaps he would grant them their freedom. The good senator could not let that happen.

"Two men to see you, Senator, a Fabius and Artorius."

"What do they want?"

"They won't say, only that it is worth a lot to you."

"Search them first and then have the guards escort them in."

Shortly, the two appeared at the edge of the spacious garden of the senator's villa. Several large men surrounded them.

"Gentlemen, welcome. I am a busy man, so to the point and be brief."

"You'll want to hear this, Senator Flavius. Privately," Fabius said.

"These men are loyal and trusted, more than I can say of you two. Speak now, or they will remove you."

"Very well. We have information that is worth a lot of money to you."

"Well, go on. What is it?"

"First, there is the matter of payment."

"Payment? Payment for what? Guards, remove them."

"Okay, wait!" Fabius called out as the guards grabbed his arms. "Our work is to help people eliminate problems, and we had an offer to eliminate you. For a price, we will give up his name."

A feeling of dread came over the senator. Was this another rumor or was it from Tiberius? Caligula wasn't emperor yet; Tiberius still held the reins of power. Could this possibly be a real threat to his life?

"Very well, 100 sesterces for the name."

They looked at one another. "We were thinking 1,000. Certainly, your life is worth a thousand sesterces?"

"Yours will be worth nothing if you don't give me the name!"

"Then you'll know nothing."

The senator's anger was only superseded by his fear. "Very well. One thousand if your information proves true. Now, what is the name?"

"It is the Master, the lanista. He came to us and asked us to kill you for him. He even offered a bonus if we did it right away."

The senator stared at the two men, then burst out laughing. "You expect me to believe a former slave, a man with few resources who, but for my generosity, would be bankrupt, wants to have me killed? Gentlemen, do you have any idea how many times we have sat face to face, he with that dagger hidden in his sleeve, and clasped hands in friendship? On any number of these occasions, he could easily have killed me. No, gentlemen, the Master has no intent to see me dead. We are old friends."

Standing, the senator moved close to the men. "But, gentlemen, I would be careful if I were you. Spread rumors like that, and you might be the ones to disappear. The Master may not have the resources to do something like that, but I do."

"But it's true. I swear by the gods, it's true," Artorius pleaded. "We came here out of concern for you. We refused, but he might have found someone else, and we wanted to warn you."

"Warn me! Exploit me more like it! Guards, show them out. And here, a few coins for your trouble." The senator gestured to his secretary, who tossed a handful of coins at the men's feet. They scrambled to pick them up before the guards grabbed them and escorted them out of the villa and off the grounds.

"What do you make of that?" the secretary asked.

"That bastard! After all I have done for him, he tries to hire someone to kill me? We will see who ends up dead. And I want his money, understood?"

* * *

For the first time in his life, he felt like a free man, though he knew he would have to do something terrible to earn that freedom. He would have to live with the deed on his conscious forever. But being free, if only for the short remainder of his life, was worth it. His palms were sweaty, and beads of perspiration clung to his forehead as he waited for the senator to arrive. He stood as the senator entered, swallowed hard, then bent to kiss the senator's ring.

"I come to you with all due respect," he said nervously.

"Please, sit. I'm not a formal man in such matters. Wine?"

"No."

"You have a request, as I understand it?"

"I request you grant me my freedom," he stammered, barely able to get the words out.

"That is a huge request. There must be a special reason to grant such a request, and a favor expected in return."

"I can do what you need done."

"And what proof do I have? It seems beyond your capabilities."

"I offer no proof, but once done, you grant me my freedom. That is all I ask."

"When?"

"When the opportunity arises."

"It can't be too long."

"Leave it to me. I will require your protection upon completion."

"That can be arranged. Send a message when it is to take place, and an escort will be by your side. When you return to me, I will grant your freedom. Now, if there is nothing else?" the senator asked while rising from his seat. "My servant will show you out."

***

The Greek was adjusting to his new surroundings and, while he missed the Nightman and Murena, it felt good being away from the old school that was filled with so many terrible memories. Julius was extremely wealthy, and that was reflected in the accommodations and training the Greek received. He had two trainers, both former dimachaeri: Delicatus, a gruff German whose personality contradicted his name, and Purpurius, a fellow Greek. Both had won many victories and were excellent teachers for the Greek. They were able to take his existing abilities and push him to new limits.

Delicatus had been a German warrior who was captured by the Romans and sold into slavery but rescued by Julius' father and trained to be a gladiator. He had fought thirty-four bouts with only two losses and retired with his freedom at the age of thirty. A talent for teaching brought him back to the school, where he had successfully trained two other stars, including the dimachaerus the Greek had killed in Venusia. But he held no grudge. That was the nature of the game, and he was happy to have the opportunity to work with someone as talented as the Greek. Simply being associated with such a fighter increased one's prestige.

Purpurius was a rarity among gladiators, a free, but poor, Greek man who had entered the arena voluntarily and signed away his freedom for a bonus of 3,000 sesterces. The money was enough to help his family, but they eventually deserted him, driven away by the shame of his chosen profession. He decided to continue fighting when the contract expired and had fought for seven years and amassed twenty-two wins and one loss. Julius had hired him as a trainer three years ago, and he was honored to be chosen to work with the Greek.

The Greek's body was becoming more that of a man each day. They worked on building up his strength, a factor that could mean the difference if he was to meet Beryllus, as everyone expected. It seemed the logical match should Caligula become emperor. The reputation of the Greek was second only to his, and with just one obstacle to overcome, the match at Pompeii, it appeared more than likely to occur.

The Greek liked Purpurius and Delicatus. He longed for companions as a terrible loneliness gripped him. He thought more and more of his family back in Thessaly. He had changed so much he wondered if his family would even recognize him. The thought caused him grief.

Most gladiators had company for a short period, but Julius realized how lonely the Greek was and thought a woman might comfort him. He wanted the Greek—needed the Greek—to be at his best for Pompeii and the fact Sperata spoke Greek was to her benefit. She was about his age, maybe a bit younger, but well-schooled in life. She was very different from Murena—tougher and more self-assured. Though a slave, she had always seen herself as achieving something more in life than being a whore and, knowing the reputation of the Greek, believed he was her chance at a better life. Everyone was sure that the Greek was on his way to Rome and freedom. If she could cling to him, maybe she would be free, too.

***

It was a few hours before the light of dawn had spread across the land when a terrible noise woke the sleeping individuals housed in the tiny abode. Decima called out to the children. They ran in different directions, screaming in fear and confusion. A large man grasped Decima and clamped a damp palm tightly over her mouth. Three others scooped up the children and threw them into a cart.

Decima was destined for a brothel in Brundisium near the docks, though, given her age she didn't bring as much as Scelestus had hoped. As for the children, the oldest boy fetched a fair price, but the other two went for a mere pittance. All were sold to the slave market in Brundisium and ended up in separate homes, their futures bleak.

***

Lucanus stood next to the Master, who stared out of the tower into the training yard. He had purchased several new young men with the assistance of Lucanus.

"That Thracian, he reminds me of the Nightman when he first came here, don't you think?" the Master asked.

"He definitely has promise."

"We have a bright future, Lucanus. Selling the Greek and the Nightman was what we needed to fix our financial problems. By the time the Imperial games begin again, we will be well on our way with some promising gladiators and those two will be retired or dead."

It was the most difficult thing Lucanus had ever done, and much worse than he ever could have imagined. He thought it would bring a sense of relief, even hope, but it seemed to bring only despair and doubt. There was no turning back.

Of those the Master trusted, and the number was few, he would never have suspected Lucanus. He searched vainly for the dagger in his sleeve, the one Lucanus had deftly removed earlier and now stood holding, the blade sunk deep into the Master's back, the tip piercing his heart. As Lucanus released his grip on the blade, the Master turned to him.

"Why?"

Lucanus stood in silence and watched him gasp for breath and sink to the floor. No one had ever been able to do this to him in the arena, but now a mere slave had brought him down.

Lucanus' hands shook as he hurried from the tower room, locked the door, and ran down the stairs as fast as his bad leg would allow. He stopped at the bottom to catch his breath. His heart was pounding so hard he nearly blacked out as the realization of the deed sunk in. After a few minutes, he walked out of the gate and ordered the guard to lock it and not allow anyone to go up to the tower, no matter who it was, until given the signal by the Master.

Next, he went into the villa, entered the Master's bedroom, and secured a leather traveling case from under the bed. He had not realized how heavy 100,000 sesterces would be. From there, he walked through the atrium into the back garden and went out a side door to the stables where a mule and cart were waiting for him. Instructing the grooms that he was on a special mission for the Master and that the Master was not to be disturbed, Lucanus placed the leather traveling case under the seat, mounted the cart, and drove out the gate.

Every noise, every passing horse or cart, caused his hands to shake with fear and apprehension. About two miles from the school, he noticed four riders in formation heading straight for him.

"Lucanus?" one of them shouted upon nearing the cart.

"Who asks?"

"We are sent by Senator Flavius to escort you safely to his side."

The answer cheered Lucanus. He felt a wave of relief, and disbelief, that he had been successful. A case full of coins lay beneath him, security surrounded him, and most importantly, freedom awaited him at the end of this journey.

With a wave of the Captain's hand, the guard directly behind the cart thrust his spear through Lucanus' back and quickly pulled it back out. He rolled out of the cart onto the road, and a small cloud of dust rose where he landed. Two of the guards dismounted, dragged the corpse off the road, and hid it in the nearby bushes. The captain reached under the seat, pulled out the leather traveling case, secured it to his horse, chased off the mule and cart, and turned back in the direction they had come.

***

Scelestus lived in the largest villa in Venusia. It was situated on the west road leading directly to Beneventum. Every morning, well before dawn, a line of clients would form before his home to pay homage and collect their pittance in coins. The entire city of Venusia owed allegiance to him; a gang of ruthless strong-arms prevented that loyalty from straying. The gladiatorial school lay on the eastern edge of the city near the amphitheater. Many wondered where the funds for his extravagance originated, but no one dared inquire. Such was the dedication of the people of Venusia to their native son that even a senator would be foolish to venture too near the man.

Preparations were under way for a banquet, but not one of Scelestus' massive orgies that lasted for days on end. This was for his prestigious guest, Gaius Julius, nephew of Emperor Tiberius and successor to the throne. The two had met years before when Scelestus, a struggling entrepreneur, had been moved by the young Gaius' funeral oration for his grandmother. They had struck up a friendship. It seemed the two had been conceived in the same pod with a passion for torture and executions, as well as indulging in gluttony and lascivious behavior. The latent evil of both would serve them well and form a lasting bond.

But this meeting was different. Gaius arrived late in the evening and wished to conceal his presence.

"Brother and friend," Scelestus said, grasping Gaius' hands as he entered the triclinium where a feast was set out for the two.

"Scelestus, closer to my heart than blood kin. It has been too long."

"Too long indeed. Please, be seated. Our meal awaits."

They reclined on two couches placed at right angles to one another so that their heads might be close for intimate discussions.

"How goes the situation in Capri?"

"Not well. My uncle surrounds himself with loyal guards even a cart load of silver cannot dislodge. The problem, and solution, is Macro, commander of the guards. If I could secure his assistance to allow me unattended access for the briefest of moments, enough time to slip some poison between my uncle's lips, the deed would be done."

"Ah, Macro, my incorruptible brother. Child of the same mother, but a righteous father. Men like him make it difficult for men like us to profit."

"So true. But a brother's love has the power to corrupt, and the prize is enormous—the Empire. And for you, there is no limit."

"All Macro has to do is turn his head?"

"Briefly, that's all I ask."

"My brother has a weakness. His lovely wife, Ennia Naevia."

"I know her. How could she help?"

"You are unattached at present?"

"Yes, following the tragic death of my beloved wife, Junia, in childbirth."

"Offer Ennia the throne at your side and sign in blood if need be. I am positive she will betray Macro to be Empress."

"You are sure of this?"

"The woman is impressed with power and wealth. The limits of a commander keep her wanting. She can be bought."

"But what could she do?"

"Macro is devoted to her. Few men have lost themselves to a woman like him. She can make him do anything. At a dinner I hosted a few months ago, he fawned over her and even served food to her! With a room full of whores and slaves to choose from for his entertainment, he stayed true to her. Such devotion is unhealthy. A man can't screw only one woman. He'll end up with some disorder! She is your answer. Dangle power before her, and she'll betray Macro. He'll look away for her."

"My heart is gladdened by your information. The deed will be done soon, and after the power is mine, you will be rewarded to your heart's delight. You must come to Rome. I will secure a station to match your considerable charm and talent. The world will be ours!" Gaius laughed.

"To power!"

"To corruptible women!"

Their wine goblets crashed together, sending a spray across the room. They laughed and joked long into the night, but before dawn, the shadowy figure of Gaius departed to return to the island of Capri and destiny.

***

The senator was furious. The four guards he had sent to escort Lucanus had not returned and it appeared Lucanus had vanished as well. That lowlife slave had double crossed him. That money should be his! The Master didn't deserve it, and Lucanus most decidedly didn't; it was rightfully his, and he planned to find it and those worthless cowardly guards. Lucanus must have decided he wanted the money instead of freedom and was fleeing for his life. He wouldn't make it far.

***

News had come to the Nightman from Scelestus that his family was safe and sound and had been placed in a comfortable cottage on the outskirts of Venusia, but his repeated requests to visit were denied on the grounds he must concentrate on preparing for his next match. Scelestus assured him there would be plenty of time for reunions later. The Nightman had a bad feeling he couldn't shake, but Scelestus seemed genuine in his statements. Perhaps the rumors about him were exaggerated.

Scelestus held the leather traveling case as if it was a precious vase that had come from the markets of Athens, turning it over, feeling the weight, and breathing in the scent. After examining it with such care, he undid the flap and poured its contents onto the table in front of him.

"How much do you think is here?" he asked the Captain, giddy from the sight of so much money.

"More than fifty, probably close to seventy."

"You shall be rewarded handsomely for this, Captain. Your information was indeed accurate. And timely, I might add."

"How do you think the senator will react?"

"With his thumb up his ass for all I care."

Scelestus refilled the traveling case, latched it, and turned around to face the captain. "Any good plot requires planning...and a lack of witnesses. Only you and I know about this, and I will never tell."

"You can count on me, Scelestus. I wouldn't say anything. In fact, why don't you keep it all? Never mind my share. I was glad to be of service."

"Don't fear, my loyal comrade. I mean you no harm. I'm sure you will be of service to me in the future. Why don't you return to the good senator with my regards?"

"Yes, immediately. I'll tell him there was no money, that Lucanus didn't have it. It must still be at the Master's school. He'll believe that."

"I'm sure he will. Now, be off."

The Captain turned and started to walk out of the room. He never saw the sword that ran through his back.

"I should have been a gladiator," Scelestus said, admiring the blood on the blade.

***

The Greek had never trained as hard as Delicatus and Purpurius were pushing him. Days were long, and they unforgiving of any faults, but his improvement was unmistakable. Julius would occasionally stop by the school to gauge his progress, though he was cautious not to get too close. The Greek enjoyed training and was glad for the company of the new woman, Sperata. She wasn't doting on him as Murena had been. She was demanding and pushy and expected better treatment due to her connection with him. Everyone knew he was a star, and she was his woman and should be treated accordingly. The Greek tolerated her behavior as he needed her company to lessen his loneliness.

Julius Tullius Pontus lived in a modest villa near the center of Capua. He chose not to be too conspicuous, despite his wealth and power. Some of the best gladiators in the empire came out of his school. It was also the residence of Gaius' stable. It wasn't often that Gaius passed through Capua, but when he did, he never failed to greet his ally.

It was late in the afternoon when word reached Julius that Gaius, on his way back to Capri, had stopped for the night at his estate, but was traveling under cover of secrecy and wished his arrival to be confidential. Julius returned home to find his guest strolling through the gardens.

"Gaius, how are you?"

"Well, Julius, as the gods smile on me."

"And the Emperor?"

"Ill, I fear. I was away on business, at his insistence of course, as I would never have left his side if I believed him ill, when word reached me of a turn for the worse. I am rushing back to be by his side."

"Tiberius is indeed lucky to have a nephew as loving and caring as yourself. You must be a great comfort to him."

"I do try to honor my family. They mean more to me than the gods."

"You are a respectable man. Be assured no one will know that you were here."

"Much thanks. I will hasten to leave before first light. I wish to be by my uncle's side before nightfall tomorrow. Your hospitality will be remembered should the untimely passing of my uncle render me Caesar."

"The empire could do worse than having you as emperor. But enough talk of gloom. Rest for a while, and then we will dine."

Julius ordered a lavish feast. As they dined, the conversation turned to their mutual love of gladiators.

"Rumor suggests you have acquired this young gladiator, the Greek, the one who haunts my stable and has already killed two of my finest."

"Your rumor has legs of truth. I purchased him recently from the Master for the sum of 60,000 sesterces."

"Sixty thousand! You put even me to shame! I would be hard pressed to consider an offer such as that."

"True, it was a large sum, but worth every sesterce. All I need is a promise from you that he will fight your man in Rome when the Imperial games commence. I'm sure you have every intention of following in the glorious footsteps of Augustus and bringing them back."

"Yes, I intend to restore the games' prominence for the people. You believe the Greek is ready to fight Beryllus?"

"He fights in Pompeii in a few weeks."

"I will have eyes at Pompeii. When are the games?"

"March 18."

"I fear that I will be otherwise occupied, but I will review the outcome carefully and consider your request. You know Scelestus has asked the same for his man, the Nightman, another deserving soul."

"True, but only one can fight, and I am betting it will be my Greek."

"Betting 60,000 sesterces! On a more serious note, I wish to ask your council."

"I am humbled you should seek my advice."

"Are you familiar with Senator Marcus Flavius?"

"Yes, I know the senator."

"And your opinion?"

"I do hate to disparage those of lesser abilities than myself."

"Please, indulge me. I have heard certain things about this man and would not wish to base opinion on rumor and innuendo."

"I have known the senator for many years. His father and mine were friends. Unfortunately, the good senator seems to have fallen far from the tree. His father was a noble and just man, but Senator Flavius appears low-bred and greedy. He is more interested in acquiring for himself than assisting his people. One rumor—but no, I shouldn't be spreading such nonsense."

"Please continue. Sometimes the truth lies hidden in rumors."

"It's just that, well, even for someone of the character of the senator, this seems unbelievable. The rumor, to which I pay little heed, is that the senator ordered the assassination of the Master."

"And has it been carried out?"

"But a few days ago, if my sources are reliable."

"But why would someone in his position want a lanista dead, a former gladiator at that? What possible threat could this man be to the senator?"

"It seems to be the result of that ugly business in Tarentum, and the most bizarre rumor of all is that you yourself ordered the death of the senator for arranging the Greek's bout with Maximianus."

"Preposterous!" Gaius said, bursting into laughter. "Surely the senator couldn't believe that I would order his murder over the loss of a gladiator? It's part of the game. Everyone knows his man might be killed. I would never hold it against anyone as long as the victory was legal. But even to consider that I would do such a thing! I am an honorable man!"

"Fear does things to a man's mind."

"And you suggest that the Master was responsible for this story?"

"Senator Flavius spent two months in hiding."

"Two months! It seems that if he did the deed, he has suffered the price and no further punishment is required. Besides, I have more important matters to consider than kicking the ass of some country senator. Now that our bellies are full, I should require but a few hours of sleep to refresh me for the remainder of my journey. Sleep comes hard to a worried mind, concerned as I am for my uncle's health."

"You are indeed a good man. Sleep well and farewell."

***

The two men waited anxiously in the atrium of Senator Flavius' villa. Fear gripped their nerves.

"This way," the senator's secretary said, and led them through to a small room where the senator sat alone. "Fabius and Artorius to see you, Senator."

"Leave us. Gentlemen, sit." He motioned to two chairs. "I'm sure you are curious as to my bringing you back here, but fear not. I mean no harm. In fact, it is good news. I have a mission for you."

"A mission? It can't be for the Master. We heard you already got to him."

"What? Where did you hear such a ridiculous lie? I would never harm a friend, and the Master was a dear friend. I'm afraid you're mistaken. It was his trusted slave, Lucanus, who murdered the Master, stole over 100,000 sesterces and then vanished. My guess is he went north into Gaul. Killed the Master for his money, a terrible business indeed. No, I have another task for you. Do you know Scelestus of Venusia?"

"Only by reputation," Fabius replied.

"I'm afraid he is involved in many unscrupulous endeavors. He has a reputation of being brutal. Unfortunately, his bad behavior brought him into conflict with a close friend of mine who now seeks my help in retribution. Which is why I brought you two here," the senator said.

"You couldn't possibly want us to," Fabius hesitated, "eliminate him?"

"Such a harsh word, eliminate, don't you think? I merely wish for you two to make a problem go away."

"But he surrounds himself with guards."

"As far as those 'loyal' guards are concerned, a bag of gold coins can change ones' loyalty."

"But where could we, I mean, how could we get close to him?"

"In a short while, there are to be games in Pompeii where one of his gladiators is to fight. This is an important match for him. He will be amongst the spectators. My sources will inform you where he sits and give you tickets to nearby seats. At the appropriate time, you will be able to get close to him without worrying about his bodyguards."

Artorius cleared his throat nervously. "If we decide to do this, the price would be high, and we need your help in leaving the region. Maybe to the north or even Greece."

"That could be arranged. As far as the fee is concerned, I think 5,000 sesterces is adequate."

"Five thousand? For Scelestus? If we fail, he will kill us."

"And if you refuse, I will send a message to him that two assassins are after him with your names and descriptions."

"That's a death sentence!" Fabius shouted.

"Not at all. If you leave the country, perhaps go to the far eastern provinces, he might not find you."

"We should get at least 10,000."

"Seven thousand and transport to Greece."

"Could we discuss it?" Fabius asked.

"Certainly," the senator said. He stood and left the room.

"We should refuse," Artorius said.

"Refuse? If he tells Scelestus we're after him, we'll be dead! At least this way we have a chance. Seven thousand is good, and we can be free of this region."

"If he keeps his word."

"He's a senator. We can trust him. Besides, if he turns us in, we say who hired us. We've never made this much money before."

"We've never had to kill anyone the likes of Scelestus. Word is he's friends with Caligula."

"The senator must know Caligula. Scelestus isn't even a politician. We have no choice. We can't refuse the senator," Fabius said.

"Made a decision?" the senator asked upon reentering the room.

The two men looked at one another, then turned to the senator. "We want half now and the balance when you take us to Greece."

"I'll give you 500 now to cover any expenses you have and the rest when you embark on the ship to Greece. My secretary will give you the money on your way out. And gentlemen, not a word of this to anyone or you will not live long enough to spend the deposit, understood? And if you're caught, keep my name out of it. Now, if you'll excuse me, I've other business to attend to."

The two men left the room and returned to the atrium where the secretary handed them a bag of coins before ushering them out the door.

***

Julius decided to move the Greek to a close relative's home in Pompeii for the last week of training. This would be the most important bout of his career, and probably the most difficult. Julius wasn't taking any chances. He had ordered extra security at his relative's home, which was situated a few blocks from the amphitheater. The house was large and airy with decorated walls and an open garden surrounded by rows of columns on three sides where the Greek could train and spar. A Thracian had also been brought along for sparing, though he wore extra armor when practicing.

The Greek was fascinated by his surroundings. Bronze statues of gods were displayed throughout the house, and it seemed every inch of wall was covered with brightly painted images of soldiers, goddesses, or fanciful architecture. He wondered whether it would be possible to live in a home like this when he became free. Maybe he could bring his family to Italy. Julius had promised not only his freedom if victorious in Rome, but a purse beyond what he could comprehend. Plus, unlike the Master, Julius would see that he received the winnings from Pompeii.

Two days before the match, a sudden noise spread through the city. It began as a dull roar and slowly increased to a crescendo of celebration as rumors flew on light wings with the news of Tiberius' death. Many feared retribution if the story proved false, but nothing could turn back the tide. The news was confirmed by midday; Tiberius had died of natural causes and Gaius was named in his will as successor. Julius arrived at his relative's home that evening buoyed by the news. Now nothing could stop his Greek from fighting in Rome. His gamble would pay off; he would own the best gladiator in the Empire.

The Greek had never attended the *cena libera*, the extravagant public dinner the night before the games. Julius was nervous about bringing him, but a huge outcry had surfaced among the population to see the Greek and, for the lucky few, to dine with him. In the early evening, Julius, followed by the Greek and surrounded by a large number of bodyguards, left the house and turned east on the Via dell'Abbondanza. After five blocks, they turned south onto a short street that led directly to the palaestra next to the amphitheater where the *cena libera* was held. Several other gladiators who would be fighting the next day were already seated at tables set up on the infield.

A feast fit for a senator was brought out, but there were no politicians in attendance. This was an opportunity for the common people to see and meet the performers. For some of the gladiators, it would be their last meal. The Greek, as the honored guest, was led to the head of one of the long tables. Everyone stared at him as he took his place. Most marveled at how small and harmless he appeared without the swords, but they knew what he had accomplished in the arena.

Everyone wanted to see him, to touch him, or simply be near him. A few bold individuals asked him questions. He sat in silence, awed by the spectacle, while Julius deflected the questions and asked the people to allow the Greek to eat.

And eat he did, for he had never seen such a selection of foods. He couldn't name half of the dishes that were offered to him. It was certainly a change from the barley porridge they lived on at the school.

For appetizers, the guests enjoyed lettuce, strong leeks, and tuna garnished with sliced eggs, cheese, and olives. This was followed by more fish and eggs, sow's udder, stuffed wild fowl and farm hens, as well as small sausages on a bed of pale beans and red bacon. For dessert, there were nuts, figs, dates, plums, fresh-picked purple grapes, Syrian pears and chestnuts, and, finally, sitting on the table near the Greek, a shiny honeycomb dripping with golden nectar. The Greek had never seen such fare. He ate with delight and forgot for a brief time what faced him next day.

**

News that Gaius was Emperor added to the excitement of the games and the amphitheater was packed. Several talented gladiators were scheduled for the preliminary bouts, but everybody knew why they were here; they had come to see the Greek. If he fought in Rome, he would most likely retire. That meant chances of seeing him were growing slim.

The Greek was confident. He was in the best shape of his short life, experienced in the arena, and possessed impressive skill in the art of killing a man. This, together with the anger that seethed in his heart, made him a very dangerous man. He knew the crowd would be cheering for him. The people adored him, and he wouldn't disappoint. This was going to be his best show ever.

The guard unlocked the cell as he nervously eyed the Greek. The young gladiator was in high spirits as he walked along the dim corridors toward the entrance gate, rounded one last corner, and caught the first glimpse of his opponent. The man stood stoically by the closed gate, a shield on his left arm and a helmet perched on the right. The Greek's steps slowed as a wave of recognition washed over him like a tidal wave. He stopped and leaned heavily against the wall.

It couldn't be. There must be some mistake. His feet wouldn't move. His heart pounded. He could barely breathe. This must be another nightmare. That was the only possible explanation.

Then his opponent slowly turned his head and stared at the Greek.

CHAPTER XI

HIS MIND WOULDN'T ACCEPT WHAT WAS HAPPENING. THE NIGHTMAN couldn't be his opponent. Maybe they were to fight together again. Yes, that was the explanation or perhaps...his mind shut down. They couldn't possibly expect him to fight the Nightman. It was *sine missione*. He couldn't do it.

"You must enter with me, Greek."

"No! I refuse! Let them kill me!"

"If you refuse to fight, they will kill us both. If you fight, at least one of us will survive."

"I can't! I can't!"

The Nightman sighed. "The Master was behind the beating of Murena. He set it up."

"The Master? But why?"

The Nightman hesitated. "Because I told him to. It was my idea."

"You're lying!" Tears welled up in the Greek's eyes and flowed down his cheeks.

"You were getting arrogant and needed to be put in your place. All you are is a gladiator, like me, like so many others. You're nothing, just a piece of human waste like the rest of us to be sacrificed to the people for entertainment. I did it to prove that to you!"

"I don't believe you!"

"Believe it, Greek! I spit on you! I spit on her memory! Fight! I don't intend to die for your sake. You ripped out Probus' heart. Now fight the man who made it happen!"

The Greek couldn't think. He wouldn't believe the words he heard. It wasn't true. They were brothers. How could the Nightman have done such a thing?

"Fight, coward! Revenge Murena's shade! If you don't, I will beat her again and again when I cross the Styx! Fight!"

The Greek rushed at the Nightman, but he sidestepped the onslaught, and the Greek fell into the dirt. The Nightman turned and entered the arena.

The Greek lay on the ground, wiping tears from his cheeks. Slowly, he raised his head toward the sunlit arena. He could hear the roar of the crowd and the cry of his name. He stood, brushed off the dirt, and walked into the warm March sun.

The arena exploded. He walked around the outside of the arena while he continued to digest the Nightman's words. The Greek knew he couldn't let it go. If the Nightman was telling the truth, he must revenge Murena. He blinked to clear the tears and went before the editor to pick up his swords.

The Nightman was waiting near the center of the arena. Killing the Greek would be easier than having to tell him that.

The Greek walked to one end of the arena and stared at the swords he held. He knew what was expected of him, but juggling seemed like such a hollow gesture this time.

Julius was sitting with the editor. He felt confident of his man's chances, but he harbored a few doubts as to whether or not he would fight the Nightman. Perhaps he would simply lay down his swords.

Scelestus sat far to the right, not having been invited to sit with the editor, and was surrounded by a legion of bodyguards. Rumors had begun circulating that Senator Flavius was plotting revenge, but anyone would be a fool to try something here. He observed both gladiators; the small boyish Greek playing with his swords like toys and his towering man, who stood stoically in the center of the arena waiting for the show to finish. Chances seemed much better for his gladiator.

The Greek stopped juggling and stared at the Nightman, the swords clutched tightly in his hands. He thought about his love for Murena and how painful her death had been. But the Nightman was like his brother. The turmoil tore at him. The Greek began to advance. The Nightman raised his shield and sword and moved to meet his opponent.

They began tentatively trading light blows. The Nightman struck at him but the younger gladiator dodged the sword easily. He had forgotten the Greek's speed. They circled the arena, intent on what was required, but they shared a mutual respect and a hesitancy to engage.

The Nightman was an impressive gladiator but, at the age of thirty-one, he was past his prime. He knew it would be a struggle to defeat the much younger Greek, but it was still a possibility. He had years of experience, and he was fighting for the security and future of his family. What was his opponent fighting for?

The Greek came hard at the Nightman. Killing Probus had given him great pleasure, but this...this wouldn't be pleasant, but it was necessary. The only thing that mattered was revenge and freedom, and he had to pass over the Nightman on the road to Rome.

The Greek struck several blows in a row but the Nightman only needed one hit to draw blood. He pierced the Greek's left side, a glancing strike. The two were evenly matched and the bout continued with neither able to gain the advantage. Both struck blows that drew blood, but experienced viewers knew they weren't serious wounds. The Nightman thrust his shield and parried with his sword, but the Greek countered the attempts and sliced at him with both swords. Sweat ran in streams as fatigue began to set in. Age started to take its toll on the Nightman. When he slipped, the Greek was quick to take advantage of the mistake and stabbed him under his shield. It wasn't fatal, but it was enough to slow him considerably. In a normal bout, he would have surrendered and hoped for a favorable decision from the editor, but today he knew better.

Scelestus jumped up and screamed for his man to attack. He was so preoccupied with the bout, he failed to notice the stealthy approach of two spectators. Fabius and Artorius positioned themselves behind him. When the Greek struck the Nightman's left side, the crowd jumped up as one and began shouting. At the same instant, the two men plunged their daggers into Scelestus' back.

Scelestus pulled the dagger from his belt and turned to slash at the men. He managed to nick the throat of one while calling for his guards, all of whom had disappeared. But it wasn't enough to stop the attack. Scelestus was stabbed several more times in the side and stomach before the men fled into the pressing crowd. Scelestus again shouted to his guards, but his cries for help were drowned out by the noise in the arena.

He clutched at the man in the next seat while sinking to the floor. As the Greek's sword found its mark once more, the crowd surged forward and stepped on the helpless Scelestus. Blood gurgled in his throat as he struggled to regain his footing. The trample of many feet held him fast as he bled to death.

The battle was nearing its end. The Greek realized his advantage and pressed the Nightman harder. The Nightman was backing away, trying to postpone the inevitable.

He staggered as the Greek's sword pierced his flesh again. He could feel a weakness creep over his body. Death would be welcome, but the thought of seeing his wife and children again drove him back into the fight. In one last surge of energy, he rushed at the Greek, swinging his shield and striking hard with his sword.

His efforts were futile. The Greek seemed to gain strength from his growing weakness and pressed him back and slashed at him. The deadly blades were only a hair's breadth from his exposed neck. A blow caught him mid-section. The Greek stepped back as the Nightman bent over. His shield dropped to the ground, and his left hand grasped his bleeding stomach.

The Greek stared into the crowd, looking at everyone and no one, while the Nightman staggered sideways. He dropped to one knee, pulled off his helmet, and leaned on his sword. The Greek moved closer. The Nightman raised his head, and their eyes met.

"Finish it! Make it quick!"

"Tell me the truth!" the Greek screamed over the noise of the crowd. "Did you order the death of Murena? Tell me the truth!"

"No. You have your answer. Now spare me any more pain. Kill me!"

With the last of his strength, the Nightman raised his chest and exposed his neck. Tears flowed from the Greek's eyes so that he could barely see the point of his sword as he leaned in close for the final blow.

"When you see Murena on the other side, tell her I love her and that you died an honorable death."

"I will." The Nightman turned his head to the right and waited.

The Greek plunged his sword into the Nightman's chest and pierced his heart. "I'm sorry."

He pulled the blade back as the Nightman's body sank to the ground, dropped his swords, and knelt beside him. He grasped his brother's body in his arms and wept.

Fights had broken out in the stands amongst the rival supporters. A few fans jumped into the arena, but they were quickly killed by the guards. Julius was gravely concerned for the safety of the Greek and called to the editor for the guards to remove him. He motioned to one standing directly below the editor's box, grabbed Julius' arm, and fled through the tunnels of the arena.

A few fans had reached the Greek and were touching him and stroking his hair. Four guards moved to protect the Greek, who remained hunched over the body of the Nightman, oblivious to the spectators. Two guards dispatched the fans while the other two grasped the arms of the Greek and pulled him to the exit against his protests. They hurried through the maze of tunnels and emerged onto the street where a waiting cart whisked them away to safety.

***

Artorius and Fabius forced their way through the crush of the crowd. It was late afternoon when they finally made it out of the amphitheater. They headed west, snaking their way through the city. Most streets were deserted. Shouts could be heard from the arena, but the two men didn't care about the games. They had succeeded. Scelestus was dead and a rich payday awaited. When they reached the Via di Stabia, they turned into an alleyway emerging onto Vicolo del Lupanare Street and entered the door of a nondescript building.

"Fabius, Artorius, back so soon? You like my girls?" the Madame asked enthusiastically.

"Not now, Victoria. My friend is hurt. Do you have some bandages?" Artorius asked.

"Let me see. That's a lot of blood, but it doesn't look serious. What happened?"

"Muggers near the forum. Can you help?"

"Yes, take him into room two and tell Amelia to get some water. I will fetch some strips of cloth to wrap the wound," the elderly Madame said as she hurried to the back of the brothel.

After washing the wound, they tied a length of cloth around Fabius' neck. The short respite and the fact that Fabius' wound was superficial helped to calm their nerves. The pair departed and headed to the stables to retrieve their horses.

Six days later, they stood on the docks of Brundisium under cover of darkness.

"Fabius? Artorius?" a voice called out.

"Here," Artorius responded. "Have you brought the money?"

"Not here. Follow me." The figure led the men through the darkened street into an alley. The dim light from a window illuminated the figure as he pulled a pouch out of his cloak. "There is a ship called the Neptune leaving for Greece at daybreak. You have passage. Here is the remainder of the payment in gold coins. Never speak of this or mention the senator's name, or you will both join Scelestus, understood?"

"Don't worry. We don't want anyone to know what we did. Tell the senator he can trust us."

"He knows that he can. Good luck," the figure said as he handed the pouch to Fabius, turned, and disappeared into the night.

No one paid any attention to the two bodies lying near the dock; it was too common a sight. When the authorities arrived, they determined it was only some ex-gladiators. No investigation was necessary. What they did find odd was the pouch full of small flat stones one of them had inside his cloak.

***

Senator Flavius was in a better mood of late. Caligula was the new Emperor and, despite his earlier fears, the senator believed he could gain financially under this man. And then there was the tragic news of the death of Scelestus who had been crushed in the melee at Pompeii. The Master's death had presented an opportunity for the senator, even though he hadn't been able to find that 100,000 sesterces. He had claimed the school for debts owed, though, in fact, there weren't any. The remaining gladiators were sold for a handsome profit. And, as a bonus, it turned out the Master owned considerable land holdings that the senator distributed to several families in the region to help secure their loyalty. Life was good again for Senator Flavius.

"A messenger, Senator," one of his slaves called from the entrance to the garden.

"Bring him to me."

The servant motioned for the man to come forward.

"What is it? More good news?" the senator asked.

"An invitation from Julius Tullius Pontus of Capua to dine at his residence in one week."

"Julius? What is the reason, boy?"

"To discuss the fate of a gladiator, sir. The Greek."

"The Greek? Does he wish to sell him?"

"That is all I know, sir. I am to wait for a reply."

"The answer is yes, of course. Tell Julius I will be there in one week."

The messenger nodded and left.

"You know this Julius?" his secretary inquired.

"His father and mine were friends. I was never close to Julius, but he is influential in the Capua region and friends, so the rumor goes, with Caligula. Certainly not a man to make your enemy. And the mention of the Greek intrigues me. He is headed to Rome without a doubt. It would be a great coup for me to own the best gladiator in the Empire. Prepare travel plans for Capua."

***

The Greek had fallen into depression upon returning to Capua after the match in Pompeii, and Julius was concerned. Emperor Gaius was sponsoring games in honor of his deceased parents in three months at the amphitheater of Statilius Taurus at Rome. The purses would be enormous and the victor against Beryllus, if there was one, would be awarded his freedom. Julius knew the honor and fame of owning the winning gladiator would spread his family name far and wide in the Empire, and this had brought him to the Greek's cell.

"Open it," he instructed the guard, "and then lock me in."

Keys jingled, and then the door swung open. Julius walked in and sat opposite the Greek, who was lying on the bed.

"I have secured a match for you against Beryllus, in Rome, in three months," Julius began. "Win, and you will be free. Plus, there is a substantial prize. Together with what you won in Pompeii, you will be able to return to Thessaly if you desire. You can retire. No more fighting. No more bloodshed. You'll be free. Is that what you want?"

The Greek sat up on the edge of the bed and faced Julius. "Why did I have to kill the Nightman?"

"Only one could fight Beryllus, and it had to be decided in the arena. Don't take it personally. It's just business. You're a gladiator. Don't you know what that means?"

"It means I'm a dead man."

"What? No, it means you are part of an honorable profession that has rules. You always fight to win, no matter who your opponent is. That is how honor and respect are gained. You are the most honored gladiator in the Empire, possibly more so than Beryllus. Death is part of the game. It's a part of life. Everyone crosses the Styx. It is the will of the gods. Only they are exempt. If you hadn't fought, you would be dead. Winning is life. Don't dwell on death. You will soon be free. Concentrate on that."

"The Master once promised I would be free if I won. I won, but still live in chains."

"The Master was not an honorable man. This is not the word of a former slave. I'm the finest member of an old and distinguished family. Gaius is descended from no lesser a man than Augustus himself!"

The Greek thought of his family in Thessaly and how he longed to return home. There was nothing left for him in Italy.

"You promise I will be free when I win in Rome?"

"By all that is sacred to me and my family, I promise you will be free when you win."

The Greek wanted desperately to believe him. "I will fight one last time."

Julius rose and called to the guard. "I'm going to move you to a small training facility outside the city. You'll like it there. Delicatus and Purpurius will accompany you, and there will be many guards to protect you. About that woman, do you want her? I can send someone else if you prefer, or no one."

"Send Sperata to me."

"You'll move in a few days."

Julius departed and returned home to begin preparations for the move. The Greek was one of the most valuable gladiators in the Empire; precautions were needed to assure his safe arrival.

When Julius arrived home, a stranger was waiting for an audience with him.

"Julius Tullius Pontus?" he asked.

"Yes. To whom do I have the privilege of speaking?"

"Who I am is of little consequence. This is to remain in confidence."

"Rest assured what you say will not pass these walls."

"The one I represent wishes to know if all is well concerning a certain senator who is to dine here in five days."

"Everything is set."

"Thank you and may the gods be with you."

The man left without another word.

***

Sperata was reunited with the Greek two days later, but her attitude had changed because she had feared that she would be returned to the brothel. She hugged and kissed the Greek as a wife welcomes home her wayward husband.

"I feared you might be injured or not want me anymore."

"You're all I have left. You and my family in Thessaly."

"When you win your freedom, will you return there?"

"Yes."

"Will you take me?" she asked tentatively.

"Yes, if you wish. I will be a farmer again, not a gladiator."

"But you will be free. That is what matters. You promise to take me? Men have made promises to me in the past but never kept them. They just threw me away. You won't throw me away, will you? You promise?"

"I promise you will go to Thessaly with me. You will go home. You will be my wife."

***

Senator Flavius decided to leave two days early for his dinner with Julius. He stayed in Beneventum, a short distance from Julius' home, with a close ally. The talk always turned to Gaius and the optimism caressing the Empire with his ascension. The senator had plans to bring up the subject with Julius.

The senator arrived at Julius' villa to a cordial greeting by the owner himself, which boded well for him. Julius allowed him to freshen up after the journey and told him they would meet in the triclinium. The room was deserted when the senator arrived; the bare tables seemed strange and a bit unnerving to him. Then he noticed them—three large men walking across the garden. When he turned toward the entrance, he spotted two more. His hands began to shake. His eyes scanned the room for a means of escape but there was none.

As the men neared, he began to plead with them for mercy. When only silence answered him, he braced himself for the inevitable. But it didn't happen. There were no daggers. He called to Julius in vain as the men led him out of the house and into a waiting carriage that was shrouded in heavy curtains. They began the journey north to Rome.

Soon after ascending to the throne, Gaius had ordered a series of various entertainments to take place in the amphitheater of Statilius. These would last for a duration of three months culminating in the gladiatorial games. Prisoners and enemies of Gaius were rounded up in large numbers and directed to the arena to be executed for the amusement of a weary population. It had been years since such extravagance was displayed by an Emperor, and it was welcomed by the people. It seemed that Gaius could do no wrong.

The senator arrived in Rome after dark and was hustled into the tunnels under the amphitheater. His fine toga set him apart from other prisoners and brought shouts and insults as he was paraded along the corridor. His howls of protest fell on deaf ears.

Shortly after dawn, crowds began to fill the amphitheater in search of the best seats. Excitement was in the air. Emperor Gaius would not preside over the events of the day, but there was a special treat in store for the audience. Rumors of the mystery spectacle flew through the crowd.

The day's entertainment began with the execution of some slaves. The first group of twenty was sent into the arena. Each had been equipped with a shield and sword and given the promise of freedom to the last man left alive. The inexperience of most produced laughter among the people as bets were placed. It quickly became apparent one man had a bit of experience with a sword. He stood on the edge of the group while others flayed away and dispatched one another. When only three remained, this man attacked and killed the other two. He raised his sword in triumph, acknowledging the crowd. He never saw the arrow that penetrated his back and pierced his heart.

An intermission followed and then the next group of prisoners was herded into the arena. Sightless helmets were attached to their heads, and each was given a sword. They swung their weapons in every direction, seldom hitting an opponent, but providing the audience with a comical presentation. When the crowd began to grow bored, the editor realized the problem and called for a gladiator to enter the arena.

Instead of killing the prisoners, he toyed with them. One man ran past the gladiator, who simply held out his sword, and he impaled himself. But it wasn't long before all the prisoners were dead.

There was a long break, after which was the promised highlight of the morning's executions. A wooden pole was inserted into the center of the arena. A length of chain with hand irons on the end was attached to it. Special netting along the top of the arena wall was raised into place. The audience grew restless because they knew the purpose of the netting—execution by beasts. The roar of lions could be heard under the seats, but the spectators knew there were other species down there as well. Their anticipation was growing.

Senator Flavius stumbled as he was pushed along the corridor. He had witnessed enough executions that it was apparent to him what was about to take place. For two months he had lived in fear for his life because of the rumors spread by the Master; now it was true. Not expecting an answer, he asked the gods what he had done to deserve this fate.

As the senator stepped into the arena, a shout of recognition spread through the audience. A man came up to him carrying a sign that read "I ordered the death of a free citizen" and hung it on his back.

The senator held his chin high and tried to conceal his shaking body as he shuffled to the center of the arena. The guards attached his hands to the shackles and hastened out. He stood alone in the vast space as people jeered and threw objects at him. He despised these people; they wouldn't get any satisfaction from watching him die. He would face death like a Roman with his head held high and tongue silent, no matter what kind of beast they sent after him.

A gate opened and, after a short delay, a bear strolled into the arena. Instinctively, the senator attempted to run but was held fast by the shackles. His knees began to shake, beads of sweat rose on his forehead, and the people screamed for his blood. The bear walked around the arena, nose sniffing the air. He ignored the senator, who continued to move around the post away from him. When the bear neared the senator, his bowels voided.

"I don't deserve this!"

Another gate opened, and three men entered. Two carried long spears; the third held a bucket. They approached the senator while keeping an eye on the bear. The man with the bucket poured most of its contents of rotten fish onto the senator and threw the remainder at the bear. He caught the scent and began licking up the bits from the sand.

When he was done, he lumbered toward the senator. In a panic, the senator tried to climb the smooth pole. The bear charged the senator, who screamed in fear and tried to kick the animal. It grasped the senator's leg and viciously shook his head. His toga shredded and blood sprayed in the air. He cried out to the gods, screamed, and cursed as the bear's claws dug into his back. Senator Flavius continued to kick at the bear as his long claws cut through his belly, spilling his intestines onto the sand.

The bear grasped the flaying man's shoulder, crushed the bone, and shook his body, then released his grip on him. The spectators cheered as they watched the bear consume pieces of Senator Flavius, but they soon grew bored

***

The Greek liked his new training facility, but the place made him long for Thessaly. He walked through the fields with Sperata and pointed out the different plants, explaining to her what each was, what they would sow when back home, and how much he wanted a family. The arena was another world, a world of death and blood. Here it was pure and simple. But doubts plagued the Greek. Would his family accept him back? Would they still be there? Could he ever wash away the blood?

And what of the terrible nightmares that arrived every time his eyes closed? The Nightman begging to die, the screams of Murena, and his opponents' blood. Training gave a respite, as did these walks, but the nightmares always returned, and the blood remained.

Julius visited often. He was anxious to follow the Greek's progress. He had wanted to observe Beryllus in training, but Gaius had moved him to Rome as soon as he became Emperor and then to an unknown location. The Emperor remained confident in his man, at least in public, offering long odds to those who wanted to bet, but, in private, he began to have doubts. Beryllus had never lost, but this Greek...there was something about him. Maybe he was truly the son of a god, or perhaps Fortuna sat on his shoulder.

The days leading up to the main event between the Greek and Beryllus were filled with executions, beast hunts, and minor gladiatorial bouts. Julius had been summoned to Rome by the Emperor, an ominous invitation to most, but he believed that his friendship with Gaius protected him. It was a connection that would fail him less than one year later, but for the present, there was no danger. Gaius met him in the palace with great fanfare.

"Julius, I'm glad you could come. How is the family?"

"All are well, Emperor."

"Come now. No formal address is needed."

"As you wish, Gaius. All is well with you? I have heard nothing but good things since the untimely death of your uncle."

"I will not lie. The burden of leadership bears heavily on me. But I am making progress. Enough of such matters. Let's discuss the reason I brought you here."

"The match, I suspect. Do you wish to concede victory?"

"A lesser man than yourself would pay for such a remark, but I know you jest. In fact, I thought you might be having second thoughts and wished to spare the life of your man."

"The Greek does not need my help to live."

"All in fun, dear Julius. I wish to inquire upon his health. No problems, one hopes?"

"The Greek will be here, much to the humiliation of Beryllus."

"You boast!" Gaius laughed. "But are you willing to match your confidence with a wager?"

"Perhaps. Should we say one sesterce?"

Again laughing, Gaius replied, "One would seem a bit excessive! Does your man limp?"

"Only after carrying out your massive prize. But, if you wish to proffer a real bet, might I suggest 50,000 sesterces?"

"That sounds better," Gaius replied, now serious.

"What prize the victor?"

"Perhaps 20,000 sesterces. And his freedom."

"Make it 50,000. Plus, when the Greek wins, he receives my winnings from the bet."

"You offer him 100,000 sesterces? Why?"

"I have my reasons."

"After paying 60,000 for him, now you offer all your winnings! You truly are a good man, Julius. I will give the Greek 100,000 sesterces and pay you your share of the bet if he wins. But there will be no need for my generosity."

"Augustus would be proud of you. You are a model to the Roman people and a fine example of the Julio-Claudian family. It is set then. In three weeks, our men meet in the arena, gods willing."

"Gods willing. Though I hope for Beryllus' sake, none of them are the parents of the Greek!"

***

Sperata was bored. She wasn't used to the quiet country life. She longed for the city, though not her old life. Maybe living the life of a goat farmer wouldn't be too bad, but then, once the Greek bought her freedom, she could simply take her fair share of his money and disappear. It wouldn't be difficult to separate him from that money. She didn't know how much he would earn in Rome, but rumors suggested at least 50,000 sesterces. That small fortune would allow her a comfortable living.

Sperata persuaded the Greek to ask Julius if she could attend his bout. She could offer to protect the Greek's winnings for him and vanish in the crowd the first chance she got.

The Greek's trainers were at an advantage. They had seen Beryllus fight and could prepare the Greek for his usual tricks. He was a better gladiator than even Maximianus had been, and certainly far above the Nightman. It would take exceptional skill and stamina to defeat him. However, they believed they had found a weakness that the Greek could exploit.

Emperor Gaius sent guards to escort the Greek to Rome. He arrived two days before the match and was housed in the state gardens where the beasts that supplied the games were held. This was a secure facility where the public was not allowed. The Emperor took pride in his stable of gladiators. The match had to be fair if he wanted to prove he had the best.

Early the next morning, the Greek was brought to the arena for the pompa. The stadium was packed. Everyone knew they were going to see one of these gladiators for the last time. Perhaps both, if the winner retired. Beryllus led the procession around the arena, and thunderous cheers rose when he entered. He was past the editor's box when the Greek walked in, last in a long line of gladiators. Spectators reached over the wall trying to touch him. It seemed everyone, even supporters of Beryllus, were cheering for the Greek. He didn't want to leave the arena.

The afternoon sand began with equites. A silence fell over the arena when two riders burst into the stadium on brilliant white horses. Each rider carried a long wooden spear, wore a broad-brimmed helmet with a visor and feathers on each side, and held a small round shield. One wore a bright blue tunic. His opponent wore a green one. They came into the arena at a full gallop and headed for one another. The sound of wood splintering caused a deafening shout to rise from the spectators as the horsemen's spears smashed into one another. The rider in the green tunic was thrown from his horse. The other circled around, dismounted, and threw away what remained of his spear. The two men pulled their swords and met in the center of the arena. The man in the green tunic was still dazed from the blow, a fact that the other fighter used to his advantage. He only needed a few strikes to knock his opponent to the sand.

Emperor Gaius extended his arm, fist closed, and turned his thumb down. The man in the blue tunic celebrated his victory while the man in green struggled to his feet and staggered out of the arena with his head hung in disgrace.

The show continued through the afternoon until, at last, it was time for the Greek to fight. Arrangements had been made for Beryllus to enter first and circle the arena before the Greek entered. Beryllus strolled around the amphitheater confident to the point of arrogance. A deafening roar greeted the Greek.

As the crowd began to settle down, the two men went before the editor, collected their swords, and walked to the center of the arena. Beryllus waited while the Greek put on a show for the people and even attempted to juggle his sword, which drew laughter from the crowd.

Beryllus fought as a Thracian, and his style was aggressive and unforgiving. The two moved together in the center of the arena. Beryllus charged the Greek, who sidestepped him and slashed at his strike, but Beryllus refused to retreat. He gave no ground and pressed the Greek hard.

They moved with blurring speed, like panthers struggling over the last morsel of a kill. For most of his career, Beryllus had won by overwhelming his opponents with superior strength and skill. They usually submitted, or were dead, after a few minutes. Beryllus was relentless in his attack on the Greek. The younger gladiator moved backward while parrying his blows. Each thrust was met with a counterblow as the Greek shifted from side to side, his feet a blur as he glided over the sand. He held his swords low and dared Beryllus to strike, but he was too fast. Beryllus' sword never hit its mark.

Even the spectators who had witnessed the Greek perform in other arenas had never seen him move like this. It was like trying to hit a shadow. A cloud of dust rose from the sand beneath their feet.

As the match continued, the Greek began to sense a weariness in his opponent. There was less force behind Beryllus' sword, but he remained cautious and patient. Beryllus was growing frustrated as his strikes missed flesh. He attempted to force the Greek against the boards, but the younger gladiator kept slipping away. The Greek's antics not only thwarted Beryllus, but endeared him to the crowd, and even though he wasn't injured, it appeared that Beryllus was outmatched.

Beryllus had been unstoppable in the arena, but this match was taking its toll on him. And, as the momentum shifted to the Greek, so did the support. Beryllus' anger grew. If only the Greek would stop moving and fight like all the others had. But the Greek wouldn't stand still. He danced left then circled to the right, always a step ahead. When the Greek did move close enough, it was his swords that hit their mark.

As Beryllus became more frustrated, he got reckless. The Greek sensed this was the moment. He began to pommel Beryllus with both swords. It was what Beryllus had been waiting for, had hoped for, but it was too late.

The Greek was cutting Beryllus to pieces. Blow after blow found flesh; his body turned bright red. Beryllus summoned the last of his strength, lunged at the Greek, and aimed a deadly blow at his heart, but the Greek sidestepped the sword. His counterblow found its mark. The Greek withdrew the sword as fast as he had driven it in the flesh and stepped back.

It was over.

The audience did not realize what had happened until Beryllus dropped his shield. He staggered back another step and the sword slipped from his fingers. His eyes found the Greek's face, and they stood gazing at one another. A grim smile tugged at the corners of the Greek's mouth.

Beryllus' legs could no longer hold up his weight, and with the next step he fell backward onto the ground. A cloud of dust rose around his body. The Greek thrust his swords into the air and began to walk around the arena.

Everyone was on their feet. His name floated through the crowd. Even Emperor Gaius and Julius, who stood by his side, were shouting in appreciation of the performance. After several minutes, one of the gates into the arena opened, and a slim, well-dressed man entered nervously. The Greek lowered his swords and faced the man, who visibly shook.

"I am the Emperor's translator. He wishes to address the people and wants you to understand his words. I am unarmed and offer you no harm."

The Greek thought how easy it would be to run his sword through the man's chest and the pleasure it would give him. He pointed his swords at the ground, and the man let out a sigh of relief. The translator motioned for the Greek to face the editor's box where the Emperor remained standing, then caught the eye of Emperor Gaius, who raised his hands in an attempt to silence the people. Quiet engulfed the arena like a heavy blanket.

"My fellow Romans," he began, "great thanks to you for attending these special games presented in honor of my deceased father, Germanicus! We have been witness to a wondrous combat today by two noble gladiators, the defeated no lesser a man than the victor!"

A roar filled the stadium as the Emperor pointed to the body of Beryllus.

"But there can be only one victor!"

A chorus of *Graecus* surged through the amphitheater.

"For his victory, I grant the Greek, from this day forth and for the rest of his life, his freedom! And," Emperor Gaius continued, when the noise subsided once more, "for his new life as a freedman, I pledge 100,000 sesterces prize for his victory today!"

Sperata couldn't believe what she had heard! One hundred thousand sesterces was more than even she had imagined possible! Perhaps she could learn to be a goat farmer for that kind of money!

"Do you understand everything the Emperor has pledged? Your freedom granted immediately and 100,000 sesterces?" the translator asked the Greek.

"Yes."

The Greek raised his swords high, and the crowd exploded with chants of *Graecus*. Slowly, he turned in a circle, soaking it in. Thoughts of his parents and sisters flashed through his mind. He realized that this was his life; there could never be anything else. His family and home were from another time, another life, and one he could never return to. He stared at the lifeless body of Beryllus and remembered the Nightman and Murena. And freedom. The arena with its pain and death were all that was left for him. Tears flowed down his cheeks as he knew he would always, and only, be of sand and blood.

The ones who saw it believed it was another sword trick or some way of saying farewell to his fans. But when the sword in his left hand, still raised high, slipped from his grasp and fell to the ground, the crowd realized something was terribly wrong.

The Greek struggled to breathe. Blood gurgled in his chest. He fought to remain on his feet until, suddenly, he dropped to his knees, the other sword buried deep in his chest. Silence filled the arena. As he drew his last breaths, the Greek collapsed face down onto the ground, and a cloud of dust rose around him as his lifeblood stained the sand red.

THE END

Beneventum

Capua

Venusia

Pompeii

Barium

Brundisium

Capri

Paestum

Tarentum

LIST OF CHARACTERS

(* indicates historical figures)

Actius: a fan and follower of gladiators

Alexandros, the Greek: a sixteen-year-old Greek peasant who is kidnaped by Roman soldiers and forced to become a gladiator.

Amandus: a Thracian opponent of the Greek.

Amelia: a prostitute in Pompeii

Artorius: a former gladiator, a bodyguard and assassin, partner of Fabius

Astus: the Cunning One, a murmillo and an opponent of the Nightman

***Augustus**: (Octavian) (63 BC - AD 14) The first emperor of the Roman Empire. He defeated Marc Antony in 31 BC to become the sole ruler of Rome and its provinces. He was possibly poisoned by his second wife Livia.

Bassus: a gladiator owned by the Master, crucified for his attempted escape.

Bearman: a murmillo owned by the Master.

Beryllus: a Thracian owned by Gaius.

Blandina, Fabius, Rufinus, Paulus, Martinus: slaves on the estate where the Greek finds refuge after his escape.

Boarman: a hoplomachus owned by the Master.

***Caligula**: see Gaius Julius.

Callistus: a Thracian opponent of the Greek.

Cassius Victorinus: one of the Greek's trainers.

Catalus Paulus: nephew of Senator Flavius.

Charon: in mythology he was the boatman who ferried shades (souls) across the River Styx, which could only happen if the person was dead and had been properly buried. A man in costume as Charon had the task of confirming the death of gladiators by striking them with a large hammer before they were removed from the arena.

Cuspius: a carpenter and fan of the gladiatorial games.

Decima: a slave and the wife of the Nightman.

Delicatus: a trainer of the Greek.

Drusus Atius Longus: son of Lepidus.

*Ennia Naevia: wife of Macro.

Fabius: a former gladiator, a bodyguard and assassin, partner of Artorius.

Fortuna: a goddess of luck, both good and bad.

Frontis: a fan of gladiatorial games and client of Senator Flavius.

*Gaius Julius: (Caligula) (AD 12 - 41; Emperor AD 37 - 41) A member of the Julio-Claudian family, nephew of Tiberius. When Gaius became emperor in March, AD 37, he was hailed by the people as a great and just ruler but later that year he became deathly ill. Upon his recovery, his personality changed completely and he became a psychopath.

Giant: a gladiator owned by the Master.

Hera: (Roman Juno) The queen of the gods.

Jantinus: a former gladiator, trainer of the Greek.

*Julio-Claudian family: one of the most influential of the ancient Roman families that began with Julius Caesar and continued to Nero.

Julius Tullius Pontus: son of a senator, a wealthy and powerful man who buys the Greek.

*Junia: Gaius' first wife who died in childbirth in AD 33.

Lepidus Salvius Capito: a wealthy businessman from Brundisium.

Lucanus: a slave and assistant to the Master.

*Macro: Praetorian prefect. The praetorians were an elite unit of soldiers whose task was to protect the emperor.

Maecenas Canuleius Zosimus: a free man who becomes a gladiator.

Marcellus: a baker in Brundisium and client of Lepidus.

Marcus Quintus Flavius: the senator from the region of the Master's school.

Master: a former gladiator and owner of a gladiatorial school.

Mercatus: a slave seller in Brundisium.

Murena: a slave given to the Greek.

Nemesis: a goddess of vengeance. Her attendants were; justice, punishment, and vengeance. Her cult was popular with gladiators.

Pinna: the Featherman, trainer of the Nightman.

Priscus: a fuller and fan of gladiators.

Probus: the Good Man, a gladiator owner by the Master.

Purpurius: a trainer of the Greek.

Scelestus Nothus: a wealthy businessman from Venusia, friend of Gaius.

Silvanus: a god of the woods and fields. His cult was popular with gladiators

Sperata: a prostitute and slave given to the Greek.

*Tiberius: (42 BC - AD 37) Emperor from AD 14 - 37. Stepson of August, he reluctantly agreed to follow August as the second emperor. He spent the last ten years of his reign in seclusion on the island of Capri. Possibly poisoned by Gaius.

Trebius: a goldsmith and fan of gladiators.

Victoria: a Madame in a brothel in Pompeii.

Vinicius Flaminius: owner of the estate where the Greek seeks refuge after he escapes.

Vitalis: a former gladiator, a guard at the Master's school.

LIST OF TERMS AND PLACES

apodyterium: the changing room in a Roman bath.

Beneventum: a city in south-central Italy.

Brundisium: a port city on the southeast coast of Italy. One of the main ports for trade with Greece.

caldarium: the hot room of a Roman bath.

Campania: the region of west central Italy centered around Pompeii.

Campus Martius: originally outside of Rome proper, it was used for military exercises and training.

Capri: an island off the west coast of Campania.

Capua: a city west of Beneventum.

Celt: a person from the area of modern France.

cena libera: a celebratory dinner given for the gladiators the night before they were to fight.

dimachaerus (s), **dimachaeri** (pl): a gladiator who fought with two swords and little or no armor.

frigadarium: the cold room of a Roman bath.

griffin: a mythological creature with the body of a lion and the head, wings, and talons of an eagle.

Hades: the underworld where the shades (souls) of the departed reside. Not to be confused with Hell which is a Christen concept and not Roman.

hoplomachus: a type of gladiator who wore a helmet, greaves, cloth wrappings on the right arm and used a spear and/or dagger and a small round shield.

lanista (s), **lanistae** (pl): the owners of gladiatorial schools and gladiators.

libellus munerarius: the program for gladiatorial matches that included the names, pairings and schedule for all combatants.

medicus: a medical doctor

murmillo: a type of gladiator who wore a helmet, short greave on the left leg, an arm-guard or cloth wrappings on the right arm, used a large rectangular shield and a straight sword.

Paestum: a city southeast of Pompeii.

palaestra: an exercise area that was usually situated next to, or nearby, an amphitheater.

Parvus Aureus: Little Goldy

pompa: a parade of gladiators and dignitaries that opened the games.

Pompeii: a city in west central Italy. Destroyed by a volcanic eruption in AD 79.

Porta Libitinensis: the Gate of Death where the dead were carried or dragged out of the arena.

questor: an official in charge of finances for a city. In many cases, he had to approve any gladiatorial games that were held.

retiarius (s) **retiarii** (pl): a type of gladiator who used a trident, dagger, and net and wore cloth wrappings on his left arm and a shoulder guard.

seats among the togas: seating was segregated in amphitheaters with the best seats, the ones for the upper classes who wore togas, closest to the action. The lowest class, female slaves, stood behind the last row of seats at the top of the arena.

secutor (s), **secutores** (pl): same as a murmillo except his helmet was close-fitting and had two small eye holes.

sine missione: literally, without mercy. In these matches the loser always died. It was banned under Augustus but the law was regularly ignored.

Statilius Taurus amphitheater: located in the Campus Martius and built by Augustus in 29 BC. It was the main amphitheater in Rome before construction of the Colosseum in AD 80.

Styx: a mythological river that one must cross to reach Hades.

Tarentum: a city in southeastern Italy.

tepidarium: the warm room in a Roman bath.

Thracian: a type of gladiator who wore a helmet, greaves, cloth arm-guard and used a curved sword and small round or rectangular shield.

Triton: a personification of the roaring sea, a sea god, son of Neptune.

venator: a gladiator who only fought and/or hunted animals.

Venusia: a city in south central Italy.

SELECT BIBLIOGRAPHY

Baker, Alan. *The Gladiator: The Secret History of Rome's Warrior Slaves*. Cambridge, MA: Da Capo Press, 2002.

Barton, Carlin A. *The Sorrows of the Ancient Romans: The Gladiator and the Monster*. Princeton, NJ: Princeton University Press, 1993.

Dunkle, Roger. *Gladiators: Violence and Spectacle in Ancient Rome*. Harlow, UK: Pearson Education Limited, 2008.

Fagan, Garrett G. *The Lure of the Arena*. Cambridge, UK: Cambridge University Press, 2011.

Grant, Michael. *Gladiators*. New York, NY: Barnes and Noble Books, 1995.

Meijer, Fik. *The Gladiators: History's Most Deadly Sport*. New York, NY: St. Martin's Press, 2003.

Nossov, Konstantin. *Gladiators: The Complete Guide to Ancient Rome's Bloody Fighters*. Guilford, CT: Lyons Press, 2011.

Shadrake, Susanna. *The World of the Gladiator*. Gloucestershire, UK: The History Press, 2010.

OTHER TOUCHPOINT PRESS TITLES BY MICHAEL ROYEA

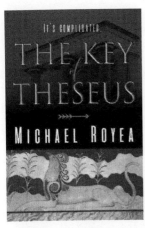

Benny Shay, an archaeologist, arrives on Crete to authenticate an ancient Minoan artifact supposedly discovered by a tomb robber. Within twenty-four hours of arriving, the tomb robber is murdered, Benny's friend and financial supporter is killed in a car accident, and Benny is being followed. After hiring a tour guide, Tara, who believes Benny is searching for a treasure, the two discover a Minoan tomb with an inscription that leads them to the Minoan palace of Phaistos. Here they find a system of tunnels under the site that ends at a secret room where they discover a gold bull pendant.

Following a series of clues they begin to believe the pendant is the mythical key of Theseus that opens the treasury of King Minos. They deduce the treasury must be in the labyrinth under the palace of Knossos, home of Minos, and the Minotaur. But others seek the prize and their van is forced off the road, Tara is kidnapped and then rescued by Benny when he blunders onto the kidnappers. And more bodies turn up.

Available at most major online retailers and through from TouchPoint Press.

Made in the USA
Columbia, SC
09 February 2018